Ben took a deep breath.

"Okay, I admit I'm at a disadvantage to get the information I need. But I can't ask you to risk your career to help me."

"You didn't ask. I offered."

"That's what I don't understand. Why?" But he didn't give time to answer. "How do you know I'm not guilty?"

He looked away from her as if her response to that question didn't matter.

Oh, it mattered, all right. She hated that she couldn't tell him what he needed to hear. If only she could announce her fervent support the way the other troopers had. But she wasn't built that way. She needed proof. Police and lab reports were like the building blocks of her constitution, the glue bonding them together. Indisputable proof.

That Ben Peterson even tempted her to step away from what she knew and trusted scared her more than any domestic or shots-fired call ever could.

Dear Reader,

I am so excited to introduce you to my True Blue miniseries and to me, since this is my very first Superromance book. True Blue tells the stories of the brave men and women of the Michigan State Police Brighton Post. They are members of a different type of family, one based on shared sacrifice and ultimate trust rather than common genetics.

This project has been great fun because it has allowed me to delve into one of my favorite topics: law enforcement. From my college criminal justice electives to the weekend cops beat from my newspaper reporter days, I have loved learning about these honorable officers, who perform heroic acts daily. The miniseries gave me an excuse to attend the Citizen's Police Academy, go on several police ride-alongs, learn to shoot a Glock and be Tasered by choice (ouch!). I hope all the research will lend credibility to my fictitious world so you'll indulge my creative license in the stories.

In *Strength Under Fire*, reluctant hero Lieutenant Ben Peterson is forced to question the foundation of his state police family when he is falsely accused of evidence tampering. Because he no longer knows who his friends are, Ben must rely on help from non-team player Delia Morgan, a trooper with much to prove...and so much to hide.

I love hearing from readers. Contact me on Facebook or by snail mail at PO Box 5, Novi, MI 48376-0005, or follow me on Twitter, @DanaNussio1.

Dana Nussio

DANA NUSSIO

Strength Under Fire

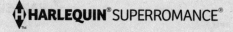

HARLEQUIN® SUPERROMANCE®

Recycling programs
for this product may
not exist in your area.

ISBN-13: 978-0-373-60947-5

Strength Under Fire

Copyright © 2016 by Dana Corbit Nussio

Printed in U.S.A.

Dana Nussio began telling "people stories" around the same time she started talking. She has been doing both things ever since. The award-winning newspaper reporter and features editor left her career while raising three daughters, but the stories followed her home as she discovered the joy of writing fiction. Now an award-winning fiction author as well, she loves telling emotional stories filled with honorable but flawed characters. A pair of *almost* empty nesters, Dana and her husband of twenty-five years live in Michigan with two overfed cats named Leonardo (da Vinci, not DiCaprio) and Annabelle Lee.

To my dear friend and fellow author Nancy Gideon,
who always knew I could write the tough stuff and
pushed me relentlessly so I could get it right.
I hope I made you proud.

A special thanks to the law-enforcement and
public-safety professionals who helped make the
Lakes Area (Michigan) Citizens Police Academy
possible for information junkies like me.
I am especially grateful to Patrolman
Tim Farrell and Officer Shawn Penzak of the
Novi Police Department, and Officer Ken Ayres
and Officer Rebecca List of the Wolverine Lake
Police Department for answering my relentless
questions and opening your law-enforcement
world to me. Thank you to Rebecca, in particular,
for helping me bring Delia Morgan to life.
All of you are the real heroes.

CHAPTER ONE

"THERE'S OUR HERO."

Ben Peterson froze in the squad room doorway as a collage of smiling faces and uniform sleeves reached out to haul him in by the shirt collar. The cheers, the thuds of applause—a wolf whistle thrown into the mix—squeezed the cramped space even tighter. Insides pleading for retreat, Ben crossed the room as if he didn't mind being right there at center stage. Even a goldfish had no choice but to keep on swimming when its bowl turned cloudy.

"No, Lieutenant Peterson is *my* hero," Vincent Leonetti called out in a flawless falsetto, a grin splitting his already ugly mug.

Once a class clown, always a class clown. Even if Bozo had been promoted to sergeant.

"Yeah. Yeah. Yeah." Ben gestured downward with his hands, wishing he had a mute button. "Knock it off, Vinnie."

"Admit it. You done good."

Ben shook his head, but finally he shrugged as he faced the dozen afternoon-shift troopers spaced around the room's perimeter and huddled on the desks at its center. They were already in their navy uniforms, silver ties knotted, heavy jackets at the ready for their trips out into the frostbitten southeast Michigan January. These were the men and women of the Brighton Post. His teammates. His friends.

Maybe it had been too much to expect that they would leave him alone to do his job today, but that hadn't stopped him from hoping. Didn't they see that yesterday's events still felt more like fiction to him than any facts reported on *News 3 Breaking Live*? And didn't they know by now that he preferred to stay in the background? He was good at it. Until he'd stepped inside that bank and shot the delicate balance of his professional life to hell and then some. The chances of getting back to his safe little norm appeared to be slim to *forget it, buddy*.

Pushing his glasses up on his nose, he crammed his sweaty hands into his pockets. "Thanks, everyone, but—"

Lieutenant Scott Campbell stepped close and rested a hand on Ben's shoulder.

"We all know that this guy enjoys being singled out about as much as getting a root canal, but moments of heroism like his deserve recognition." Scott gestured toward him. "So on behalf of the Michigan State Police Brighton Post,

I would like to congratulate Lieutenant Ben Peterson on a job well done."

Ben opened his mouth to try again, but the other lieutenant raised a hand to stop him.

"Even on his day off, Lieutenant Peterson single-handedly took down two suspects in a bank robbery attempt, and at the same time he—" Scott paused, winking "—made a deposit into his interest-bearing checking account."

"Are you kidding? Interest-bearing?" Vinnie's eyes were as wide as his grin.

"Thanks for protecting the greenbacks," someone called from the back of the room.

"Can you get me a preferred rate on a sixty-month CD?" another chimed.

As the punch lines continued pinging around the room, Ben finally let go of the breath he'd been holding. Compared to the awkward accolades his coworkers might have given him for those thirty terrifying minutes at Brighton Bank & Trust, this gentle ribbing was a gift.

When the laughter filtered down to chuckles, he jumped in. "Thanks again. But I was only doing my job. Just as any of you would have done."

"But would we?"

Scott's words cut him off and ended the other conversations in the room. "We want to believe we'll be ready if called upon to act, even when off duty. And Lieutenant Peterson *was* ready. Good to know, especially for those of us who drive desks more often than patrol cars."

He gestured toward Ben to indicate whom else he included in that sedentary *us*.

"Glad you remembered to show off your good side on Channel 3," Vinnie started again.

"Thanks." Ben winced at the memory of last night's interview and the others he would have to endure for the benefit of the post. The media attention hit too close to a home he never planned to visit again by choice. Not that he'd chosen it the first time, either.

"You're one lucky asshole," Trooper Grant Maxwell called out.

"That coming from a guy who narrowly escaped a bullet last spring," Vinnie quipped. "Now there's some luck."

"Just another day on the job," Grant said with a smug grin. "Anyway, I'm not the one who's gonna get his own comic-book character. He leaped right into hero mode without breaking a sweat."

"I'm no hero." Ben's words were automatic. A reflex. He cleared his throat. "I mean, I just did what I had to do."

The sense that he was being watched was so strong that the hair on the back of his neck stood up. Of course someone was watching. They *all* were. But he had no doubt that one individual would be studying this scene more carefully than the others. Sure enough, a petite brunette stood at the edge of the activity, always as an observer, but never quite a participant.

Trooper Delia Morgan couldn't have looked more uncomfortable, her posture as stiff as the unforgiving bun she always wore in her hair. Though a competent, by-the-book new recruit and a skilled, left-handed sharpshooter, from the start she hadn't fit in well with the Brighton Post team, and she'd made no effort to change that.

Deep blue eyes, heavily lashed and so huge that they seemed to see everything and more, caught Ben's gaze and gripped tight. Of course Trooper Morgan would be suspicious of him now. For months, he'd preached teamwork to her like a televangelist, and here he was basking in the spotlight of individual praise.

"Congratulations, Lieutenant," she said after what must have been the most pregnant pause known to mankind.

"Uh. Thanks."

Strange, she'd been obliged to say something nice, and yet she'd almost sounded sincere. That couldn't be right. She was the last person he'd expect to get caught up in this hero nonsense. Did Delia see him differently now? Would he enjoy it if she did? As Ben pushed away those disconcerting thoughts, Delia tilted her head and a tress of shiny hair escaped its clip, falling across her jawline. It came to rest along the fair skin of her neck.

The impulse to test the feel of those silky-looking strands struck him so fast that his hand reached out before he had time to get his thinking straight. He stuffed his hands back in his pockets, blinking several times, his mouth suddenly dry. What was that? Never mind that the woman was clear across the room, nor that this *particular* woman would have slugged him for getting too close. Thankfully, she must have missed his idiotic move because she reached up and shoved her hair out of the way herself.

He swallowed. What was he doing focusing on Delia like that anyway? Make that *Trooper* Morgan. Even if the overly independent officer had been an enigma to him since she'd been assigned to the Brighton Post nearly a year before, now wasn't the best time for him to try to figure her out. He had no business thinking of her in any way other than as a fellow officer, either. Especially not as an attractive woman.

"Well, I wonder who's out protecting the citizens of Michigan this morning."

Ben straightened like a teenager caught scoping out a girl during a bio quiz, which was especially awkward since he was thirty-two and Delia was twenty-six. Luckily, none of the other officers had noticed his gawking. They'd turned to the far doorway where Captain Lou Polaski stood, his beefy arms crossed, his expression stern. But then the hard line of his mouth curled, and he started clapping, setting off another round of applause.

"Well done, Lieutenant Peterson."

"Thanks, Captain."

With a nod, the post commander shifted to face the whole group.

"Yesterday's events offer the post some positive PR in a time of state belt-tightening and post closures," he said. "But they should also serve as reminders that we always need to be prepared to react. Even while off duty.

"We are first responders. Period." Polaski swiped a hand through the air to emphasize the finality of that point. "The requirement for us to carry our weapons at all times is not just a suggestion. We must always be ready. Lives depend on it."

The flash of panic that Ben had experienced inside that bank lobby rose again like bile in his throat. His pulse thrummed now as it had then, while he'd frantically tried to recall whether or not he'd strapped on his ankle holster before running errands. If he'd forgotten just that once, the post might have had little to celebrate today.

The squad room fell silent at the gravity of Polaski's words. Was Ben the only one whose insides quaked at the thought of flags flying at half-mast? Who worried that his mistakes could have grave consequences and leave grave markers in their wake? These troopers put themselves in harm's way every day. They did it for their fellow officers, who were like family, and they did it for people they'd never met. Yesterday's incident only reminded them of what the stakes were. And how high.

"So on that note, everybody get back to work." Polaski pointed with his thumb to the steel door that led to the parking lot. "The state isn't paying you to stand around, patting each other on the back."

Ben breathed a sigh of relief. The rodeo show was over. At least for now. The normal din of the squad room returned as troopers shrugged into their coats, grabbed their radios off chargers and started for the door. Some of the higher-ranking officers drifted down the hall, but Ben waited for the last few troopers to leave on patrol.

Instead of rushing out to her car to be first on the road the way she usually did, Trooper Morgan took her time collecting her things. When the door closed behind the others, she turned back to him.

"Lieutenant Peterson, you did a great job yesterday."

Ben stared at her. She'd probably felt pressured to say something kind earlier, but this was overkill.

"It's what we're trained to do," he managed over the awkwardness clogging his throat.

"But you really did it."

"Uh…thanks."

The inflection in his last word made his comment sound like a question, and he recognized that it was one. Was that shock he'd heard in her voice? Or awe? It must have sounded strange to her as well because her eyes went wide. He should have looked away. It would have been the decent thing to do when she looked uncomfortable enough to fire through the floor for an escape route. But he couldn't drag his gaze from her face. Porcelain skin without a freckle anywhere, a straight nose with one of those cute tipped-up ends that women paid good money for and a mouth as close to a perfect bow as any he'd ever seen.

Why had he never noticed those things about her before? Weren't details supposed to be the bread and butter of good police work? Maybe it was because she was behaving as suspiciously as a suspect with half a dozen crack cocaine rocks in her pocket. Or maybe because she was treating *him* so differently today. Like she admired him or something equally unbelievable.

No matter the cause, it was ridiculous to be

seeing Delia Morgan as if for the first time and, worse yet, this time he was noticing all the wrong things. As if to put an exclamation mark on that point, his gaze dipped to just below her silver badge where small breasts softened the boxy lines of her uniform. Would they be as perfect as he imagined? He averted his gaze as heat rushed to his face. He really was just a horny teenager, hiding behind a uniform and a fancy title.

The trooper must have read his mind because she lifted her chin to stare him down for his unprofessional behavior, an expression that might have been more effective if she'd been standing on the desk instead of next to him where she had to look up. Way up. Nevertheless, she was again that tough young officer, too independent for anyone's good, including her own.

"Well, Trooper—" he paused, clearing his throat "—be safe out there. Remember, call for backup when you need it."

"I will...*if* I need it."

Ben chose to let the comment pass this time. She couldn't take back what she'd said earlier, anyway. And if she really did see him differently now, then maybe she would finally listen to his teamwork message. Finally buy into it just a little. He could hope, couldn't he?

"Also, you should try to meet up with everybody after your shift. They're going to the Drift-wood instead of Casey's Diner this time. I'm sure the others would like it if you came."

"Okay. Sure."

She didn't look at him as she said it. He made a mental note to remember how she looked, acted when she was lying. She shoved open the door, allowing the frigid air to whoosh inside, and stepped outside. Either she or the wind pushed it closed behind her.

For a few seconds, Ben could only study the exit and wonder what had just happened. Their strange conversation wasn't the half of it. Twice, in a matter of minutes, he'd checked out a female trooper, something he'd better stop doing *yesterday* if he planned to keep his job. What was wrong with him?

Maybe it was simply this unusual day, surreal in *Groundhog Day* proportions, that had made him so uncomfortably aware of her. Or maybe it was that Trooper Morgan had surprised him. Only a handful of people had ever been able to do that.

In his experience, people stayed true to form, no matter what that form was. Law-abiding cit-izens kept following the rules, and convicted felons became repeat offenders with tragic regu-larity. He understood too well the collateral damage those habitual offenders left behind, not to mention the worry over apples that fell too close to their second-rate trees.

Trooper Morgan either didn't understand the rules of the game or refused to play along. Just when Ben had begun to wonder if he'd ever find a crack in her armor of fierce self-reliance, Delia had shown him a flicker of possibility.

Somehow he had to help her become a real part of the Brighton Post team before Polaski decided that her independent streak was a bigger liability than her determination and commitment to justice were assets. But how could he convince someone like her that there was no *I* in *team*? Maybe he should become more involved in her work development, while maintaining strict professional boundaries, of course. He could do that with his eyes closed, right?

As he entered his office, giving a self-satisfied nod, an image popped into his head, unbidden and unwelcome. Delia as he'd never seen her, her dark mass of hair flowing down her back, those huge eyes shining with humor and a sexy smile playing on those perfect, kissable lips. He blinked away the rest of the image because in it, besides that smile, she wore nothing at all.

On second thought, he needed to forget about doing *anything* with his eyes closed. He'd better keep them wide-open, and if he had any sense, he would stretch a barrier of bright yellow crime-scene tape between him and a certain female trooper. Tape that said Police Line Do Not Cross.

DELIA GRIPPED THE steering wheel so hard that her hands cramped as she merged the patrol car onto Interstate 96, but even focusing on her aching fingers failed to clear her thoughts. She should have felt better in the familiar black interior of her car, where the rules made sense, where she was in control, but everything was out of whack now.

Why had she said those things to Lieutenant Peterson? It wasn't like her, at least not the current her. That little girl behind the curtain of her past, *she* might have said something like that. She'd been the one prone to hero worship, who'd trusted grown-ups too easily. And she'd paid dearly for those mistakes. Delia barely remembered that silly, naive girl.

If only she could forget today's conversation with the lieutenant. Why hadn't it been enough for her to just congratulate him like everyone else had? Especially when all he'd really done was to be at the right place at the right time. Okay, maybe a little more than that, but still. As if the hero's welcome hadn't been enough, she'd heaped more praise on him when no one was watching.

But you really did it.

The memory of his chocolate-colored eyes widening behind those Clark Kent glasses had her straightening in the seat now. But her words weren't even the worst part. She had the uncomfortable feeling that she'd meant what she'd said. Despite the fact that the type of opportunity *she'd* needed to distinguish herself at the post had fallen right into *his* lap. Or that she couldn't move up to a higher-profile agency where she could focus on child-predator cases while she spent her days handing out traffic citations and investigating property-damage accidents.

I'm no hero.

She squirmed in her seat as his words echoed in her ears. With her watching and waiting for his teamwork message to implode over his fifteen minutes of fame, Lieutenant Peterson had come up with a comment like that. It didn't make sense. She knew police officers. They were cocky SOBs, who would take credit for building the Ambassador Bridge if they thought they could get away with it. The attitude came with the uniform. That edge showed up with the badge.

If Sergeant Leonetti had been the one congraluted, he would have grabbed a microphone and cued a comedy monologue. Trooper Shane Warner would have struck a pose to show off his overdeveloped biceps. Even she would have only pretended to hate the attention. After all, it was a means to a critical end.

But Lieutenant Peterson had come through for those bank customers in a highly volatile situation, and he'd done it with the kind of humility she couldn't help but admire. She'd never seen anything like it. The people in her life had never even stood up for those they claimed to love, let alone for strangers.

A reluctant hero, but a hero still.

She supposed it shouldn't surprise her that Lieutenant Peterson had reacted differently than others would have. Sometimes it astonished her that a man like him, someone with such kind eyes, had become a cop in the first place. He had "nice guy" written all over that baby face he tried to shield behind his glasses. As if those could do anything to hide that dimple in his chin or the way his smile lifted slightly higher on one side. Even his light brown hair betrayed him by curling the moment it grew a millimeter outside of its close-trimmed cut.

Not that she'd noticed those things when she'd started working at the post ten months ago. Or kept noticing them.

"Great. Just great."

Delia shook her head as she took the exit for

US 23 and continued to her favorite traffic surveillance point near Whitmore Lake. Today backing into the spot shielded by the overpass felt like
diving for cover. Why was she allowing herself to
have inappropriate thoughts about a fellow officer? And more dangerous than that, letting herself
be tempted to believe that *any* man was different.
They were all the same, and she knew it.

Delia reached for the passenger seat and flipped
on her handheld radar gun. The numbers reset on
the screen, their details clear. If only her thoughts
about a certain lieutenant were as easy to flip on
and off. She had to make them stop. Wasn't it difficult enough being a woman on the force without
her behaving like one of those vacuous females
who oohed and aahed over heroes in uniform? All
of her effort to establish herself as the most competent recent graduate of the State Police Recruit
School would be down the drain if she didn't get
her thoughts under control. She could almost hear
the sucking sound of her lost momentum.

A beep on the laptop, stationed on her console,
interrupted her pity party like a needle popping
balloons. Setting the radar gun on the passenger
seat, she clicked on the message from Gail Jacobs, the administrative assistant.

Lieutenant Peterson asked if you could make a
run through Kensington Metropark during your

shift. He wants you to take a look around the scene where that burned-out car was discovered last week.

Delia hit Reply and typed OK. It wasn't as glamorous as thwarting a bank robbery, but routine assignments were part of the job. She glanced down at the message again and blew out a breath. Obviously, she'd made a big deal out of nothing. Just because she'd made some goofy comment this afternoon didn't mean there would be some monumental change at work between her and the superior officer.

Before she could return to traffic monitoring, another beep announced a second message.

Oh. He also said thanks again. All that attention today must have been killing the poor guy.

Delia swallowed as she lifted the radar gun and pointed. Whether or not Gail had misunderstood the message she'd been asked to pass along, something had clearly changed at the Brighton Post. And it had moved as quickly as the red pickup truck that raced past Delia, clocking eighty-five in a seventy-miles-per-hour zone. But no matter what had shifted, she'd better figure out a way to move it back.

Switching on the spinning red light often called

the "gumball" on the patrol car's roof, she pulled out behind the speeding driver.

"Sorry, buddy. This isn't your lucky day, either."

CHAPTER TWO

A SCENT OF something deliciously fried and, therefore, off-limits wafted over Delia as she opened one of the heavy wood doors to the Driftwood Inn. Ignoring the urge to let the door fall shut and hurry back to her practical champagne-colored midsize, she stepped inside and wiped the snowy sludge off her shoes onto the mat.

Rich wood paneling and low lighting hinted at a hunting-lodge feel, but the mounted deer heads and the antler chandeliers clinched it. Because the place had given her the creeps on the few occasions she'd joined the group here—like dining on a cemetery plot—she scanned the length of the gleaming bar instead of looking at any of the mounted creatures too closely.

"About time you got here." Sergeant Leonetti stood up from one of the tables that had been pushed together and waved her over. "Did you go to Casey's instead?"

Before she could stop herself, she glanced over her shoulder to make sure he was speaking to her. Why had they been waiting for her? How had they known she was coming? Even she hadn't known for sure until her car had pulled into the parking lot as if on autopilot.

"Yeah, what was the holdup?" Trooper Kelly Roberts brushed back the dark blond hair she wore tied up for work but which fell in perfect waves to her shoulder blades tonight.

"Oh. Sorry. I had the place right. I was just dragging in getting out of work." Delia tried to ignore the strange temptation to pat her own hair into place. What was that about? She knew perfectly well that her bun was still right where it always was. Well, except for that one section that had refused to stay put all day.

Anyway, since when did she worry about her appearance around these people? That made about as much sense as her showing up there tonight to take part in an activity that she usually avoided just to make an odd day seem normal.

"Still dragging, aren't you?" Trooper Warner noted.

"Oh. Right." Well, she couldn't keep standing there by the door, so taking a deep breath, she forced herself forward toward their table, casually taking attendance as she went. They were all dressed in street clothes—Leonetti, Roberts, Campbell, Warner and Maxwell. A few others, too. Even the two most recent additions at the Brighton Post, Trevor Cole and Jamie Donovan, had put in appearances. Cole was a casualty of the Manistique Post closure in the Upper Peninsula, and Donovan was so new that the ink hadn't dried on his recruit school certificate.

Only Lieutenant Peterson was noticeably absent.

Delia let out a breath she hadn't realized she was holding. Of course she would be on the lookout for him. She'd avoided him throughout the rest of her shift, delaying the awkward moment when she would have to face him again after her embarrassing comments. But now she had this disturbing, heavy sensation she refused to define as anything other than relief.

Only three empty chairs remained at the far end of the table, so she took the one in the center, which gave her a buffer on either side. She was making an appearance as the lieutenant had suggested without the extra effort of actually holding up her end of a conversation. A win-win situation as far as she was concerned. No one seemed to pay attention to where she sat, anyway, so she opened her menu and started reading.

"Hurry up and figure out what you want," Trooper Warner said. "We waited to order, and we're wasting away from starvation down here."

"That'll take a while for you, Shane."

Delia's breath caught, forcing her to cough into her sleeve to cover it. She didn't need to look over her shoulder to confirm who'd spoken from somewhere behind her. The shiver feathering up her spine did a fine job of that all by itself. But she couldn't resist turning to the door any more than she could stop the unfortunate dance in her tummy when she did.

Now *that* she couldn't explain at all.

She'd seen Lieutenant Peterson out of uniform before as they all changed after their shifts, but he looked different tonight. As if it wasn't dramatic enough that he'd skipped wearing his glasses, he was also dressed like a fashion model. He'd paired dark jeans with a gray cable sweater, and his black wool coat hung open. Strange how his shoulders and chest looked broader than she remembered. That could have been the sweater. He looked taller, too, though it didn't take much to tower over her, especially when she was seated.

He would hate to hear it, but without his glasses and with his dimples flashing, his eyes crinkling at the corners, he looked even younger than normal. *Boyishly handsome.* The descriptor that popped into her head with no permission whatsoever had her turning back to her menu with a jerk.

Trooper Warner pushed his burly self away from the table, stood and crossed to the door to shake Lieutenant Peterson's hand.

"If you were trying to offend me, you failed." He did a biceps flex. "I take that as a compliment."

"Whatever gets you through the day, man." Lieutenant Peterson patted the trooper's shoulder, his eyes alight with mischief.

The lieutenant seemed as different outside of work as he looked. Not as formal. Or serious. But then everyone was more relaxed when they were here together. Well, everyone except for her.

"Glad you made it, Ben," Lieutenant Campbell called from the other end of the table.

"Guess we should feel privileged that you squeezed us in with all of your public appearances," Sergeant Leonetti chimed as he waved him over.

So much for this new, relaxed Lieutenant Peterson. He stopped at the end of the table, his posture suddenly stiff.

"Can we *not* make this a repeat of this afternoon?" He covered his face with his hands, staring at them through his splayed fingers. "If my head gets any larger, I won't be able to fit into my shoe box. Er... I mean office."

Lieutenant Campbell shook his head. "Or if you don't stop, he'll shoot out of here faster than an IndyCar at Belle Isle."

The two men exchanged a meaningful look, and Lieutenant Peterson shrugged. As if by unspoken agreement, the others returned to their own conversations. Delia might have done the same if she'd been speaking to someone or if the lieutenant hadn't started walking again. Right toward her.

The idea of having an empty seat on either side had seemed clever at the time. Now…not so much. He was left with no choice but to sit next to her. And if her stomach had been unsettled before, it now moved on to a gymnastics routine.

What was the matter with her? Their earlier conversation was no excuse. Her nerves were on full alert, and this wasn't even a crisis situation. She was vacuous, all right. What would she do next, bat her eyelashes at him?

He stopped behind the seat to her left and shrugged out of his coat, hanging it over the back of the chair. The sporty, masculine scent of his cologne drifted in her direction. She had this ridiculous temptation to close her eyes and breathe it in until her lungs ached when she should have been holding her breath. She didn't care about things like cologne, whether it smelled incredible or not. She didn't even *own* a bottle of perfume.

Without looking her way, he opened his menu.

She cleared her throat. "Lieutenant Peterson."

"Delia."

He caught her sidelong glance and smiled. "We don't have to be so formal off the clock."

"I know."

Not that she would ever be comfortable addressing any of them informally. Skipping titles was like ignoring the chain of command. Something she never did. Yet now she found herself rolling *his* first name around on her tongue. *Ben.* Because it tasted a little too nice, she again returned to her menu, deciding between a ham-and-Swiss panini and a Caesar salad.

"Glad you decided to come."

She blinked. Of course, she'd said she planned to come, but he'd been right to doubt she was serious. She searched madly for a safe topic and then blurted the first thing that came to mind.

"I've never seen you in contacts before." That wasn't what she was going for. She'd just admitted to watching him when he *wasn't* wearing them.

"Yeah, I just wear them when I want to look about eleven."

"Are you kidding? You look every bit of thirteen." Why couldn't she stop herself? Now he knew she'd noticed his baby face. And maybe even that she liked it.

At the brush of his arm against hers, Delia startled and whacked her other elbow against the side of the table. She crossed her arms, as much to brush away uncomfortable tingles as to rub her smarting joint, and give her nervous hand something to do.

"Sorry."

"No big deal."

He leaned in close and spoke again in a low voice. "Just promise you won't compliment me again."

She tried not to shiver as his warm breath tickled her ear and neck. She forgot about the pain in her arm altogether. "Oh, I promise," she choked out.

If only she hadn't opened her big mouth earlier today, then maybe she wouldn't be on sensory overload now. She wanted to believe that, but she had the uncomfortable feeling that even if she'd shut down her primary senses, she would still be every bit as unsettled by his nearness.

"Good. Of anybody, I knew I could count on you to keep this in perspective."

Of anybody? His words ripped her right out of her off-limits daydream, leaving a path of irritation in the gaping tear. Was he praising her or slamming her? Did he know that she'd been watching him to see how he would handle his moment in the spotlight? She expected him to look back to her with a knowing expression, but instead he turned to the waitress and ordered a bacon cheeseburger.

Without saying more, he leaned in to listen to a conversation farther down the table. Apparently, this was just like any other day for him. She was the only one who'd worried that there had been a shift in their professional relationship. Had she overreacted? She might as well have called in the bomb squad for a one-block power outage. With a frown, she turned to the waitress and ordered the salad.

Ben, whom she'd suddenly started thinking of as *Ben*, was oblivious to her discomfort as he spoke to the other lieutenant across the table.

"What did you think about that Red Wings game last night? Killed the Avalanche, didn't they?"

Lieutenant Campbell shook his head, chuckling. "A man with five kids? When would I have time to watch pro hockey?"

Delia rolled her eyes. Not that she cared, but male officers often used sports talk to exclude women from their conversations. Just another reminder that it was a mistake to think of any man, Lieutenant Peterson included, as different from the others. Using sports to shut *her* out only proved what little he knew about her. It would serve him right if she spouted sports statistics until his eyes crossed.

"Don't let him kid you," Sergeant Leonetti piped in. "His whole gang was watching that game. And doing the wave on their couch."

"Who do you think started the wave?" Lieutenant Campbell said.

She was dying to talk about last night's over-time goal or how much the team had suffered since their star player's retirement, but she held back. Then Ben gestured toward her.

"Delia, you're a Wings fan, aren't you?"

His words startled her as much as his touch had earlier. Maybe more. "How did you—"

"Just a guess."

But he reached down to the purse at her feet, her car keys resting on top. When he lifted his hand, her winged-wheel key chain, the symbol for Detroit's professional hockey team, dangled from his fingers.

"I'm a cop. They pay me to notice details."

He jiggled the keys until she reached for them, and then he lowered them into her hand, accidentally brushing her fingers.

"Well, you blew that case wide-open." She ignored another round of tingles as she stored away the keys.

Ben had made a point of including her in the conversation. It shouldn't have surprised her, given that he'd been suggesting ways for her to become more involved with the team for the past few months, but it did.

"He's on a roll this week, then," Sergeant Leonetti piped. "First the bank and now this."

Ben pointed at the team's comedian. "Come on. No more."

His warning only started the ball rolling, though, and soon hero jokes were shooting from both ends of the table. He accepted several jabs with good humor before putting up his hands.

"Enough already. I thought we were talking about hockey."

"Were we?" Trooper Warner lifted a brow, but as if he realized they'd pushed the lieutenant far enough, he turned to Delia instead.

"Fair-weather or die-hard?"

"Excuse me?"

"Fan. Which kind are you?"

She shrugged, her gaze shifting among the others, who were suddenly focused on her. Was this how Ben had felt that afternoon after the big announcement, like a bug under a microscope, smothering between the slide's glass panes?

"Die-hard, I guess. I mean, the Tigers and Lions are great, too, but there's nothing like the Wings during playoffs."

"You've got that right," Ben agreed.

The waitress and a second waiter appeared then, carrying trays laden with food. Delia was relieved to be forgotten as everyone got down to the business of distributing and inhaling their late-night meals.

Even as she took tiny bites of her salad, Delia couldn't help but to steal glances at the man beside her. Because she wasn't even sure that she needed his help to fit in with the team—or if being enmeshed in a team was critical to her job—she found her rush of gratitude toward him unnerving. But she did find his actions awfully sweet. He'd gone out of his way to invite her tonight and then to include her in the conversation. She couldn't remember anyone who'd done something just for her. Was it only for her sake? Or was he just paying her back for the things she'd said earlier? Maybe he wanted to even the score. Or have her *owe* him.

Delia shifted in her seat, pulling her elbows tightly against her sides, her closed hands pressed against her hips below the table. He might have done something nice, but that didn't mean she owed him.

She would never owe any man. Anything. Ever.

She drew in a ragged breath and let it out slowly. Now she was really being paranoid. If Ben did have an ulterior motive for directing attention to her, it was probably just to deflect some of it away from him. And who would blame him for that after the day he had just spent?

If only she didn't always have to question people's motives. Didn't have to suspect that there was an evil grin lurking behind every smiling face. But she couldn't help it. Some hard-learned lessons couldn't be forgotten no matter how much she wished she could whitewash the gate guarding her memories.

She risked one more peek at him. One too many. He was looking back at her, watching so closely that he could have described each of her pores. Only this didn't feel like an examination. More of a caress, really. One that smoothed from her temples to her baby toes. And from the heat building in her private places, that touch hadn't missed any tourist stop along the way, either.

Hell, even her arches tingled.

Then it was over. Well, on his end, anyway. He turned away as if nothing had happened. She, on the other hand, was too shocked to do anything but hold herself perfectly still, as her frayed nerve endings still snapped with sparks. Obviously she was out of practice at reading signals from men, not that she'd been all that good at it when she was *in* practice. But her reaction now was not just inappropriate, it was downright indecent.

You know you wanted it.

She swallowed, ice water dousing the heat that had radiated along her skin. Those words and their speaker shouldn't still have been able to reach out from the past to club her, but they could and had. The few bites she'd managed to swallow turned to acid in her stomach. Swirling. Clenching. She couldn't go back there. If she allowed herself to slip down those shadowy halls and become lost in that maze of lies and blame, she might never find her way back.

"You okay, Delia?"

It took her a few seconds to decipher the concern creasing his brows. What had he seen? Had she given herself away? "Oh. Just a headache." She rubbed her temples with her thumbs for effect. If only it were that easy to rub away those thoughts.

He indicated farther down the table with a tilt of his head. "Let Kelly know if you need something for it. She carries a whole pharmacy in that big bag of hers."

"Hey, I resent that." Trooper Roberts showed off a large lime-green purse without a bit of shame and then stowed it under the table.

Delia pushed around a piece of chicken on her salad. There was no way she'd be able to eat another bite. She wanted to believe that the past could no longer break her, but it was sure giving it the old college try.

At least Ben didn't try to start another conversation because she couldn't look him in the eye now. If she dared, she might do something unforgivable like melt into a puddle on the floor. Or, worse, tell him about her past. She squashed that thought immediately. That it had even crossed her mind was unacceptable. She would never again tell anyone. She'd shared her story once, and look where that had gotten her.

What was going on with her, anyway? For someone who prided herself on having an absolute immunity to men, she needed a booster shot where Ben Peterson was concerned. No, make that *Lieutenant* Peterson. Impersonal. Distant. The way it was supposed to be. Until she built up some resistance to this particular strain of male, she needed to avoid the exposure zone.

CHAPTER THREE

BEN STOMPED UP the front steps to the 1930s farm-house his friends had deemed "the project." To him it was just home. He grimaced as a loose floorboard creaked when he reached the wrap-around porch. Something else to fix. Just like the mess he'd made at the Driftwood. As if things between him and a certain trooper hadn't been awkward enough today, he'd just made them a whole lot worse.

His freezing hands fumbled with the keys, and they dropped to the snow-dusted wood with a *thunk*. It just figured he would have forgotten to leave the outside light on tonight. Why did he continually forget when he knew how dark it was out in the country? Grumbling, he crouched near the door and patted around him until his fingers closed over the keys. After several of his misdirected jabs, he finally slipped the key into the lock.

He pushed the door open, welcoming the rush of heat that struck his face even before he could reach inside to switch on the light. With the corncob-quality insulation in these walls, this would be the only time he felt warmth in this place all night. He kicked the door shut harder than he'd planned to and then braced for the sound of breaking glass. The near complete silence that only those who live outside of city limits ever experience filled the space instead.

As he rounded the corner into the formal living room, a collection of faces stared back at him, their photo frames askew but still clinging to the wall. Enlarged color snapshots featured a silver-headed couple with a boy at various ages, but most of the images were in black and white. A portrait of the great-grandparents he'd only known from their stories took the center spot in the display. They weren't smiling, either.

"Your week must have been as bad as mine."

As Ben hung his coat on the antique coat tree and zipped on the sweatshirt he always wore inside the house, his gaze followed the lines of the Victorian furniture that had been there for as long as he could remember. There probably wasn't a single piece that had anything more than sentimental value, but they all had plenty of that to spare. Except for the goldfish bowl on the bookshelf, nothing in this room had changed in thirty years.

On his way through the house, Ben smoothed his hand along the dark wooden doorway molding. Admiring some of the woodwork he'd restored himself usually calmed him after a stressful shift, but there was nothing usual about this week. He braced himself for another onslaught of images he would never forget, shouts ringing again in his ears, the pungent scent of his own fear still fresh in his nostrils. He'd hated the stink of it, even then.

He shivered, telling himself it was only from the cold. He could lie to himself if he wanted to. The house felt chillier tonight, anyway. Bigger. And emptier. The hollow echoes of his own footsteps chased him on the creaky floors as he continued into the kitchen. As he'd done so many nights before, he washed vegetables, diced chicken and sprinkled spices. Only after the chicken in the wok had turned white and the pea pods and water chestnuts were sizzling in the sesame oil did he remember that he'd already eaten.

Slamming a plastic container on the countertop, he poured the meal inside it to refrigerate for later. He should have known better than to show up at the Driftwood tonight after his crazy day at work. And not just because of the pep session, either. If he'd known that Delia would be there, he would have headed straight home. Technically, she'd warned him that she planned to show up, but he'd had no reason to believe her. He could count on one hand the number of times she'd joined them at either of the haunts where the officers gathered after their shifts, so he couldn't account for her presence any more than he could explain the spike of his pulse when he'd seen her there.

Even now, he wasn't sure how he'd made it across the restaurant to sit next to her without falling over his feet like in a B-rated comedy flick with a D-list cast. Worse yet, that clumsy approach had been the most acceptable thing he'd done all night. He'd whispered close to her ear so he could sneak a whiff of her lavender shampoo, and he'd made up so many excuses to *accidentally* brush her arm that it must have looked like an elbow fight. He probably would have copped a feel right over her oh-so-proper black turtleneck if he could have gotten away with it. He'd sure helped her out of that sweater with his eyes.

Suddenly thirsty, he threw on the faucet and poured himself a glass of water. With his eyes squeezed shut, he took several gulps. What had happened to him? He used to be a professional. He knew the rules, and until now, he'd followed them. So how had he gone from finding ways to bring one of the troopers more fully into the post team to wanting to frisk her in all the best ways right there on the table?

It didn't make any sense. He'd passed by Delia Morgan every day for months, wearing the same uniform, finishing up reports at the same desktop computer, and he'd never once suffered from a case of dry mouth. Until today. He couldn't recall a single case of sweaty palms over her nearness, either. Until... But that was the thing. Something had tripped a switch in him today, and no matter how hard he tried to click it off again, she kept showing up in his thoughts, accentuated by nothing less than ideal lighting.

He took another drink and then held the cool glass to his cheek. Unfortunately, his face wasn't the only thing that felt too warm over just the thought of her and that sweater.

This situation had disaster written all over it. He couldn't be attracted to a trooper, even if he wasn't her direct supervisor. He didn't *do* interoffice romances. He wished he could make the excuse that it had been too long since he'd dated, but that disastrous blind date from last weekend probably still counted. As for "afternoon delights" as Vinnie would have called them, though, it had been a long, dry year in the whole delights department, afternoon or otherwise.

"Get your head on straight, Peterson," he grumbled.

Polaski definitely would tell him that if he saw him now and probably with more colorful vocabulary. Whether or not Ben had sought out attention when he'd entered the bank yesterday, he'd become an object of curiosity. A *hero* in some people's minds, even if he would never see himself as one. Well, he'd better start behaving like one. A hero would always be his best, most professional self, not someone who only thought about his own needs as his father had. A hero wouldn't allow himself to see a coworker as anything more than a brother or sister in blue. He would work solely for the good of the public and the post.

Yes, he still wanted to help Delia Morgan better assimilate into the post family. It was the right thing to do for the team, after all. But if he couldn't put his plan into action without crossing that firm line, then he needed to back away for his own good…and hers.

THE EIGHT PCs positioned around the squad room were deserted, except for the one where Delia sat typing information into the blanks of an electronic arrest report form. She would have been just coming off patrol herself soon if not for a routine traffic stop earlier that ended in an arrest. That stop had changed when her Law Enforcement Information Network database search had shown an outstanding arrest warrant.

Sensing that she was no longer alone, she lifted her head and glanced over her shoulder. Not hoping it would be anyone in particular. Just curious.

Sure enough, Lieutenant Peterson leaned casually against the door frame. His pose and the way he startled, as if he'd been caught doing something he shouldn't have been, had to be the reasons for the tickle that skittered up the back of her neck.

She cleared her throat. "May I help you?"

He smiled then, and Delia's tummy did an unfortunate jig the way it had so many times around him lately. She tightened her jaw and crossed her arms over her stomach to still those dancing feet. Why couldn't she just get past these inappropriate reactions to him?

Sure, Ben Peterson had never been invisible to her. Far from it, no matter how hard she'd tried *not* to see him. But everything was magnified since his shining moment last week.

Since she'd noticed him staring back.

She'd probably imagined that, too, so it was downright annoying that the sparks she felt around him continued to crackle and pop.

"I just wanted to get a good look at the trooper who arrested Mary Poppins in there." Ben pointed with his thumb toward the door to the cinder-block holding cell where Delia's suspect sat awaiting transfer to Livingston County Jail.

Frowning, she spun her office chair to fully face him. "I would expect that a lieutenant would take an arrest seriously. Any arrest."

"Seriously? Even this one?"

As much as she wanted to hold on to her stern expression—this was their job after all—she didn't stand a chance when facing off with Ben's silly smirk. He had a point. It was pretty funny. "Why are you so interested in *this* arrest, anyway? Are you a closeted Poppins fan?"

"So what if I am?" He pursed his lips. "Er… was."

She finally gave in and grinned over his joke about him giving away his secret. "'Practically perfect' and all of that?"

He grinned again. "You know it."

It was amazing how easily she bantered with Ben now, but she shouldn't have been surprised. As often as he'd struck up conversations with her during her shifts in the past week, how could she not have become more comfortable around him? She shouldn't make too much out of it, though. Ben was friendly with everyone at the post, from the commander to the lady at the front desk. But he'd focused on Delia lately, seeming determined to roll past that awkwardness between them and to really become her friend.

Strange how she wanted to give in on both things. Having someone to talk to at work certainly hadn't been all bad. She'd found herself looking forward to the moments he would stop by, curious what interesting thing he would say next. Even if he'd probably only made the effort to further his plan for making her *team-worthy*. Of course he had an agenda. Everyone did. People didn't do things without a motivation of some sort. Even Ben. She should know better than to believe he was doing it just to be nice.

He stepped closer to her desk and glanced at the report over her shoulder. "This has to be a good story. Tell me how you broke this case."

Immediately, she stiffened again, a reflex when anyone moved too close to her, but she forced a smile and continued typing. Maybe he hadn't noticed.

"Okay, I'll admit I didn't expect to find anything on LEIN when I pulled over a white-haired lady for driving thirty-two in a seventy."

Whether he shifted to the next PC to ensure that the machine was working or to signal that he'd noticed her discomfort, Delia couldn't tell.

"Usually a good bet," he said finally.

Delia swallowed, sliding a glance his way. Though he could have been answering either her comment about senior suspects or the thoughts she'd kept to herself, she chose the safety of the earlier topic. "But then doesn't that make me guilty of profiling? Or *un*-profiling?"

"Probably just of being human. No one wants to think of anyone's grandma as a suspect."

"Don't let me off the hook so easily."

He pointed to the closed door. "Come on,

Delia. That woman in there is proof that looks can be deceiving. She looks more like an escapee from a library convention than a suspect with an outstanding warrant for failure to appear on an impressive list of check-fraud charges."

"Maybe it was just a clever disguise."

After another look at the holding cell, he shook his head. "No. I bet she always looks like that. Sensible shoes and all."

"Then clever career choice?"

He gestured toward the arrest report on her screen. "If that isn't a pink slip for that particular job, I don't know what is."

"No unemployment line for that one, either."

"After an arrest like that, taking down a wanted fugitive and all, you'll be the next one to make the local news." He paused, chuckling. "Viewers will be relieved to see your pretty face after having to look at mine for so long."

Pretty face? A startled laugh escaped before she could stop it. Was Ben Peterson flirting with her? Would she like it if he were? Of course he wasn't, and no, she wouldn't. He was only joking with her the way all of the officers did with each other, and she was making too much out of it. Again.

"In my interview, I'll give credit to the team like—" Delia stopped herself, glancing over at him. She hoped he didn't think she was making fun of him over the banking incident. She cleared her throat. "Anyway, nobody makes the news for bringing down Mary Poppins. Or maybe Mrs. Doubtfire, who—"

"Wasn't who she seemed to be," they both said at the same time and then laughed.

"A senior-citizen fugitive or big bad bank-robbery suspects." She held out both hands, palms up, weighing the two options in an imaginary scale. "Those two arrests don't compare on the if-it-bleeds-it-leads scale for TV news."

He tilted his head back and forth, considering her words. "Guess not, but they should."

"Thanks."

"Anyway, there was no blood in either of those arrests," he pointed out.

"Which is a good thing."

Ben shifted from foot to foot, clearly uncomfortable with the turn in their conversation. He hadn't spoken about the incident at the bank at all other than the details he'd listed in the report. Was there more about the case that he hadn't disclosed? Something critical that he'd left out of the report?

But he spoke up again before she had time to ask. "We were both just doing our jobs."

She had returned to her own report, but now she couldn't help but to look back at him, waiting for answers.

"Some cases get more attention than others—" he paused, shrugging "—but all of our work is important as we serve and protect the people of southeast Michigan."

The words were out of her mouth before she had time to edit them. "I was wrong about you."

His eyes widened behind his glasses. "You mean you no longer think I'll forget about the team now that I've made the six o'clock news?"

Delia was just standing up from the chair, but his comment caused her to pop up so quickly that her holstered weapon bumped the desk. "What do you mean? I never said—"

He shook his head. "Forget I said that. I meant to ask *how* you were wrong about me."

Because she didn't want to confess that he'd already hit on the exact answer like a nail driven home by one perfect strike, she scrambled for another reason. "I was wrong to think you'd tried to avoid speaking to the media because public relations wasn't your forte."

"Oh. Then you were right the first time."

He tipped his head to the side, his chuckle low and sexier than it had any right to be, especially right there in the squad room where just anyone could hear it. Delia refused to think about other locations where a sound like that would be perfect. Places with low lighting and soft music—

"Nope," she said to the both of them. She shook

her head as much to clear it as to disagree with him. "Not buying it. Just listen to you. You're a walking, talking public-service announcement. 'Serve and protect the people of southeast Michigan'? In front of a camera, you could convince residents that they *want* us to give them speeding tickets."

"Thanks, I guess. But let's hope I don't have to prove it now that the media attention has died down."

Delia needed to finish the report before her suspect was transported to jail, but she was stalling. She had a job to do, and she could only stand there searching for something clever to say that might keep him there longer.

"You're a good cop, Trooper Morgan."

She swallowed. Those were the words she'd worked so hard to hear. Words that meant everything to her. She sneaked a calming breath, exhaling in slow puffs. Maybe she should have expected that he might be the first to say those words to her, but she couldn't have guessed how much they would humble her.

"Thanks. Um, you, too, uh…Lieutenant." Strange how she was tempted to call him Ben, even here where it would be frowned upon. The way she would talk to a friend.

The side of his mouth lifted. "I wasn't fishing for compliments, but if you're handing them out, I'll be happy to take a few big ones, please."

"I'm serious. Really."

And she was serious, even if he was determined to deflect the praise. Stranger still, she was suddenly tempted to say more. Thoughts she should keep to herself. Like that he was a *real* hero. And how incredibly rare people like him were. Maybe even how lucky she was that someone like him wanted to be her friend.

But someone threw open the door to the parking lot then, a strong-arm invasion of winter gusting inside. Kelly Roberts and Grant Maxwell hurried into the squad room, still laughing over some earlier joke while they brushed snowflakes off their covers and uniforms.

Delia straightened, gripping the edge of the desk. She appreciated the jolt from the frigid air almost as much as she did the interruption. At least both gave her a chance to rethink what she'd been about to say.

Things she'd had no business saying. She was grateful for the growing collection of witnesses and the comforting hum of conversations other than the tape repeating inside of her head. The one that demanded to know why she was tempted to let down her guard with Ben Peterson. But most of all, she was grateful for all of these things that saved her from saying words she couldn't take back.

CHAPTER FOUR

"Perfect timing."

Delia turned toward the voice to find Jamie Donovan next to her as they sloshed toward the post building. Nearly soaked after just stepping out of their patrol cars, they didn't bother sprinting for the door.

Jamie shook his head, spraying more droplets in Delia's direction. "What's with the downpour in January? Isn't this supposed to be snow? In the Upper Peninsula where I grew up, this would be snow."

"You're not in Kansas anymore, are you, Toto? Here sometimes it's snow, and sometimes it's rain."

"This is so not Oz," he grumbled.

She had to agree with that. "It's going to be a nightmare tonight. When all of that freezes…" She shook her head, imagining the work ahead for the midnight-shift troopers. That shift was the only one where troopers were partnered for patrols, and they would definitely need their partners tonight. "Let's just hope drivers slow down."

"That's not gonna happen."

"Well, maybe nonfatality accidents, then."

He nodded. "Let's hope."

Delia smiled as she pulled open the door, waved Trooper Donovan in and entered behind him. She'd had an actual conversation with one of her fellow troopers, if weather and traffic counted as valid topics. Would Ben be impressed that she'd tried anyway? Not that she worried about what he thought or agreed that all of this "connecting" was necessary, but still. Who knew? Maybe there was something to his team theory. If it helped her make the right impression at this post, playing along with his idea wouldn't be all bad.

"Nothing like driving through a monsoon—"

Jamie's words cut off, and he stopped so quickly that Delia bumped into him. When he didn't move, she stepped around him as she shed her soggy jacket. That several troopers were spaced around the room, coats still in their arms, wasn't all that surprising given that they were all coming off their shifts. Only the superior officers, Ben included, were there with them, but out of place, lined up along the back wall instead of at the front of the room where they usually presented updates at the *beginning* of their shifts.

All of them were preoccupied with the tiny flat-screen mounted high in the corner. Even Gail

Jacobs, who never hurried anywhere, rushed into the squad room, took a spot along the wall and stared up at the television. Without saying more, Jamie crossed the room and took a place near the a few troopers on the opposite wall.

Delia slipped into an empty spot in the back and brushed some of the water from her bun. Her stomach was tight, as if it knew something she didn't. Just down from her, Ben frowned, looking as confused as she felt. The ten o'clock news from one of the Detroit stations filled the TV screen, a graphic of a state police shield and a photo of the Brighton Post building flashing behind the news desk.

Ben groaned. "It can't be that slow of a news week."

Whatever the cheery newscaster was reporting must have been a teaser because the station went to commercial, leaving them staring at an ad for basketball shoes.

"I thought we were finished with this," Ben said in a low voice. "Don't they have anything else to report on? A road-rage incident maybe?"

A few murmurs and shifting of feet prevented the room from being silent, but Gail remained eerily quiet, which was no more like her than hurrying was. She stared at the screen as if willing the newscast to return from the commercial break.

Delia rubbed at the gooseflesh beneath her uniform sleeves. Her throat felt dry. Something definitely wasn't right. She didn't know what was going on, but this wasn't another follow-up on the bank-robbery story. The guarded expression on Lieutenant Campbell's face confirmed her suspicion that this report would offer no good news.

Ben glanced from one officer to the next, his hands pressed to his sides. "Would one of you tell me what this is all about?"

Lieutenant Campbell's gaze flitted to the screen and then back to him. "We're not really sure yet, but—" As the newscast flashed on again, he stopped and gestured toward the screen.

"In a *News 3* exclusive," the newscaster began, "two Detroit attorneys have filed a class-action lawsuit in response to the Department of Human Services's use of what has been called the 'rocket docket' to determine…"

Ben frowned at the TV and turned to Sergeant Leonetti. "You know anything?"

The funny man wasn't even grinning this time. "Sorry, man. I don't."

A loud click came from the steel door behind them, and Trevor Cole rushed inside with Kelly Roberts close behind him hurrying to get out of the rain. Both paused inside the door to shake off their coats. Trevor glanced from the officers to the television.

"Another meeting of the Ben Peterson fan club? Who interviewed him now?"

"You'd think he'd get better at giving interviews after so many, but he looks miserable every time," Trooper Roberts said as she slid out of her coat.

At the almost imperceptible shake of Lieutenant Campbell's head, the two troopers stopped talking. What did some of them know that they weren't sharing? Instead of paying attention to the conversations that were shrinking to curious whispers, Captain Polaski stared at the television, his posture so straight that he appeared cemented in place.

"Up next is our report coming out of Brighton," the reporter said to segue to the next news story. "From the same post where just last week we reported on an incident of bravery and heroism comes disappointing news. What can you tell us about this, Laura?"

A field reporter, next to the big blue "State Police Brighton Post No. 12" sign, appeared on a split screen.

"Yes, Kimberly, I'm here at the Brighton Post, where an investigation is underway in evidence tampering and larceny regarding drugs confiscated during a series of arrests." She paused, her expression becoming somber. "Sadly, a person of interest in the case appears to be the same officer recognized last week for bravery in a thwarted bank robbery. Will this be the downfall of a hero? We'll let you know as *News 3* investigates."

If the others hadn't been hauled into an uncomfortable silence, Ben's gasp might not have sounded so loud. But in that vacuum, the sound pierced the quiet like the click of the magazine in a .40-caliber Glock.

"A person close to the investigation tells us that Lieutenant Ben Peterson..."

Delia barely heard anything the woman said after that as the reporter cited convenient, unnamed sources. She couldn't pull her gaze from Ben, who stared, wide-eyed, at the screen, his arms stiff at his sides.

The urge to run to the TV, smack its power button and shout to anyone who would listen that the newspeople were wrong was overwhelming. And yet her feet must have been buried in ice. The other troopers appeared frozen, as well.

Delia shook her head to get out of the deep freeze. The suspicion surrounding the lieutenant was incomprehensible, but her reaction to it made even less sense. Without her knowing the details of the investigation, or having any proof, her gut reaction was to eliminate him from the suspect list. How could she even call herself a cop? How did she know he wasn't guilty? What did she even know about him really? Nothing.

The scene shifted on the screen, and Captain Polaski stood next to the reporter in a taped segment.

"Captain Polaski, what can you tell us about the investigation and the independent state investigator appointed to oversee it?"

The commander cleared his throat. "Sorry. I am unable to comment on an active investigation. I can only say that the Brighton Post will cooperate fully with the state investigator."

"Can you confirm or deny the tip we received that Lieutenant Peterson is a person of interest in this case?"

"Again, I can have no further comment on an active investigation."

The reporter only smiled. "Captain, then can you confirm if Lieutenant Peterson is the same Ben Peterson, son of Leonard J. Peterson, a—"

"That matter doesn't pertain to this—"

But she continued as if he hadn't tried to interrupt her. "—a career criminal, who died in prison after a vehicular homicide conviction involving the death of his own wife."

Delia stiffened. Had she heard that correctly? Ben's dad was responsible for the death of Ben's mother? She was right. She didn't know Ben at all. She hadn't even been aware that she wasn't the only one with ugly secrets. Unfortunately for Ben, his secrets had just been aired for the entertainment of the entire Detroit metro viewing area.

From some faraway place, Polaski repeated the standard response that he couldn't comment, but silence in the room swallowed the sound. It didn't matter that the captain cut off the interview right then. The titillating details were already out there, just as the newswoman had planned.

Sergeant Leonetti grabbed the remote and hit the power button, sending the screen back into darkness. The other officers seemed to hold a collective breath, waiting for Ben to respond. Seconds ticked by in the rhythm of Delia's pulse that pounded in her ears. Finally, Ben turned to the commander.

Polaski held his hands wide. "Sorry, Lieutenant."

Ben only shook his head. "I don't know where all that's coming from."

Although some of the others looked as shell-shocked by the news as Delia was, Lieutenant Campbell stalked angrily toward Ben. When he reached him, he squeezed his shoulder.

"This is shit, Ben. You know we'll get it cleared up."

"We're behind you," Sergeant Leonetti added.

"Sorry, man." Trooper Cole paused, clearing his throat, "And, uh, sorry to hear about…the other stuff."

The others didn't speak up, pretending not to

be watching Ben. Gail swiped a sneaky tear from the corner of her eye.

"Thanks, guys," Ben said after a long pause.

The hitch in his voice sliced through Delia. She had this irrational, unprofessional urge to gather him in her arms and tell him everything would be okay. What was wrong with her? She not only didn't know if he was guilty, but she also had no idea whether anything would be *okay* for him again. She needed to take hold of her emotions before she did or said something stupid.

Polaski looked at Ben and gestured toward the hall. "Guess we'd better talk about this in my office."

"Yes, sir."

The lieutenant's lack of emotion bothered Delia as much as the break in his voice had. Why wasn't he more upset over what had just happened? Or furious at the reporter for sensationalizing his family's dirty laundry?

Ben hadn't looked at her once since the news report had aired, but as he followed his superior officer from the room, he glanced her way. Gone was the laughter that had always danced in his eyes. His gaze was raw now, his glasses only magnifying the bleakness. She'd seen that dazed look in the eyes of accident victims before. Was Ben a victim or just someone shocked that he'd been caught?

Her lips opened as she searched for words of comfort, but none came. His gaze narrowed, and then he lifted his chin, continuing into the commander's office. The door closed with a final-sounding click.

The others slipped from the room as if driven to the protective havens of their offices or locker rooms. Delia couldn't bring herself to go with them. Other officers who were just coming on duty emerged from the locker room, the questions on their faces left unanswered.

Delia took a seat at one of the desktops and opened a report she had to complete before she went home. She didn't want to leave yet. Not without knowing what had happened to Ben. Muffled masculine voices came from the distant office, but she couldn't make out the words. Though it was none of her business, she couldn't help herself. She had to know.

Part of her sensed that no matter what Ben was accused of, he was innocent. That it was all a mistake. In the end, he would be cleared, if he was even ever charged. But an unsettling feeling that formed deep inside her brought a truth along with it: she'd been wrong about people before.

CAPTAIN POLASKI'S OFFICE was smaller than Ben remembered as he settled into the visitor's seat, the closed door making it feel like a cell. Only this time he was on the inside. Ben brushed damp palms on his trousers, refusing to listen to the voice inside telling him he wouldn't wear this uniform for much longer. He couldn't think about that. But he couldn't stop the pain in his chest, unwelcome hands squeezing it from inside.

How was this happening? One minute everything was good at work—better than it should have been since he'd been manufacturing daily excuses to talk to Delia—and the next minute… *this*. He focused on the wall, covered by certificates and framed photos of recruit classes, but the images only washed together in a swirl of muted blue. Then the images shifted into a pile of twisted metal and shards of glass. The screams. Pain everywhere at once. So much blood. The relief, then the guilt, of realizing it wasn't his blood.

No. He blocked the backward journey of his thoughts. He forced himself to breathe. Even if none of what was happening tonight made sense to him, these were different news stories than those from his memories, about different crimes with a different suspect. Namely him.

He shifted at the sound of the door opening. Captain Polaski squeezed past him, shutting the door and settling into the seat behind the desk. Ben leaned forward, toward what he hoped would be answers, but his boss didn't fill in the blanks quickly enough.

"Do you know what they were talking about out there?" Ben gestured toward the squad room. "Because I don't."

"No," Polaski said, but his nod contradicted his words. "I would've guessed you didn't."

"Well…"

"I'd been hearing murmurs for a few weeks, but I didn't know any of the specifics until today."

Meaning either he hadn't been told who was being investigated, or he hadn't been given details of the allegations. Polaski knew all of those things now if that closed brown file he kept touching on his desk was any indication.

Ben stared at the file, willing it to open, until his boss's words filtered in. He looked up. "Wait. Weeks?"

"As I said, we didn't have the specifics."

Those words Ben accepted with a nod, no matter how frustrating they were. Of course Polaski couldn't share information about a possible investigation. He knew that. So why was Ben taking it so personally that he hadn't? His boss couldn't exactly tell him, *Yo, dude, keep your head low.*

"So what's it about? The reporter said something about evidence tampering and theft."

"That's right. You know how we've been making more drug arrests in Oakland and Livingston counties over the past few years?"

"Yeah. The numbers are up."

Polaski held his hands wide. "Well, strangely, our conviction rate has barely risen."

"How can that be?"

"That's what state officials wanted to know when they started looking at our arrest records."

Instead of asking more, Ben crossed his arms and waited for the captain to explain.

"They wanted to figure out how the drugs confiscated during traffic stops kept disappearing before trial," Polaski continued. "How dirtbags were getting off scot-free when the arrests were clean. What they found were several discrepancies involving our evidence room. Someone's been messing around with the evidence if not removing it altogether."

Someone like *him*? As he considered the likelihood of that, Ben started shaking his head. "What does all of this have to do with me?"

"Do you remember what a common denominator is from elementary-school math? Well, you're it. You signed off on the evidence chain in several of the cases in question. Investigators are still looking at the other cases, though."

"But my name could be found on hundreds of evidence chains." As soon as the words were out of Ben's mouth, the reality of them hit him squarely in the head. He'd been set up. How? Why? By whom? And again…why?

"I can't be the only officer who signed off on

those pieces of evidence." He wasn't even sure why he'd said that. Even if someone had set him up, how could he wish for one of his friends to be falsely accused just so he could avoid the headache of it? That was further proof that he was no hero, if anyone had ever been fool enough to consider him one in the first place.

"So far, you're the *only* common denominator."

This time Ben nodded. The last thing he needed to do was make this worse. "You do know I would never do anything to help drug dealers, don't you? Never."

"I know," Polaski said simply.

But did he know? Did any of them? Sure, they'd all spoken words of support, but were they all looking at him with the same suspicion they did a suspect in custody? Unlike in the court system where defendants were considered innocent until proven guilty, guilt was never ruled out until suspects were cleared.

"With my dad..." he began but let his words trail away. His family's story of addiction and tragedy was hardly news to those who'd been around the post for a while. Drugs had stolen too much from his life for him to ever see them in any way other than black-and-white.

"Yeah, I'm really sorry about that part." Polaski frowned. "I didn't pick up on where the reporter was headed with her questions quickly enough.

She was determined to get those juicy details out there no matter what I said."

"I know. It's okay."

"But the other…" He touched the file again. "You understand that we'll have to cooperate fully in this investigation, right?"

"Of course. I wouldn't expect any less."

"With as much scrutiny as police departments have been under lately, we can't afford to allow any suspicion that we're showing favoritism. We have to conduct this investigation completely by the book."

Something about the way Polaski said it made Ben shift in his seat. "You're not saying that you're putting me on a desk job, are you? Because, uh, I already have one of those."

Instead of picking up on his attempt to lighten the mood, the commander shook his head. "No. But I am going to have to put you on paid administrative leave."

"Leave?"

"I need you to stay away from the post while state investigators are digging around here."

"But, Captain, you can't do that." Ben's eyes widened just as his boss's narrowed. "I mean *if* you do this, I won't have any way to prove my innocence. Someone has set me up, and I need to figure out who. I won't have any access to LEIN or any of the databases to investigate."

"I don't want you anywhere near LEIN or any-thing else in this investigation." He shook his index finger at him, losing patience. "Stay out of it. Let the system work."

Ben nodded, his acceptance settling heavily inside of him. He'd said the same thing to suspects who'd claimed to be innocent. Only now could he truly understand their skepticism. The system didn't always work. Not for everyone. With the possibility of serious charges hanging over his head, could Ben afford to trust the system with his freedom?

"Yes, sir." He pushed forward in his seat, intending to stand.

"Relax, Peterson." Polaski stood first. "Think of it as a vacation. Do some things around that project house of yours."

"I'll try" was all he could manage.

"And we'll take care of the rest."

It was the commander's way of saying they would look for the truth, no matter what it was. He wouldn't promise any more than that, and Ben would never expect him to. A fierce commitment to justice was something the two of them shared.

"Thank you, sir."

Pulling open the door, he started down the hall. At least no one was still in the squad room as he made the walk of shame to the locker room and then to the parking lot. Even Delia was finally gone, which was probably good. He wasn't prepared to see her right now, especially not with accusation in her eyes.

He scanned the half-filled water bottles and coffee-shop cups spaced around the room, suggesting that the others had left in a hurry. As much as he appreciated his fellow officers giving him space, the empty room made him feel abandoned. He was so used to being able to count on his Brighton Post family. And now that he was in trouble and could use a little help from his friends, he no longer knew who his real friends were. He cared about these people, would lay down his life for them, but he couldn't escape the truth that one of them had targeted him.

Yesterday, he was surrounded by friends. Part of the only real family he'd had in years. Today he'd never felt more alone.

CHAPTER FIVE

"WHAT ARE *YOU* doing here?"

Delia tried not to bristle at the way he asked the question. She couldn't blame him for wondering, though. Not when she was asking herself the same question as Ben Peterson stared out at her through the narrow opening of his front door. Make that *frowned* out at her, squinting behind his glasses.

Okay, it was too early in the morning by ordinary standards for her to show up on anyone's doorstep, especially his. An address she wouldn't have known without snooping in personnel records. But it didn't seem too early to be there when she'd been up all night repeating the reasons she should steer clear of Ben. And the logical case for keeping her nose out of his current situation altogether. She'd lost the arguments around sunrise and hadn't been able to wait another minute to do something she would regret.

Ben clearly wasn't happy to see her. His hair stood at odd angles, at least to the degree possible with a cut so short. Blue flannel pajama bottoms showed beneath his navy bathrobe, and a pair of what had to be freezing bare feet peeked out from those. She definitely did *not* notice that he was bare-chested beneath that cinched bathrobe or wonder if that tiny tuft of chest hair at the opening was as soft as it looked. And she absolutely wasn't imagining how he would look if that belt magically untied and how it would feel to press herself against all of that skin.

Delia blinked. Despite the chill, her cheeks burned. She'd never had thoughts like that, and starting to have them now would be a worse idea than even coming here was. So she pushed the images away, refusing to acknowledge the warmth that had spread from her face to her neck and downward.

"Hello, Lieutenant," she managed and then dampened her suddenly dry lips. "I mean…uh… Ben."

He crossed his arms and rubbed one foot against the other, probably to fend off frostbite. She was shivering just standing on his porch with a full armor of winter gear.

"Well, are you going to answer my question?"

She gripped the rickety handrail tighter with her gloved hand and shifted forward, the wood creaking beneath her boot, her step smearing the pristine dusting of snow.

She didn't do things like this, either. She didn't

bend rules, let alone break them. For anyone. Yet these days she was breaking them like it was her job. Too bad the career that meant everything to her was what this sabbatical of her good sense could cost her. Forget hunting child predators, if this didn't go well, the only thing she would be tracking down was a good spot in the unemployment line. As if sticking her neck out wasn't foolish enough, she was doing it because of a *feeling* that Ben might be innocent. A vague notion that was in no way based on fact. Feelings and hunches didn't belong in a solid criminal case. Or in her life.

"I just wanted…" Delia let her words fall away because she didn't really know what she wanted or why she couldn't follow her own advice to stay away.

"Well, you shouldn't be here. Didn't Polaski tell you that?"

He studied her, his gaze so narrow his eyes had to hurt. Little red lines snaked out from his irises, and purple half-moons had settled beneath his lower lashes, suggesting that the game he'd played last night had involved too many bent-arm throws. His liquor-store-Dumpster cologne confirmed her suspicion. This was so unlike the man she'd thought she knew. But then the responsible man who'd nursed just one beer at the Driftwood was the same one who'd neglected to mention that his father was convicted in his mother's death. Could he also have failed to mention ties to a suburban Detroit drug ring?

"Oh, he told us. He was pretty clear."

"Then why would you—" Ben stopped and sighed. "Well, I guess this is going to take a while. You might as well come in. Can't afford to heat the outdoors."

Heating bills would be the least of his worries if he faced charges in the state probe, and they both knew it, but neither bothered saying so.

Just as Ben pulled the door wide, a gust of wind dumped a few dozen snowflakes on the wood flooring in the entry. Delia grimaced at Ben's automatic frown as she stepped into the place she never would have imagined him living. It appeared to have been decorated in *Early Floral Explosion*, from the dated wallpaper and the welcome mat to the wreaths and swags on the walls near the staircase.

Closing the door, Ben rubbed his hands together. He didn't bother offering to take her coat. Clearly, she wasn't staying. Delia pulled off her hat anyway, hating that she worried about the static in her hair. What did she care what he thought? She wasn't here to impress him.

"Well? I don't have all day."

"Another appointment with a bottle?" She immediately regretted stating the obvious. Still, if she found the word *hangover* in the dictionary, she would find a selfie of Ben in his present state next to it.

His jaw ticked, but he shook his head. "It was a rough night."

"I see that."

Instead of answering, he tromped away through a formal living room that was every bit as much of a flower garden as the entry. She had no choice but to keep standing on the doormat as chunks of snow dropped off her boots. She was starting to sweat, so she unbuttoned her coat, but left it on. She couldn't risk startling him and having him throw her out before she'd had her say.

He passed through a doorway into what was probably the kitchen and returned several seconds later, a drink in his hand.

She shook her head. "I don't need anything. Thanks."

"It's not for you."

He opened his other hand to reveal a pair of white pills, popping them in his mouth and chasing them down with his drink.

"Oh. Right." Her gaze caught on the inch of clear liquid in the glass. Could it have been…? He jiggled his hand so the liquid swished.

"Water. Want to smell it?"

"No. Thanks."

He grimaced. "Stop shouting, okay?"

Her lips lifted. "I wasn't."

Even so, he squeezed his eyes shut. When he opened them again, he pinched the bridge of his nose as if pressing against a monster headache.

"I don't know why I thought that would help last night. It's not a regular thing for me."

"I didn't figure."

He studied her as if trying to decide if he believed her. "I knew better."

The poor guy did look miserable. Delia could relate to that next-day pain and regret. She'd allowed social lubricants to help her make poor decisions a few times. Ben had been drinking alone, though. And she knew what it was like to feel truly alone. Without anyone in her court. She wouldn't wish that black hole of the spirit on anyone. But the temptation to reach out to Ben, offering comfort and a soft place to land, that was new and disconcerting. And wrong. Did she need a bigger sign that it was a mistake to come here?

She cleared her throat. "Cut yourself some slack," she managed to say. "It was a bad night."

"Why would you say that? You don't cut anyone slack."

"I guess not."

At first she was surprised that he'd noticed that detail about her, but it was hardly a secret. She'd never been comfortable with the grays in life or in the law. Not when black and white were purer neutrals, without the untidy smears of mixing paint. As for breaks, she hadn't met many people who deserved one. And she certainly had never been given any.

They weren't here to discuss her, though, so she stepped out of her boots and padded away from the mat in her heavy socks to get a better look into the living room.

"So…nice place." She turned back to him. "Funny, though, it doesn't seem to match you."

"As if you know me so well."

She pressed her lips together. How could she answer that when the information she'd learned in the past twenty-four hours had suggested that she didn't know him at all? Why hadn't he told her about his parents? Of course, she had no right to expect him to confide in her when she'd shared nothing with him.

"It was my grandparents' house. They raised me." He glanced around the room as if trying to see it through her eyes. "Grandma liked flowers. A lot."

He wasn't kidding. Petals and stems showered the drapes, the throw pillows, even the settee. Ben Peterson owned a settee?

"Haven't gotten around to updating the place since they passed," he said.

When had they died? Recently? Had they passed away years apart or close together? She had so many questions, but none of them had anything to do with why she'd come today, and she couldn't get sidetracked.

"Hey, it was nice of you to stop by to see if I was okay. I am." Ben's gaze lowered to the glass in his hand. "Well, relatively. You must've drawn the short stick if they sent you here. Vinnie cheats, you know. You can tell him I said so."

"Can't do that. Nobody knows I'm here."

"They didn't send you?"

"That would be a no."

"Then what's going on, Delia? Tell me why you're here. If you need to gloat, could you save it for another time? I'm not up to it today."

She couldn't fault him for thinking such a thing. Not so long ago, it wouldn't have been far from the truth.

She took a deep breath and dove in. "Look, I'm here because I want to help."

"Not a good idea. I don't need—"

"Help?" she finished for him. "Oh, you're going to need help all right."

"I was going to say…pity."

Of course he would hate that. She waved away his suggestion with a brush of her hand. "That's good because I wasn't offering any."

But Ben kept shaking his head. It was probably emasculating enough for him to accept help from her, but pity? That had to be like ripping his Man Card to shreds.

"What I am offering is the chance to have someone working with you, but on the inside."

"I can get answers," he insisted. "I'll just have to be more...creative."

"Creative? You're going to have to be a freaking magician to do this on your own. A crime has been committed here whether you're willing to admit it or not. Someone is guilty. If you claim it isn't you, then who is it?"

He opened his mouth to argue, but she was on a roll. She couldn't stop now, not when she hadn't yet convinced him to let her help. She couldn't slow down long enough to ask why it was so important to her, either. What would she say? That it was the right thing to do? That he'd tried to help her, too? That he seemed to be a good man? It was more than any of those things alone, but she couldn't tell him that.

"Stuck at home, you won't have access to the databases to help you clear your name. Technically you shouldn't be accessing LEIN for personal use, anyway, but—"

"No, but—"

"And how will you observe the other officers while at home in your bunny slippers?"

"I'm not."

"Wearing bunny slippers?"

She glanced down and was surprised to find that he was no longer barefoot. At some point, probably while he was in the kitchen, he'd put on old hiking boots, their well-worn leather etched with the hard work of their rugged, capable owner.

The jolt that shot through her system was so sudden, so unexpected, that she was surprised she didn't land on the floor. Forget the heat in her face earlier—she was warm all over now. Even in places where heat wasn't allowed, she simmered like a teakettle just getting started.

"What?" He stared down at his boots. "The floor's cold."

She nodded, not trusting herself to speak. Had it been anyone else reacting this way, she would have called it lust, but that wasn't a word she'd ever applied to herself. And over a pair of work boots? Or did it have more to do with the man wearing them? Either way, it needed to stop. She didn't have feelings like that. Not for anyone, but especially not for a coworker.

When she looked up again, Ben was shaking his head.

"Listen, Polaski told me to stay out of it and let the state investigators do their job. And that's what I'm going to do."

Any remnants of her unacceptable thoughts evaporated with that comment.

"Pfft!" When he lifted his chin, she continued, "Sorry, but are you planning to wait until the cell door locks with you on the inside before you advocate for yourself?"

"Well…"

"Then do you believe that justice always prevails? Well, it doesn't." She shook her head harder than was necessary, but then not everyone knew how malleable justice was when tapped with the tools of money and power. "Just tell that to those who've been wrongly found guilty and sentenced to Death Row. To the one hundred and fifty of them who've been exonerated and released since 1973."

"I never said I wouldn't check out a few things."

"So at least now I know you were lying to me before?"

Ben opened his mouth and then shut it again. Had he forgotten that it was part of their job to separate the truth from the bull?

"Either you're too proud—and dumb—to accept help or you just don't want it from me." She held up her hand to stop him when he tried to argue. "But the way I see it, you don't have many options. I didn't notice your other friends lined up out there offering to help you."

She indicated the front porch, refusing to wonder whether he'd thought of her as a friend instead of only the subject of his teamwork experiment.

"How do you know some haven't already called?"

"Have they?"

"Scott did. I told him to stay out of it." He shrugged. "He has a wife and five kids."

"And the others?"

He lifted his chin and pinned her with his gaze. "Maybe they're not used to disobeying direct orders from a superior. Maybe they're not in the habit of acting alone."

"Are you saying that I am?"

Instead of answering, he waved around her to indicate her presence in his house.

"You might have a point."

Ben took a deep breath, puffing up his cheeks and then releasing it slowly. "Okay, I admit I'm at a disadvantage to find the information I need. But I can't ask you to risk your career to help me."

"You didn't ask. I offered."

"That's what I don't understand. Why did you?" But then he didn't give her time to answer. "How do you know I'm not guilty?"

That was definitely the question of the day. He looked away from her as if it didn't matter to him how she answered. Oh, it mattered, all right. She hated that she couldn't tell him what he needed to hear: that she believed he was innocent. But she couldn't do that. Not when she didn't know for sure yet that he was.

If only she could announce her fervent support for him the way the other troopers had right after the news segment. But she wasn't built that way. She needed proof. Police reports and lab evidence reports were like the building blocks of her constitution, and proof was the glue bonding them together. Indisputable proof. She had to have it.

That Ben Peterson even tempted her to step away from what she knew and trusted scared her more than any domestic or shots-fired call ever could. At least with them she had guidelines to follow.

"I don't know," she admitted finally. "Are you guilty?"

Something raw flashed in his eyes. Then it was gone. But the mask of nonchalance he used to replace it was something she understood.

"No, I'm not guilty."

"Neither are most of the suspects I've arrested. At least the way they tell it." It was supposed to make him laugh, but he only pressed his lips into a grim line. "Anyway, you don't know if I'm the one who set you up, either."

He studied her for several seconds. "I guess I don't."

"Then we're even."

Where her previous attempt at humor fell flat,

this one must have rubbed his funny bone because he grinned for the first time since she'd arrived.

"Not exactly," he said. "Only one of us is on a paid holiday of sorts and has been banned from the place he's been working for ten years."

"More time to watch cooking shows."

"Why cooking shows?"

"Well, that's what I'd do. I like to cook," she said with a shrug. "I record the shows and watch them after work. They're my secret addiction."

He smiled again. "I guess everyone has a few secrets."

Delia only nodded. He was probably just talking about the shows and about her being a rule breaker, but his comment unsettled her just the same. She knew his secret about his family now. But he didn't know her secrets, the ones she'd kept so carefully walled off that they seemed like someone else's life.

She'd never told anyone. She'd never even been tempted to. And yet this reluctant hero, who just might have been moonlighting as an accomplice to a ring of drug dealers, tempted her to hammer through the brick and mortar and let her secrets pour out. Of all the things that scared her about helping Ben Peterson, that one terrified her most.

That truth, and the fact that they'd run out of things to say, had Delia buttoning her coat and slipping her gloves back on. She moved past him toward the door. "I'll get back to you when I know something."

At his nod, she opened the door and stepped through it.

As she took a few steps toward her car, he called after her, "Are you gonna tell me why you're going to all of this trouble?"

The many reasons rushed into her thoughts at once. This was Ben, who'd made an effort to help *her*. And he was alone right now. If only someone could have helped her when she was alone. Anyone.

But as she turned back to him, she chose only one of the reasons. "It's the right thing to do."

He nodded as if accepting her words this time. "But then we both know how seldom people do the right thing."

Delia just stared at him. He was probably just talking about how in their career they often saw people at their worst. But it seemed like more than that. Did he know about her? How could he? Did she *want* him to know?

CHAPTER SIX

DELIA'S HANDS TREMBLED as she watched the face staring back at her from the women's locker room mirror only a few hours after her conversation with Ben. Fisting and unfisting her hands, she tried again, finally managing to button her uniform shirt over a Kevlar vest.

Attention to detail was critical in her career, and she usually checked the items on her duty belt a couple of times before heading out into the squad room. Weapon, expandable baton, extra rounds, flashlight, pepper spray, Taser. But she usually didn't come to work with the express intention of deceiving her coworkers and defying a direct order from her commander. So today she'd checked each item three times, and as she buckled the belt over her uniform, she couldn't resist doing another inventory.

She'd pinned her badge in place, but she still found herself patting that spot above her heart to make sure it was there. Two more times.

How was she supposed to pull this off with her coworkers when she couldn't even fool the woman looking back at her in the mirror? These officers were trained to recognize when someone was lying or hiding something. There was no way they wouldn't figure out that she was trying to pull one over on them.

She shook her head hard enough that she had to resecure a section of hair that fell loose from her bun. She was so nervous that anyone watching her would swear this was her first day on the job. A chill shimmied up her spine at the possibility that someone *could* be watching. Her gaze slid to the side, just to be sure. Maybe Ben was right. It was too risky. He recognized it, even if he really needed her help.

She could lose everything.

But then so could he.

Why had she gone to so much trouble to convince him that he should let her help? Sure, it was the right thing to do, but could the fact that her pulse raced every time he came within a twenty-foot radius of her have something to do with it, as well?

Whatever her reasons for offering, she'd given her word, and she would honor it. But in order to be Ben's eyes and ears on the inside, figuring out which of their coworkers might have set him up, she needed to move under the radar. As fidgety as she was at present, she might as well have been carrying a sign that said "I'm investigating the rest of you."

At least Trooper Kelly Roberts, the only other female officer on second shift, was running late so Delia was alone in the locker room. That would give her a few minutes to pull herself together.

Delia straightened, smoothed her hair in the mirror and adjusted her hairpins. Deciding she looked better after the slight adjustment, she nodded at her reflection.

But just as she reached for her hat, called a "cover," her cell phone started clanging with its obnoxious ring. Figuring it was a telemarketer, she sent the call to voice mail. The icon that appeared on her screen surprised her though. A message? She never received those. Curious, she clicked into her voice mail.

"Sweetheart? It's Mom and Lloyd."

With just five words, Delia's past overwhelmed her present like a gorilla attack from behind. The cover she'd tucked under her arm slipped out and thudded to the floor. They had her cell number now?

"You're one hard lady to get ahold of," her mother's voice droned on, just as she would have done if they'd been face-to-face. Marian would never have noticed that her daughter was suffocating, her lungs having forgotten how to expand. Delia needed to hang up. Just one click, and these sounds, these awful, crippling sounds would quiet again. A least for a while.

"Your answering machine at home must not be working. I've left so many messages. Thank goodness one of the other stylists at Helen's old shop had your cell number. Well, maybe you've heard by now that we've moved back to the area."

As a matter of fact, she hadn't. She'd deleted several messages in the past few weeks without listening to them, her finger automatically hitting the delete button the moment she heard the squeal of her mother's voice. She'd hoped they would get *her* message that she didn't want to talk to them. They hadn't, and now were not only close by, but they also had two numbers for her. They would never leave her alone.

"…and we're dying to see our successful lady cop—"

"They know?" The words whooshed from her lungs. She didn't hear the rest of her mother's message as she madly pressed the buttons on her cell, searching for Delete. Whether she hit the right one or not, she wasn't sure, but at least the sounds stopped.

She set the phone back on the bench and stared at it as if it could reach out and bite her the way her past had. How could she be of help to Ben when her own problems were creeping ever closer no matter how hard she'd worked to chain them to the past? How could she chase his demons when hers were touching her with filthy hands?

She jerked at the sound of approaching footsteps, caught in the act of remembering. Kelly Roberts swished through the doorway, black peacoat open, silver scarf and all of that blond hair fluttering as she moved. She stopped and glanced from the phone on the bench to the hat Delia was scrambling to collect from the floor.

"Glad to see I'm not the only one running late today. That construction on US 23 is killing me."

Stripping off her sweater, Kelly pulled on a base layer over a too-lacy-for-work bra and slipped her padded vest over her head. She turned to Delia expectantly, as if to ask, *What's your excuse?*

Delia rested her cover back on the bench and gestured toward the phone. "I had a call." It was a half-truth, but closer to reality than the stories her suspects told her.

Kelly nodded as she pulled her hair into a ponytail and deftly twisted it into a barely neat knot.

"Not bad news, I hope." But she didn't wait for an answer before continuing, "My mom's always calling me when she knows I'm at work. 'Kelly, you have to hear what your crazy cousin did this time' or 'Could you drop by with a gallon of milk on your way home?'"

She pointed to her own phone on the bench, the

one with the hard floral case. "That thing feels like a tether sometimes."

"Don't I know it." As if Delia knew anything about being hounded by calls. At least until lately. Now *tether* wasn't a strong enough word. It felt more like a pocketful of rocks, threatening to pull her under if she let it.

But she couldn't let it. Perverts like Lloyd Jackson deserved every bit of the misery they endured in prison, and she intended to be one of the people sending such people there by the boatload.

Laughter from the squad room filtered through the locker room door, interrupting them.

"Guess at least one of us had better get out there," Delia said.

"I'll be right out." Kelly was checking the contents of her own duty belt. "Have to make a pit stop."

Delia nodded, despite the clash of thoughts in her mind. Kelly was the only other officer on this shift who could relate to the slight differences female officers worked with every day. Simple things like restroom breaks, which meant a trip back to the post since the procedure required them to remove their duty belts. They couldn't exactly hang those things on restroom stall doors, given that they weighed about twenty pounds and had a gun in them and all.

She and Kelly might have shared those little

inconveniences, but they sure as hell never mentioned them to anyone, including each other. That would have been like admitting that there were differences between male and female officers, and Delia wasn't about to do that.

Kelly might have felt the same way, but they'd both kept those thoughts to themselves. In fact, this conversation was the longest one they'd ever had. That would need to change now, with Kelly *and* with the other troopers, if Delia planned to discover information that would help Ben. Just listening to others' conversations wouldn't be enough. She would have to really become a part of the team if she hoped to find the answers she needed.

Pushing open the door, Delia stepped out into the squad room, trying not to freeze as the others turned to face her. She could handle this.

"Glad at least one of you could join us," Sergeant Leonetti called out. "Some kind of party going on in there?"

"Something like that." She waited for the dig about women always going to the restroom together, but it didn't come. "But the party's over, so let's get started already."

Kelly, who had slipped in next to her, winked at Delia.

Lieutenant Campbell stepped in front of them,

appearing oddly alone without Ben next to him. It just didn't feel right.

"Hello, everyone," he said with a nod. "I realize that things are in an uproar around here. But we all need to stay calm. The best thing we can do for this investigation and for Lieutenant Peterson is to continue doing our jobs. Captain Polaski wanted me to remind you all that no one is to have contact with Lieutenant Peterson for the duration of the investigation. We have to stay out of this one for all of our sakes."

Murmurs of disagreement spread through the room, but Lieutenant Campbell ignored them.

"As you're probably aware, we will be under extra scrutiny now. Media attention is on us. Reporters are smelling an even bigger story. Let's not give them more fodder by offering special treatment to one of our own."

"But we can't just leave him hanging there," Trooper Donovan insisted.

The room quieted as everyone waited for Lieutenant Campbell's reaction. As a newer recruit, Donovan was taking a risk by sticking his neck out that way. Delia could relate.

The lieutenant turned his way. "We'll do what we need to, and what we need to do is follow orders." He sighed, holding his hands wide. "Lieutenant Peterson would tell you the same thing and then say something about the team."

"Then let's do this for Ben…and the team," Trooper Maxwell called out.

"For Ben and the team," the rest of them said in unison.

Although she repeated the comment with them, the words grated on Delia. One of those officers announcing solidarity with Ben might have been the reason that the lieutenant was at home now, waiting to be charged with a crime he didn't— Well, a crime he *might* not have committed. Though if he was guilty, she intended to prove that, too.

Lieutenant Campbell hadn't joined in with the others to chant, but he hadn't stopped them, either, though his gaze slid toward Captain Polaski's office a few times. Ben had said that Campbell was the other officer who'd offered to defy orders and help him. The only other one. And as the only officer on their shift with a spouse and kids, he also had the most to lose if caught. Ben had been right when he'd said that doing the right thing was the exception, not the rule.

And this didn't seem right.

Ben deserved to be there with Lieutenant Campbell, leading the troopers and reminding them about the importance of teamwork. She still didn't know if she agreed with him on that front, especially when a member of this team might have failed them all.

Delia glanced surreptitiously at the officers one by one as they put on their coats and checked their radios. Which one of them had something to hide? Was it Trooper Warner? Had he needed anabolic steroids to build that physique that mattered so much to him? Had he made an agreement with drug dealers to secure his own supply? And what about Lieutenant Campbell? Sure, he'd volunteered to help, but was that just a cover? Did he have financial problems at home with all of those mouths to feed, something that would make him susceptible to businessmen with deep pockets?

What about Trooper Maxwell or Trooper Roberts or Sergeant Leonetti? They all looked like decent people, but how much did she know about them? They definitely didn't know her, though they probably thought they did. They all seemed to have the same commitment to public safety and the citizens of southeast Michigan, but one of them had fooled them all. She intended to figure out who the liar was. Even if it was Ben.

Her gaze shifted again, this time to Trooper Cole, who'd been standing near one of the desktop computers. But she didn't have the chance to consider him a possible suspect. Because when she peeked back at Trevor Cole, ready to study him without being noticed, she found him staring right back at her.

BEN AWOKE WITH a start, his heart thumping in his chest, his T-shirt as soaked as a marathon runner's though the house wasn't any warmer than usual. He didn't need to turn on the lamp to know that his blankets and sheets would be caught around his ankles as if he'd been trying to race away from a pursuer only to be trapped in a tangle of cotton and wool. This nightmare had invaded his sleep too often lately, and each time he hadn't been able to run away fast enough.

Craving light, he flipped on the lamp and sat up in bed, reaching for the water bottle stationed next to the clock. The digital display read 1:43 a.m. He took several deep swallows from the bottle before putting it aside. If only he could push away the images that lingered in his thoughts as easily. But the faces of terrified bank customers and employees continued to flit through his mind in a high-speed slide show. The shrieks. The pleas. The fear in the customers' eyes. Probably in his own.

Get on the ground! Now.

Do you want to die today?

The words were clearer now than even when the two suspects had shouted them, their voices muffled behind latex horror masks with hollowed-out eye sockets and blood-smeared gashes that promised death. His moment of panic was as familiar as the words, a visceral ache that started at his center and fanned out in all directions.

He had to make it stop.

Ben shoved both hands through his hair. He could have missed the narrow window of opportunity to take down those two suspects. But he hadn't. He could've forgotten his training and allowed his fear to paralyze him. He hadn't let it. He could have failed the people he'd been assigned to protect the way he'd always expected he would and could have ended up surrounded by victims as innocent as his mother was.

Those things hadn't happened, either.

Somehow the two suspects had ended up handcuffed and in the backseats of separate patrol cars, and no shots were fired though one of the suspects had been armed.

"Man, we were lucky," he breathed to the empty room, his shiver having nothing to do with the cold.

So darn lucky that his chest still ached from the weight of the what-ifs he'd dodged. So why did he keep returning to this memory? Especially when he had other things to worry about now that his reputation had taken the trip from that alleged "hero" to a more fitting *zero*.

With a wistful glance at his pillow, he threw back the covers, sat up and shifted his legs over the side of the bed. Since he was as likely to go back to sleep as he was to discover that the suspicion swirling around him had been just a bad dream, he decided to get to work.

Tugging on a pair of heavy socks, he slid on his hiking boots. But as he yanked a T-shirt in place, he recalled Delia's gaze yesterday when she'd noticed that he hadn't been wearing a shirt under his robe. As if she was offended or something. If she hadn't been already, she definitely would have been if she'd known what he'd been thinking. She'd come to offer her help, and all he could do was wish she were the topless one wearing that robe. Then he could have unwrapped her like a birthday present. The *favorite* present.

What was wrong with him? Lust was about the last thing he had time for right now. He blinked to exorcise the image of all that perfection, but the painfully hard result of his peep show lingered, darkening his mood. Where was his sense of self-preservation? His career and his freedom were on the line. Worse yet, he'd allowed Delia to risk her career, as well, something he never should have agreed to no matter how convincing she'd been or how much he needed her help.

He shook his head. This was a bad idea. How was he supposed to work with Delia, asking her to put on her uniform and lie for him, when all he wanted to do was peel her out of it, layer by layer? But it was a little late for his crisis of conscience when she'd already started her part of the investigation during her shift last night. She'd gone out on a limb for him, so he'd better hope that the branch was strong enough to hold them both.

Frustrated in more ways than one, Ben clomped down the stairs toward much-needed coffee. He had to get his thoughts back on the investigation. Only the investigation. That would be all he could allow himself to think about when he met her later that night to discuss their progress. He wouldn't sit back and wait for her to solve the mystery by herself, either. He might not have access to databases or the opportunity to interview potential witnesses, but he had high-speed internet and the motivation to find some answers.

He carried his coffee through the living room and past the front door to the den, the one room in the house that he'd made his own by adding his collection of state police photos, a buttery-soft leather sofa and a mahogany desk. Flipping on the desk lamp and positioning his coffee on the desk pad, he switched on the laptop.

But when the screen appeared for a new search on his internet browser, he could only stare at the empty box. It shouldn't be this hard. He'd conducted hundreds of investigations over the years, and now that he was at the center of one, he was struggling with where to begin. Obviously, he needed to start with his team members. *Coworkers*. He couldn't call them a team anymore, at least not until he figured out who was the broken link.

Instead of typing, he reached in his desk drawer and pulled out a pen and a legal pad. He started a list of names, each one striking a fresh chord in his melancholy: Polaski, Campbell, Leonetti, Donovan, Cole, Campbell, Maxwell, Roberts, Warner, Jacobs and, of course, Morgan. Then there were the other shifts, too.

He'd eaten dinner with some of their families. Had been to birthday parties at their homes. Some he felt he'd known forever, while others were new to the post. He'd trusted a few with his history, and all of them with his life, and now he wondered if he really knew any of them.

Lowering his pen, he moved his fingers back to the keys. He would have to search each of them, obviously, but who would he start with? Maybe his pseudo-partner in this unofficial search should come first. She definitely gave him as many questions as she answered. Even her offer of help raised a red flag. Who took such a risk just because it was the "right thing to do"? Nobody he knew. There was definitely something she wasn't telling him.

Delia even had a motive to want to see him discredited. She was ambitious and, quite possibly, jealous of his record with the force. She'd made a few comments about his smooth trajectory through the state police ranks and had joked about his upcoming commendation—the one that likely had been put on hold. He hated to think she might have offered to help him just so she could take him down and earn special recognition, but he couldn't rule it out. He couldn't rule out anything.

The truth was that Delia had behaved more suspiciously than any of the troopers since the whole bank incident. She was one of the newer troopers and the most obsessively private. He probably knew less about her than he did any of them, other than that she was the stepdaughter of a minor political figure with a bad reputation. So everything told him he should be looking at her.

Everything but his gut.

"It isn't her," he announced to the officers in all of those photos. Most of them would have told him he should check Delia out with more reliable sources than his hormones. But it wasn't hormones telling him to look in another direction. At least he hoped it wasn't. He was using the sixth sense that he'd honed during more investigations than he could count. The one he trusted implicitly. It told him that though Delia Morgan might have secrets, they had nothing to do with him or his problems. Anyway, he knew better than anyone that people had a right to their secrets. They shouldn't have to see them on the TV news.

Of course, his hunch didn't mean he wouldn't scrutinize Delia as carefully as any of the others. Especially now that he understood intimately how the innocent could be made to look guilty. However, it did mean he could look at the others first. But as he turned back to the list on paper, making bullet points next to each name, his hand hovered over the last name.

His pen refused to make that last dot. Maybe some questions simply needed to be answered before he could move on to the others. Setting his pen aside, he moved back to his keyboard. With a sigh, he typed Delia Morgan.

CHAPTER SEVEN

DELIA WASN'T SURE she had the right place as she stepped into that crowded blue-collar bar that was positively pounding with after-work intensity. It had seemed like a good idea to meet Ben over in Warren, where neither of them were likely to be recognized, but now she wasn't so sure. With its low lights that cast all the faces into shadow and its sticky floors from what had to be yesterday's beer, Dilly's Place appeared to be the perfect location for a crime scene rather than somewhere two people might solve one.

At least the patrons were too busy blowing off Hump Day steam to notice her as she passed behind the bar stools. Good thing since she couldn't have looked more out of place if she'd put on her uniform and drawn her weapon on the bartender while he poured drafts from the taps.

The east wall was covered with yellowed posters and banners from the three Detroit sports teams. A dark wood bar stretched along the west wall with flat-screen TVs at either end providing an out-of-place bow to current technology and a long mirror bearing dated smears of a long-ago cleaning. A few tables were squeezed into the center of the room, with a line of dark booths attached like train cars all the way to the kitchen door.

"Dee. Over here."

Dee? How she heard his voice over the chatter and the brokenhearted chorus of a country ballad, she didn't know, but the sound broke through the din and kicked off a tingly hum inside her. A hum that wasn't entirely unpleasant. She tried not to make too much over the fact that he'd called her by a nickname. He'd just been trying to get her attention.

Opposite the bar, Ben had slipped into one of the booths—not quite in the back corner like in a clandestine meeting in a movie, but close. Just the thought of *those* types of meetings sent a shiver through Delia of something she was wary to define. Instead, she noted that Ben sat facing the bar's main entrance. Even if they were violating a direct order by working together, Ben had followed police procedure in positioning himself where he could monitor patrons as they entered and exited the bar.

She needed to follow his lead, focusing on the job they were here to do. That would be better than allowing herself to think about how the low lights, probably intended to cover spotty glasses, made the place seem somehow…intimate.

On rubbery legs, she approached the table and sat on the bench opposite him. *Knock it off*, she told herself as she sat, unwound her scarf and unbuttoned her coat. She'd set boundaries for herself regarding this meeting, and she was darn well going to make sure they held strong.

"Dee?" she couldn't help asking, though there were so many questions she should have asked instead.

"Thought it would be easier to hear. Besides, would you want your real name thrown around in a place like this?"

"Probably not." She glanced around once more. "Interesting location you picked to meet."

"Everyone minds their own business here."

She nodded. That did matter. "How did you find it?"

"A sting about five years ago. We were assisting several other agencies."

"Sure none of the other officers—or the commander—hang out here?"

"Not that I know of. But then I haven't been here myself in years. So we'd better keep an eye out."

When she looked up at him, a sardonic smile lit his lips. Why did her gaze have to linger on those lips? If only she could stop wondering if they were soft. She had to look away before she made a fool of herself, so she lowered her gaze to her lap and pulled her cell from her coat pocket. She held down the button to shut it off.

Not that she usually received calls, but right now it wasn't enough to just silence the ringer. Until she figured out how to block her parents' number, she couldn't risk allowing it to vibrate and tempt her to look at it. Especially in front of Ben. She would never be able to hide it from him if they called when he was there. He read her too easily.

"Expecting a call?"

"I'm turning it off."

The side of his mouth lifted. "You'll be out of contact with the post."

"Just for a little while," she said, even if the idea of it had her straightening in her seat. It would only be an hour or so.

"Good." He watched her for a tick longer than necessary. And then a little longer.

She shifted again. "What?"

"Your hair looks different."

Did it look bad? She laced her fingers together to keep from reaching for the band she'd used to tie her hair back. She'd been in a hurry. To get here. To where he was.

"I like it." He looked away as if he didn't mean it.

She licked her lips, shifting her gaze from her hands to his face and back again. Why did she care what he thought about how she looked, anyway? Oh, she cared, all right. More than she should care what anyone thought. Especially any man.

Slipping her arms out of her coat sleeves, she took her time arranging her coat over her shoulders. She needed to steady her hands if she didn't want him to notice how nervous she was. How flustered he made her.

"I know it's too soon to expect results, but did you see anything at the post last night that set off any alarms for you?" he asked instead of calling her on any of it.

Either he hadn't caught on, or he realized they had more important things to talk about. He rested his elbows on the scarred table, waiting for her answer.

It pained her to have to dash that hope in his eyes with a shake of her head. "Too soon. The place is still in an uproar. It definitely hasn't returned to normal."

He nodded. They both understood that the Brighton Post wouldn't return to *normal* for a long time. If ever. Even if it did, that would only be a "new normal" with staff changes and, possibly, an arrest.

"Everyone still seemed supportive of you."

He smiled, but it didn't reach his eyes. "That's good, I guess. Even if one of them is probably lying."

"Probably." Strange how much she hoped it wasn't him.

A waitress, dressed in a sporty referee uniform that was miniaturized from too many dryer spins, approached them. "Something to drink, honey?"

That the woman had addressed her question only to Ben grated on Delia's nerves. Was she seeing things, or had the waitress just leaned in closer to give him a good look at the melons she'd crammed in that tiny striped shirt? Delia crossed her arms over her own subpar breasts. And *honey*? Where did that broad get off calling him that right in front of her? What if they'd been on a date or something? That was rude, plain and simple. Jealousy had nothing to do with it. Not a thing.

Ben kept his gaze on the waitress's face as he ordered soda water with lime. A safer choice than whatever had sidelined him yesterday morning.

The waitress turned to her. "What about you, sweetie?"

The woman smiled down at Delia. So she had endearments for everyone. Fine. Delia ordered a soda, trying not to worry about dirty glasses and questionable ice.

"Could you throw some nachos in with the

drinks?" Ben asked the waitress before she hurried away to turn in their order.

Delia couldn't help but smile at both his suggestion and the irony of the situation. This secret meeting was the closest thing she'd had to a date in…she paused to calculate…a really long time. Of course, this wasn't a date, either. If only she could convince her hands of that. They were so sweaty that when the waitress returned with her mug of soda, Delia wrapped both hands around it to cool them off.

"Figured that now wasn't a good time to pick up any new bad habits," Ben said.

"What?" When she slanted a look his way, he gestured toward his mug with a lime slice on the side. "Oh. Right."

"Well, other than the obvious, was anything different at work last night?"

She considered telling him the truth, that everything had been different without him there, but she decided against it. "Not really. Other than Trooper Roberts coming in late. Something about construction on US 23."

His lips lifted as he sipped through his straw. "She uses that one too often. She needs a new excuse." His smile slipped away as he drew his eyebrows together. "But no one seemed to be acting, I don't know, strangely?"

She shook her head. "Sorry."

A flash of that odd look from Trevor Cole crept into her thoughts, but she dismissed it. If the other trooper had been staring at her, it was probably because she'd been too obvious while observing all of them. Great. Someone had been behaving strangely, all right. Her.

She cleared her throat. "How about you? Were you able to find out anything? I know your internet search opportunities are…limited, but maybe you found something."

"Nothing important," he said vaguely. "Just did some general searches on a few coworkers' names."

"Hope you didn't waste time looking up mine." She licked her lips. Had she spoken too fast? "I mean, if you did, you probably would have already died from boredom." At least he would have if he'd looked up her last name, rather than the name of her mother's second husband.

"I didn't find out much of anything about anyone." Ben paused until she looked up at him again. "How could I when I was working with what amounted to a chisel and a stone tablet?"

"We're both doing the best we can."

The waitress returned with a platter of nachos, plates and wrapped cutlery. Until the food had been set between them, dripping with cheese, Delia hadn't realized how hungry she was. She dished out a serving and dug in, taking several bites before she sensed that he was watching her. Looking up from her plate, she set her fork aside and wiped her mouth on a napkin.

"I forgot to eat today," she said, pushing her plate away.

He set aside his plate of nearly untouched food. "Guess I wasn't that hungry after all."

She couldn't blame him.

"Well, let's see if we can figure some of this out," she said, returning their conversation to the case. "Maybe we need to back up and look at the big picture. I'm not even sure why specifically you are considered a person of interest."

"Polaski said I was the 'common denominator.' I don't see how I could have signed off on the chain of evidence in so many of the cases in question." He stopped and made a circular gesture with his fork. "How is that even possible? We run three shifts. How could drug evidence only be collected on the afternoon shift?"

"Well, it's good to know that nobody sells drugs on midnights or mornings." She shook her head, rolling her eyes. "That has to be a relief for troopers working those shifts."

"Right? You and I obviously chose the wrong shift."

"Still, I can see how that would look suspicious," she said. "Do you know which cases they were referring to?"

"I have a few guesses. We don't have those types of drug arrests every day.

"Possession, sure, and even possession with intent to deliver, but charges for manufacture and delivery are less common."

Pulling his plate back to him, Ben stabbed his fork into a nacho chip that was likely soft by now, but he still didn't take a bite. "I would love to look at the cases, see who the arresting officers were and compare the locations. Look for things they have in common. Besides me."

"Where would you get ahold of that information?"

"The commander had a file on his desk when I was in his office. I'm not sure that was it, but he kept touching it every time he said something about the case. State investigators must have given him a copy. What I wouldn't give to get a look at that."

Delia swallowed, dread building inside her. He needed a copy of that file. Could she risk getting it for him?

"I can get it." Apparently she really did want to be fired. Or maybe be charged with impeding an investigation. Forget being "in for a penny." She was going for whole gold bars.

Immediately, he shook his head. "No. I can't ask you to do that. I was just thinking out loud."

"You didn't ask." In fact, he'd never *asked* her

to do anything for him, and yet she was already in shoulder deep and sinking fast. "As for the thinking-out-loud part, if you don't want my help, then keep those thoughts to yourself."

"I'll try to remember that. And Delia?" He waited until she looked up at him. "Thanks."

She nodded, well aware of how hard it was for him to let her do any of this. If the tables were turned, Ben wouldn't have hesitated to step up for her or for any of the other team members. That made the betrayal of one of them seem so much worse. She shoved away that thought. How could she be thinking of Ben as the victim when she didn't know for sure that he was innocent? She needed to remember that.

"I know it seems unlikely, but do you think any of this has to do with the thing at Brighton Bank & Trust?"

"The thing?" He smiled at her description of the event, but then he shook his head. "I've been trying to look at the bigger picture, too. I know it's too soon to rule anything out, but I can't make a connection there."

He held his hands out from his sides. "On one hand, you have missing evidence from a series of drug arrests. On the other, there's a botched bank robbery by a couple of punks who got their ideas from an old Keanu Reeves movie."

"You're kidding. Do you mean *Point Break*?"

His smile finally reached his eyes. "Only instead of the being the ex-Presidents, these guys wore monster masks."

She grinned back at him. "And the suspects didn't have any place to surf once they were finished robbing banks."

"That, too."

She twirled her fork around on her plate. "But the timing seems awfully coincidental."

"I think so, too. But the investigation itself could have been going on for months. The crimes in the case might go back even further than that."

"But still—"

"I know. We can't rule it out. It's Law Enforcement 101. Coincidences don't exist." He frowned, shaking his head. "This one, though, just might buck against that truth."

Strange how she disagreed with him on that, even if he had more law enforcement experience than she did. Those two news reports—about the bank robbery attempt, then the announcement of the formal investigation—a week apart, didn't sit well with her. That awful news segment replayed in her thoughts, bringing with it that same sick feeling as when she'd viewed it for the first time.

"Could it have anything to do with your past? I know, that's probably a stretch, but could whoever did this have known about, you know, what happened to you?"

Delia gripped her hands together, expecting him to refuse to answer just as she would have if he'd starting digging into her past. Some burial grounds were just off-limits.

"I don't think so." He shook his head as if convincing himself. "It was sordid enough to make for an entertaining news story, but that's it. And, yes, the suspect could have known. Nearly everybody at the post knew."

Not everybody. She and Trevor Cole hadn't known. Had it been a surprise to anyone else?

"That wasn't even the first time my family made the news. Just the first time in a long time. People love to learn about other people's tragedies."

"It makes them feel better to know that somebody has it worse than they do."

"And, for a while, anyway, my family had it pretty bad."

For a hell of a long time, as far as she could tell.

"Why didn't you ever tell me?" The words were out of her mouth before she could stop them. She had no right to ask him to confide in her when she'd never shared anything that mattered with him. Yet, she needed to hear *his* story, whether it would be useful to the case or not.

The side of his mouth lifted, but a stark vulnerability remained in his eyes. "It isn't a great conversation starter when you first meet people. Like, 'Hey, I'm Ben, and this is my sad story.'"

That she understood. The difference between them was that he'd eventually become comfortable enough to open up to some people, even if she wasn't one of them. Still, she couldn't imagine ever sharing like that. With anyone.

She waited, but when he didn't answer, she added, "I understand if you still don't want to—"

"My dad wasn't even unique, as convicted felons go," Ben said before she could let him off the hook. "A two-bit criminal. He burglarized homes and then robbed a convenience store to feed a drug habit. Even his armed robbery wasn't all that imaginative. He pulled a toy gun—mine—on a store clerk. He'd already served the minimum sentence for that one. Six years."

"During your childhood?" she asked to keep him talking. When had it become so important for her to know and understand him?

"From just after my fourth birthday until I was ten. When he was released he'd sworn he was clean. Rehabilitated. I didn't trust him at first. Didn't want *her* to trust him."

He took a deep breath as if the rest was hard to tell. "But old habits are hard to break. She'd always given him another last chance. No matter what he did. She couldn't help herself. Eventually, neither could I. We were so desperate to believe our lives could be normal that we pretended they were."

Delia's eyes burned as an image of a little boy with glasses invaded her thoughts. A child trying to shield himself and his mother from more pain. Failing on all counts.

"I know what that's like."

She didn't realize she'd spoken aloud until Ben's gaze shifted her way. She sat, frozen, while he watched her as if expecting her to explain herself. Something she just couldn't do. "I mean I can *imagine* what that must be like."

"Oh. I see."

But did he? Could he even guess that as much as she wanted to know more about his tragic past, she was just as tempted to share more about hers? She couldn't let herself be that vulnerable. Especially with a man. She couldn't let that happen. Ever again.

"Mom and I had managed not to *see* a lot of things," he continued finally. "A few painkillers popped after he'd injured his shoulder cutting wood. Or after repairing the water softener. The cash that was disappearing as fast as Mom could make it.

"So I don't know why I sensed there was something more wrong than usual that last day when we climbed in the car to go for a picnic in the park. But I did. Mom was too excited to notice, though. We were having a family outing, the kind that other families took for granted."

Delia couldn't bear to hear more, but the knot in her throat was so large that she couldn't speak. Couldn't beg him to stop. Like being stalled on a train track, she knew what was coming but was powerless to stop it. She held her breath, bracing for impact.

"We never made it to the park. It was one in the afternoon, and my father was so high that when he swerved off the road, he never thought to hit the brakes. Rammed into a tree. Old car. No passenger-side air bag. You can guess the rest."

"Oh, God, Ben. That's awful. I'm so sorry."

"I don't remember anything after that. I woke up in the hospital with cuts and a broken leg."

Absently, he stretched his neck and traced his fingers over an inch-long scar just beneath his jawline. With all of the time she'd spent watching him, how had she never noticed that?

"Mom was gone," he continued. "Dad broke his arm but went straight from the hospital to jail. The next time I saw him was in court. Driving under the influence of drugs causing death. Maximum sentence. Twenty years."

Delia had been staring down at her hands as the story grew heavier, but now she couldn't help but look up at him. The stark emotion in his eyes tore straight through her heart. She couldn't imagine that little boy's heartbreak, but her heart ached as much for the man, who still carried around scars from that tragedy. Outside and inside.

"I'm so sorry. You lost both parents that day." She cleared her throat. "The, uh, newscast said your father died in prison."

"About five years later. A body can only take so much drug use. He died in his cell one night. Heart attack."

"So you said your grandparents raised you."

"Mom's parents," he clarified. "Instead of enjoying their retirement, they took on an angry eleven-year-old, moving me from Indiana to Michigan."

"That house," she said, understanding now. "No wonder you didn't want to change anything about it."

"They were great." He smiled at some faraway memory. "They forgave my father and encouraged me to forgive him, too."

"I bet that was hard."

"Not as hard as it was living with all that anger."

He couldn't really mean that, could he? How could he have forgiven that kind of betrayal, the self-centered slaughter of a future? No one could. As if her shock amused him, he smiled.

"My grandparents were all about teaching big life lessons. Like that we should try to build a better future rather than spend time crying over the past." He shook his head as he stared down at his folded hands. "And that we can all accomplish more with the help of others than we ever could by ourselves."

He looked up from his hands then, trapping her with his gaze. The unspoken message about the lesson she'd failed to learn hung heavily in the air between them. She could see now where he'd first learned his teamwork credo, but she wouldn't mention it and give him the chance to turn the conversation on her.

She chose the cowardly way out, returning to his history instead. "When did they...uh..." She twirled her hand to have him fill in the blank.

"They lived long enough to see me graduate from Ferris State and then the academy, but not too long after that." He turned his head, suddenly interested in one of the patrons sitting at the bar. "I buried them just three months apart."

"That just doesn't seem fair."

His gaze moved back to her. "Fair? Sure, some of it stunk, but I was lucky. Not everyone has the chance to experience unconditional love in his lifetime. I had it from three different people."

Delia could only stare at him. He had as much reason to be angry as she did over the cards he'd been dealt. His childhood had been ripped away from him as surely as hers had been stolen from her, and even the silver lining to his dark cloud had been trimmed away. Yet with all of that, he didn't hold a grudge. He forgave and accepted in a way that no real human could. She suspected that even if they figured out who'd targeted him now, he would still forgive.

How would she ever understand a man like him when her own anger had been the one thing that had helped her to survive and escape? How could he be as valiant when the chips were down as he'd been when the cameras were rolling? But a bigger question than those two remained: Why was she wishing she could be more like him?

CHAPTER EIGHT

"Sorry we got so far off track tonight."

Ben pushed open the bar door for Delia as they stepped out onto the sidewalk. Her strained expression made him smile, but at least she didn't jerk the door out of his hand. Of course, Ben was pretty sure that chivalry wouldn't sit well with her. She would never see it as just common courtesy. She probably would have preferred to open doors for *him*. Or even carry him through them.

She buttoned her coat all the way to her chin though they'd already bundled up, even pulling on gloves, before braving the outdoors. It was still cold, with a few falling snowflakes glistening in the light from the street lamp, but at least the wind had died down.

"It wasn't off track, really," she said as they walked along the cleared sidewalk toward the parking lot. "As we said, we can't rule out anything yet, no matter how small."

Though Ben doubted that details from his childhood tragedy had any bearing on this case, he didn't force the issue. At least he wasn't the only one who seemed uncomfortable tonight. He'd been on edge from the moment Delia had stepped into the bar, appearing laughably out of place. And almost unbearably hot.

He couldn't explain why he thought so. She'd been wearing more clothes than most of the women in that bar. Yet he hadn't been able to keep his eyes off Delia. He wasn't the only one who'd noticed her, either. What was it about her oh-so-proper turtlenecks that made him want to yank them over her head?

Even that simple ponytail she'd worn had driven him crazy. Why had she picked tonight to loosen up and skip that tight bun of hers? It had been all he could do not to pull off the band and sink his hands into that mass of dark hair. He still itched to do that though she'd covered her head with a snowflake-dotted stocking cap.

The funniest thing was that she probably thought her questions were what had made him uncomfortable. He'd been uncomfortable, all right, but for different reasons entirely. Specifically, it was her creamy skin that begged to be touched and a mouth that promised the kind of kisses that could warm a man through many lonely nights that had unnerved him. Though her questions had stirred painful memories, they'd come as a relief, offering a break in the constant stream of electricity from the other side of the table.

"Did you park in the lot or on the street?" he asked her as they reached the parking lot.

"The lot." She pointed toward the back. "It was packed. I was lucky to find a spot."

"Yeah. I'm on the street. I got here a few minutes before you did and nearly had to wrestle someone for a table."

"That I would like to have seen."

Out of the corner of his eye, Ben caught her smiling. She was only joking, but the thought of demonstrating his best wrestling moves for her had him tightening in all the wrong places.

"She was about seventy, but I could have taken her," he somehow choked out.

When her eyes widened, he grinned.

"Are you always this gullible?"

She shook her head. "I'm off my game lately."

"Rule breaking doesn't sit well with you." He didn't bother posing it as a question. As hard as she'd tried to maintain her distance, he shouldn't know her so well, but somehow he did.

"Guess not."

He touched her coat sleeve, pretending not to notice her arm stiffening beneath his touch. He stuffed his hand in his coat pocket again. "I'll walk you to your car."

"That's all right." Her chin lifted. "I'm fine."

"Come on. Just let me go with you. It's common sense. The same thing we tell other women every day."

"I'm not 'other women.'" She took a few steps into the lot, the snow crunching beneath her feet.

No, she wasn't. She was the most overly independent, untrusting and exasperating woman Ben had ever met. And he couldn't get her out of his mind.

"Let me do it, okay? For my own peace of mind."

She stopped and turned back to him. "Well, if it will make you feel better…"

"It will."

"Fine."

He didn't touch her again as they tromped toward her car in the far corner of the lot. It was the darkest corner, with a burned-out street lamp perched above it.

"This is the spot you picked?"

"I told you it was the only one left."

"Probably would have been safer on the street."

"I'll remember that the next time I come here."

He caught her grin before the shadows of the darkened area overtook them both. She was about as likely to become a regular here as she was to throw a house party and invite the whole Brighton Post team.

"You still haven't said much about it."

He studied her darkened profile. Did she really want to know more, or was she trying to keep him talking so he wouldn't leave? His first thought was probably the right one, but he couldn't help wishing it was the second one.

"I told you I don't remember much more about the accident."

"I'm not talking about the accident. I mean the incident at the bank. You know, besides what's in the report. And besides the monster masks."

This time he stopped, his stomach tightening, and she slowed next to him.

"What do you want to know?" His voice didn't sound right in his ears, so she probably heard it, too.

"Tell me about it. Maybe something you say will be important to the case."

He doubted that. He couldn't figure out why she'd been asking the questions any more than he could understand his impulse to answer every one of them. Why did he want her to know him when she obviously didn't want him to know her? Though he'd been filleting himself like a salmon all night, she hadn't shared a single thing about herself. Judging from the articles he'd read today about the scandal involving her sleazy politician stepfather, Lloyd Jackson, she likely had some stories to tell herself.

"Or maybe you're just being nosy."

She chuckled. "There's that, too."

He took a deep breath and started talking again, sharing even more of his story with Delia. "I was standing in line like all the other customers. The line was longer than usual. I was annoyed about that. Wasting too much time on my day off.

"Everything that happened after that seemed to move in slow motion. Or maybe that was just my reaction time." His chuckle filled the air, but she didn't join in.

He cleared his throat. "The two suspects rushed through the door, wearing those gory masks and heavy coats. Everyone started yelling. Whimpering.

"One of the suspects had a handgun, but with the coats they were both wearing, it was hard to tell if they were armed with other weapons. The one with the gun waved it around and told the customers and employees to get on the floor. He shouted, 'Do you want to die today?'"

"Tell me something I don't already know."

Ben blinked. Though he'd expected some sort of reaction to what he'd just said, that wasn't it.

"All of that stuff was already in the police report."

"You read it?"

"Just trying to be thorough."

"Oh. Right." He searched his memory for something he hadn't included in the report. Only one thing stood out. "I would love to tell you that my training kicked in, and I reacted the way we were taught in those computer simulations in the academy, but it didn't work out that way."

"Why? What happened?"

"The training is supposed to make your reaction so automatic that you forget to be scared. It didn't. I was scared to death." He shook his head even though he knew she couldn't see him doing it. "Actually, that's an understatement. I was terrified. I had this moment of utter panic when I couldn't remember if I had strapped on my ankle holster."

"We've all done that, Ben. We've all had times when we've made a quick trip out and have forgotten to wear our weapons." She cleared her throat audibly. "Or have *chosen* not to."

"I just don't know what would have happened if I'd forgotten that time."

"But you didn't forget."

"Luckily, no. The ankle holster scraped against the side of my calf when I lowered to the floor, so I knew it was there. Then I was scared that I would mess up and get my weapon taken away, and it would be used on one of the other hostages."

"None of those things happened."

"I guess not. Anyway, the rest is in the report.

All I know is that I used the guy's own mask against him, pulling it over his eyes when he was taking our cell phones. While he was wrestling with that, I got lucky and knocked his gun out of the way and then somehow pinned him to the floor. When the other guy stepped in, I withdrew my weapon and aimed it at him."

"I did read that part. It sounds amazing."

"The whole thing probably looked like a Keystone Kops comedy in black and white."

"The other hostages called you a hero. I saw their interviews on Channel 3."

"I'm not…a hero." He hated that he couldn't even say it without wincing.

"Come on. You're getting a commendation."

He shook his head hard. "Believe me, I'm not. I just got very lucky that no one got hurt."

"It was more than luck—"

"Look." He breathed out a frustrated breath. "I was too terrified at that moment to ever think of myself as a hero."

Delia was quiet for so long that he wondered if she would respond at all. Did she think less of him now that he'd told her the real story? He didn't bother saying that it didn't matter what she thought. It mattered. A lot.

"Isn't that the very definition of heroism? Not

to never deal with fear, but to be truly afraid and then to act in spite of it."

Ben swallowed, his pulse suddenly pounding in his ears. Had she just said she believed he was a hero? He must have heard her wrong. She hadn't even admitted that she thought he was innocent in the post investigation case, and yet she'd just all but called him a hero.

He didn't want to be drawn in by her words, didn't want to need her approval, but the temptation was too strong this time. She believed in him. Did she understand how much he needed someone to have a little faith in him right now when he was beginning to question himself?

Before he could think better of it, Ben reached for Delia in the dark and crushed her to him, their mouths finding each other in less a dance than a frantic claiming of lips. He shouldn't be doing this. He knew better. It had *MISTAKE* written all over it in indelible marker. All uppercase letters. But Delia's lips were even softer than he'd imagined in his best dreams, her taste unbearably sweet.

The most amazing thing of all, though, was that she was kissing him back, and she seemed every bit as hungry as he was. Who was he kidding? He couldn't stop kissing her now if he wanted to. And, God help him, he didn't want to.

She moved restlessly against him, her lips parted and pliable as he tasted the corners of her mouth, flicked his tongue over her cupid's bow and nipped at the fullness of her bottom lip. He would do anything to get her to repeat that soft gasp of pleasure when he angled his head to kiss her more thoroughly.

Anything.

She seemed to want more, too, and he was happy to oblige. He slid his tongue between her willing lips, and he groaned as she drew on his tongue, shock waves shooting to every nerve ending in his body. Forget the cold. He could start a fire right next to them with just the heat coming off his skin.

Walking her backward until her backside touched her car door, Ben pressed against her, leaving no doubt just how obliging he could be. Instead of pushing him away, she gripped his waist, holding him close.

Though they were still bundled up like a pair of overdressed snowmen, his gloved hand found its way inside her coat and covered her small but perfect breast. In response to his over-the-sweater move that he'd mastered in middle school make-out parties, she arched against his hand.

His mind told him this should stop—must stop—but his body was delivering entirely different messages. Of claiming. Of completion. Of inevitability. Just one more kiss. Another touch. One last sweet taste.

And then he realized he was kissing all by himself.

Her lips were still warm, still malleable, but Delia had stopped moving beneath his touch. Her arms had fallen to her sides. All of that sweet urgency was gone. A much-deserved bucket of ice water seemed to have been poured over his head, as well.

Slowly, he lowered his hands and took a step back. What was he doing? What could possibly have told him this was a good idea, no matter how great she tasted and no matter how much he was tempted right now to start the whole thing over again? Needing to see her face, he strained his eyes against the darkness, but the shadows that had been friends before were now enemies. What was she thinking right now? Was she as furious with him as she had every right to be? Why had she responded like that?

"I'm sorry. That shouldn't have happened," he said.

Liar. Well, it was partly true. Maybe it shouldn't have happened, but there was no way he was sorry.

"You're right. It shouldn't…have."

The tremor in her voice hit him harder than a slap would have. He could understand her being mad, but her voice didn't sound angry. She sounded upset. Vulnerable. Delia Morgan? That didn't make any sense. It was just a kiss. Okay, a kiss like an Orion spacecraft blastoff and with a little more hands-on involvement than the average peck, but it was still technically just a kiss.

"I didn't mean..." He didn't bother finishing. Oh, he'd meant it, all right. In the worst way. But only if she was on board with the idea. Her distress ripped right through him.

"I don't know what you were thinking—"

"What *I* was thinking?" He cleared his throat. He was sorry for blurting, but she had to realize that he wasn't the only one involved in that kiss. With gusto. He gave her a break by not calling her on it.

"I'm sorry," he repeated. "I did a lousy job of reading your signals—"

"Well, whatever it was, it can't happen again."

"You're right. It can't."

Had the outside temperature just dropped a few degrees, or was the chill coming from Delia? Clearly, she wasn't taking any responsibility here, even for the mixed signals she'd sent. But at least she was back to her hardheaded self. This stubborn, impossible Delia Morgan he understood, but that other, more vulnerable Delia was a mystery to him. Could he have imagined her? He cleared his throat, jamming his hands in his coat pockets as his gloves were no longer keeping his hands warm enough.

"Look, I want you to know that I don't expect… uh…anything from you. Even for you to keep helping me if it makes you uncomfortable now."

"We're not starting that again, are we?"

Ben could only look at her, wishing again he could see her face. "I just didn't want—"

"To let me help you. We've already established that."

It took him a few seconds to realize she was joking, even if her voice still sounded strained. Still, the fact that she was making jokes gave him a reason to relax. Maybe things wouldn't be weird between them after all.

"But there's one thing I have to say."

"What's that?" he asked as that spark of hope was extinguished.

"This can't happen again, or I won't help you, and then you won't have anyone to support you from the inside at the post."

"Of course." He didn't bother mentioning that he'd tried to talk her out of helping in the first place. Or that she was still suggesting that he'd acted alone in the kiss.

"And you need me, Ben."

"Is that because you believe I'm innocent?"

She met his gaze and then looked away without

saying the words he longed to hear. "You need me," she repeated.

With those parting words, she clicked her key fob, opened the car door and climbed inside. She barely glanced at him, just enough to make sure she wouldn't drive over him, before backing her car out of the parking space and pulling away. Her taillights showed her path to the exit and then disappeared as she turned onto the street.

Oh, it was going to be weird between them, all right. But she hadn't walked away from him completely, no matter how easy it would have been for her to do that. As he trudged toward his SUV, he chose not to analyze why it relieved him so much that she hadn't given up on him.

At least when he'd apologized, he hadn't claimed he didn't want her. What would have been the point of lying? To her or to himself? After the little event that had just happened between them, she could have no doubt exactly what he wanted, anyway. But why Delia Morgan? Even if timing wasn't lousy and the workplace romance thing wasn't a big issue, Delia couldn't have been more wrong for him. She was as guarded as he was open, as bullheaded as he was reasonable.

What was it about her that made him behave so differently? He approached everything else with almost obsessive forethought. There were too many potholes in life, too many chances for him to make a mistake and prove he was a product of the faulty genes he'd tried to escape. But with Delia he was tempted to throw caution to the wind. Why? Did he have some sort of career-related death wish? Was one more taste of *forbidden fruit* worth losing everything he'd worked for?

The fact that he couldn't answer that question with an emphatic *no* was just another sign that he needed to get his priorities straight. Delia had hers in order. She might have blurred some lines by offering to work with him, smeared a few more by kissing him back, but now she'd drawn the precise boundaries of their relationship. He had to be just as clear about what he needed now, and that was to prove his innocence and find out who had committed the acts that had put at risk the reputation of the Brighton Post and the Michigan State Police.

If he hoped to have any help finding the answers he needed, he would have to figure out a way to keep his hands off the huge distraction that was Delia Morgan. Easy, right? He shook his head. After tonight, he wouldn't be able to get the idea of kissing her out of his mind. Worse than that, even with his career and future on the line, if Delia showed any sign of being amenable to another kiss, he would need handcuffs to keep his hands to himself.

Frustrated in more ways than he cared to admit, Ben threw his car into Drive and pulled into traffic. He was in a bad place, and he knew it. He might as well go ahead and be fitted for his prison jumpsuit because he'd come to a telling conclusion. Even prison life didn't sound as terrible as the thought of never having Delia in his arms again.

CHAPTER NINE

DELIA SLUMPED ONTO her sofa, as out of breath as if she'd been chasing a suspect. Or running from her own thoughts. Her lungs ached with the effort as she took a few deep breaths. Perspiration dampened the hair at her nape, and her underarms felt sticky beneath her coat. Dread was wedged inside her stomach as heavy as a fist-size stone, its edges sharp and cutting.

What had just happened? She covered her face with her hands, the scratchy sensation reminding her she was still wearing gloves. After peeling them off her clammy hands one finger at a time, she covered her mouth again, but her lips were chapped and sensitive. Lips that had been so thoroughly kissed that they throbbed with the memory. She dug her teeth into her bottom one to quell the tingling.

"What were you thinking?" she whispered into the empty room.

If only she could say that what had happened with Ben had been just a kiss. But *just a kiss* shouldn't have ripped through her insides and fragmented like one of those RIP bullets, leaving a path of delicious warmth instead of destruction. *Just a kiss* wouldn't have left her with skin that felt too tight, a heart that beat too loudly and the suspicion that her stepfather had been right about her all along.

How could she have let that kiss happen when she was supposed to be helping Ben? Or how could she have *wanted* it to happen and keep happening? She shouldn't have allowed Ben to take the full blame for it, either, but she couldn't face the fact that she'd responded to him with such relish. That she'd loved every touch, every taste, when she should have been repulsed or unwilling. Or at the very least, she should have felt nothing at all.

But she hadn't felt *nothing*. She'd ached for the smooth and rough of his skin, the heat and pressure of his body against hers. She'd behaved wantonly. She'd been brazen. Needy. As if she actually wanted a man. Wanted Ben.

Shaken, she glanced around her apartment, determined to replace those unacceptable thoughts and images. She'd always thought of this place as *streamlined*, its clean surfaces and minimal accoutrements making a statement. Now though, with the ceiling fixture tossing yellow light and shadows on the bare walls, the apartment just looked empty.

As her gaze slid over her unadorned tables, she could think of nothing except the doilies and bric-a-brac that crowded end tables and bookshelves at Ben's house. Her lonely pair of striped throw pillows—the ones that had come with her slouch-style sofa—only reminded her of the overgrown flower garden that was Ben's living room.

Stop. She shook her head hard enough to make her neck hurt. She couldn't keep doing this. Why did her every thought keep returning to Ben? She could no more answer that than she could explain why she'd thrown herself at him in the parking lot. Her actions had reeked of lust. She didn't *do* lust.

Delia blew out a breath as she leaned back into the sofa cushions, crisscrossed her legs and hugged one of the pillows. She was acting like someone who'd never done *those things* before. And she had. Well, a few times. When necessary. She'd even had more than one partner. Two to be exact. One from college and another just before she started the academy. Sometimes it was just easier to get it over with than to make one more excuse as to why she wasn't ready. Not that pretending had helped much. Both relationships had fizzled soon after she'd reluctantly agreed to go to that next level.

That uncomfortable history made everything that had happened tonight between her and Ben more unsettling. Agreeing to physical intimacy when she felt obligated to do it was very different from craving it like some hussy. Today she'd been tempted to crave.

That had to stop, too.

She could never allow herself to need someone that way. Need granted power, and she wouldn't give anyone power over her ever again. She refused to be that weak. Ben was only a man, after all. Hadn't he been as hungry as any man once he'd started kissing her? She knew perfectly well that all men were the same. Like animals. They used women to slake their lust and then tossed them aside like garbage.

Not Ben, a voice inside her insisted, as she squeezed the pillow tighter against her. She couldn't listen to that voice. It was as dangerous to her as the man himself was. It tempted her to believe that Ben, the most quietly heroic man she'd ever met, might be a contradiction to his gender in other ways, as well. She couldn't afford to let herself believe he might be different. It was too much of a risk. She couldn't bear to place her hope in him and have it shattered.

She'd been right to pull back from him and get her head above water, even as every cell in her body clamored for the chance to drown in him. She had to keep the boundaries of their partnership firmly in place for self-preservation. For as much as she hated admitting she was physically attracted to Ben, this was about more than attraction or even that foolhardy kiss, and now they both knew it.

That *more* had her popping up suddenly from the sofa and padding back to the table near the door. She rummaged through her purse for her phone, but when she pulled it out, its screen was black. Of course, she'd forgotten to turn it back on before she left the bar. So much for an hour. Just how long had she been out of touch with the post? Two hours? Three?

Flicking on her phone, she cringed as she waited for the texts and voice mails to download.

"Seventeen missed calls?"

She quickly clicked through screens, only to discover that, yes, she had just as many voice messages. Why had she been so careless as to turn off her phone tonight? Some police officer she'd turned out to be. What had she missed?

She checked the call log first, and though there were a few different numbers, she didn't recognize any of them. They didn't seemed to be from the station, either. But then she wasn't close enough to the other troopers to have exchanged private cell numbers.

Clicking on the first voice mail and tapping the play arrow to start the recording, she braced herself and waited.

"Delia, it's Mom." Delia deleted the message immediately without waiting to hear the rest.

The second message was from a different number, but when she clicked that one, her mother's voice cut in again. "Delia, honey, we know you're busy, but we'd really appreciate it if you would call back…"

The third message came from yet another number, but the result was the same.

"Stop it," she said, deleting the message and then clicking out of that screen.

She paced back and forth in the living room to that closet that passed as a galley kitchen. The calls were coming from different numbers, and yet— Her chest tightened. Throwaway phones? They must have guessed she would try to block their numbers. Why were they going to such lengths just to talk to her? What did they want from her?

She considered getting rid of all the remaining messages without even listening, but she couldn't do that. She might delete an important call from someone at the post, especially since she couldn't tell if some of the calls had come from her co-workers' personal cells. Maybe Ben was right that it wouldn't kill her to get to know some of them, at least well enough to have their numbers.

Returning to her voice mails, she clicked on the next message, which turned out to be another entreaty from her mother. But just as she started to trash it like she had the others, she paused, her finger hovering over the delete button. Was she destroying evidence? Just to be safe, she saved this message instead.

Of course, she was overreacting. Even if she planned to file a report, what crime would she accuse them of? Calling too often? If that were a crime, then a quarter of the parents in America could be charged with it.

Still, she listened. To every word of every message. And she continued to save them, though she wasn't sure why since she would never file a report. In each message, her mother's words were the same. Well, almost the same. Similar requests with escalating frustration and, perhaps, urgency.

"Delia, dear, it is impolite not to return our calls…"

"I know you're receiving these messages, so you need to call back right away…"

By the sixteenth message, Delia could barely listen. She didn't know what she'd expected. Well, she knew *what* she expected—an apology, a plea for forgiveness—but she didn't know why she'd longed for it. Her mother hadn't believed her then, so she had no reason to think she'd changed her mind now. Even if deep inside— in the place that she didn't want to believe still existed—she'd hoped.

A glutton for punishment, she played the final message. The last message in a series that had been left over the past three hours. She could rest assured there would be more of the same tomorrow.

But the voice this time made her breath catch, blood freezing in her veins.

"Hello, Delia. It's Daddy."

"LOOK WHO FINALLY showed up."

Delia shifted in the booth seat and looked around, but Sergeant Leonetti—Vinnie—wasn't even looking her way this time. Could she look guiltier? She'd arrived early enough to help commandeer two of the deep Formica-topped booths at Casey's Diner and to open the divider that separated them. She was grateful that Trooper Warner, make that *Shane*, was the straggler tonight.

After the extra "work" she'd completed at the post tonight, the last thing she needed was to draw attention to herself. That was the problem with starting a life of crime, or something incredibly close to it—now she would always be watching her back.

Shane didn't seem to mind the attention, but he didn't have a "borrowed" police file hidden under a blanket in his trunk, either. He grinned as he hung up his coat and shook the snow out of his hair.

"You know how bad the roads were tonight," he said.

"Yeah, those few big snowflakes were a real hazard," Kelly Roberts chimed.

"And think of the many fine young *female* members of our community you had to pass just to get here," Vinnie said.

"We all have our crosses to bear." Shane shot a glance toward the long white counter with vinyl-covered bar stools. "Speaking of which, is *she* here tonight?"

"Back off, Hormone," Grant Maxwell called out to him. "She's not going to give you the time of day."

"You think you've got a shot with her?" Shane said. "You're smoking something strong if you think she's going to climb in that new pickup you blew your whole inheritance on and ride off with you into the sunset."

"The sunset?" Vinnie said with a guffaw. "He was probably just looking for a sun*rise*. He won't be getting that, either."

Everyone laughed, but no one bothered asking who "she" was or argued that the petite blonde waitress, who emerged from the swinging door to the kitchen, would pay attention to *any* of the troopers. In fact, the young woman barely made eye contact with them as she moved around the tables, efficiently jotting down orders, and then hurried back into the kitchen.

"Thanks, Sarah," Shane called after her just as the door swung closed.

"Sorry, Sarah," Lieutenant Scott Campbell said, although she probably wouldn't hear it. He turned back to the others. "Stop harassing the waitstaff, or they won't let us come back."

"Yeah, guys," Delia chimed in. "How many all-night diners do you think there are in Brighton?"

She was surprised by how easily the words came. Maybe getting to know her colleagues wouldn't be as difficult as she'd thought. On the other hand, maybe talking with them seemed easy tonight because she was getting so used to lying that she'd bought her own story.

"Diners in Brighton?" Vinnie said as the waitress delivered their drink orders. "That would be a big, fat one. Otherwise, why would we come here? We don't even know who this *Casey* is."

Nobody mentioned that they'd been hanging out more at Casey's lately because it seemed strange returning to the Driftwood without Ben. But then there were a lot of changes they weren't talking about tonight, including that Delia had suddenly become almost part of the gang. Was it too much too fast? She wasn't sure, but she hoped Ben would be proud of her. Not only had she met with her coworkers twice this week, she'd also begun *thinking* of them by their first names. That was progress, right?

"Someone was being an overachiever today," Kelly said.

Delia waited for one of them to come up with a pithy response to that until she realized they were all looking at her. Her throat tightened before she could fully process the words. They couldn't know, right? She'd checked once, twice, three times to ensure no one caught her slipping the file from the commander's office and then returning it after she'd made a copy. Maybe she hadn't been as careful as she'd thought.

"What are you…" she began, and suddenly she understood. "Oh, you mean the arrest."

Kelly grinned. "What else would I be talking about? Nice haul. Like a mini pot plantation. How'd you pick that one out?"

"It was no big deal," Delia said automatically. "If any of us hand out enough traffic citations and run enough plates, we're bound to get lucky eventually."

Delia shrugged, stirring her fork in the scrambled eggs she'd chosen for a late-night breakfast. A few weeks ago, she would have been happy to have the spotlight focused on her. Now all she wanted to do was blend in.

"The guy made it too easy," she said. "The lesson here is if you're wanted on a bench warrant and have a trunkful of baby marijuana plants, don't drive around with a broken taillight and a car that smells like a gange bash."

"'Gange,' huh?" Lieutenant Campbell—Scott— said with a laugh.

Chuckles spread along both sides of the two booths.

"Wow, you sound just like—" Vinnie stopped himself, but it was too late. It was as if the very person they were all avoiding mentioning had just walked in and planted himself atop one of the tables. "Well, except for the drug street name."

The waitress filled the awkward pause by returning with their orders. She distributed the dishes as everyone returned to their conversations about NCAA men's basketball matchups, the upcoming Daytona 500 race and the new putters eager to be baptized on area golf courses once the snow melted.

"Has anyone heard anything about the case?" Kelly asked.

The woman hadn't raised her voice, but her question stopped the other conversations as effectively as if she'd shouted. Delia choked on her bite of eggs and coughed into her napkin.

If they only knew.

At least this time she didn't have to worry about everyone watching her. They were all dividing their attention equally between Kelly and Scott.

The lieutenant shifted, crossing his arms, and then glanced at each of them by turns. "We shouldn't be talking about it. You heard Polaski. I know it's hard, but we need to stay out of it."

"We can't do that," Grant said. "I'm sick of sitting around. There has to be something we can do."

"Yeah, something," Jamie Donovan agreed, though he barely knew Ben at all.

Kelly leaned forward so she could get a better look at her superior officer. "Have *you* even heard much about the case?"

Scott opened his mouth as if to admonish them once more, but he only closed it again and shook his head. "They're keeping us out of the loop, too." He shrugged. "Ben's a friend."

Delia wasn't the only one who nodded at him then, but she was the only one who knew the truth. After all of their pledges of support and help, Scott was the one person who'd even made an attempt to put those words into action. Well, besides her. So much for their brand of friendship. In fact, with the exception of Scott, she was annoyed with all of them for Ben's sake. If they weren't going to really step up to help him, then she wished they'd just stop pretending.

The last thought made her straighten her posture. In some way, nearly everyone there was pretending. And what about her? Was she pretending that she still wasn't sure if Ben was telling the truth? Was she sure? No. Of course not. She still had no reason to rule him out as a suspect. Yet with each conversation, every time she looked into his eyes, and with that kiss that made her nerve endings zing, she was having a harder time believing he could be guilty. And he really could be guilty.

She took a drink of her water to force her bite of food down. She couldn't lose control over her judgment. Right and wrong was all she had. The only things that made sense to her. The gray areas of this secret investigation were difficult enough for her to navigate without her betraying her black-and-white views on guilt and innocence. She wouldn't do it. Not for Ben. Not for anyone.

"Penny for your thoughts, Dee?"

Whether it was because someone had caught her daydreaming or that he'd called her the same nickname that Ben had used *that night*, Delia wasn't sure, but she startled, dropping her fork on the table. Reaching for it, she glanced up to find Trevor Cole watching her and smiling as if he knew a secret. Her secret.

"Just daydreaming. Sorry," she managed over the sudden clog in her throat.

She hoped her grin was convincing because

she was so uncomfortable she could barely sit still. Instead of looking away, Trevor just kept watching her with one of those long, slow gazes she usually reserved for suspects. So different from when Ben had stared at her, Trevor's unblinking gaze gave her the creeps.

What did he know? Her thoughts flashed back to last week when she'd been almost certain he was watching her. At the time, she'd dismissed it, figuring she'd been behaving too suspiciously *not* to draw attention. But why now—what had she done? An icy tremor flicked up her spine.

Did *he* have something to hide? Just what did she know about Trevor Cole, anyway? Did he have secrets back at the Manistique Post?

"It's always hard to decompress after a big arrest, isn't it?" he said finally.

"Did you have a lot of those back in Manistique?" she couldn't help asking.

He lifted a brow. "You know about that?"

"Yeah, of course." Delia frowned. He shouldn't have been surprised that she knew about his transfer. They all knew he'd been reassigned from one of more than twenty posts that closed due to state budget cuts. But now she probably appeared too interested in his background. Would she ever get this investigation right?

"Not that the arrest today was a big deal or

anything," she said to fill the pause when he didn't say more.

Was he trying to avoid answering questions about his time in the UP? Did it have anything to do with the investigation involving Ben? Come to think of it, when they'd all expressed their concern and support for Ben, Trevor hadn't spoken up as much as the others. Sure, he didn't know Ben as well as some of them, but then neither had Jamie, and Jamie had chimed in several times. To be fair, she hadn't said much herself, but she knew which side she was on.

"I've had my moments."

She looked up at him, surprised that he'd answered after so long. "Now you have me curious."

He lifted a shoulder and then lowered it. "The pace was slower in the Upper Pennisula. We didn't have five-car pileups during rush hour, but elk-vehicle accidents were a dime a dozen."

"Sounds a little dry."

He nodded. "We had polls around the post over how long it would take certain patches of grass to grow."

She smiled at his joke, but her thoughts continued spinning. She didn't bother pointing out he hadn't answered her question, unless he was talking about arresting those wayward elk. What was he *not* saying about his time in Manistique, three hundred and fifty miles from Brighton? Were there irregularities regarding evidence there, too? It was easy to see how a connection might have been missed since the facility was closed now.

Was she seeing connections where there weren't any? Maybe, but it was a lead, and she was desperate for one of those. At least she would have something to tell Ben when she saw him Monday night. It would also give her something else to think about besides how perfect his lips had felt when pressed against hers and how much she had loved being in his arms.

If she couldn't keep her thoughts on the task at hand instead of ways she would like his hands on *her*, she would be of no help to Ben. The clock was ticking. It was only a matter of time until state investigators determined if they had enough evidence to charge, and she suspected that they might. She had to find something, anything, to help him clear his name, before it was too late.

CHAPTER TEN

BEN TYPED AS quickly as his hunt-and-peck fingers would allow. If only he'd taken the keyboarding class that Polaski had suggested three years before. The digital time on his laptop screen told him it was after seven. Delia would be there in less than thirty minutes, so he needed to get off these sites soon.

The last thing he needed was to have her catching him researching her past when she'd made a point of hinting that there would be nothing to find there. But the more he read about Lloyd Jackson and his wife and stepdaughter, the more curious he became. Particularly since Delia wasn't volunteering any details.

As he scrolled down the page of search engine results, he rubbed his upper arms over his Henley pullover. It did nothing to stop the chill that seeped from the eight-foot windows along Novi Public Library's west side. Nothing could be done about that, though. He always sat with his back to the wall, and he wasn't about to change that now.

Just behind the carrel where he sat, the stacks

stretched to the building's south wall. Off to his right, a sprawling open area was filled with long tables, carrels and even two sofa seating areas, large enough to fit two basketball teams, complete with subs. And adults and high school students had claimed nearly every available spot. The place was loud enough to be a college library and active enough to provide anonymity to a pair of police officers who weren't supposed to be working together.

From this vantage point, Ben could see all the library patrons as they stepped off the staircase across the room onto the second-floor landing. Thankfully there was no sign of Delia yet. Even after five days, he still wasn't sure he was ready to work with her again. Would he be able to keep his mind on the case once she was right next to him, where he could smell the floral scent of her shampoo and be reminded of how incredibly sweet her lips tasted?

To distract himself, he focused on the search results and then clicked on the link for a headline.

Scandal Prompts County Commissioner's Resignation

He'd already read a few similar articles in the *Detroit Free Press* and the *Oakland Press*, but he hoped this one from a local weekly newspaper would tell him something new.

Jackson, who faces charges of racketeering and mail fraud involving Oakland County contracts...

The article began just as the others had, so he scanned further down the page.

Why hadn't Delia told him about her family history? Especially after he'd shared all those gory details about his dad. She could have said they both had criminal fathers. Unless he'd sounded too pitiful, and she didn't want to share anything in common with him.

Maybe she was just ashamed that her stepfather was a corrupt politician. But this was Michigan. Had she never heard about Detroit's notorious former mayor? Didn't she realize that after the scandals and convictions of several Detroit city officials, that her stepfather's charges weren't all that shocking or even unique? Of course, maybe she was more embarrassed that Jackson had avoided conviction. He couldn't blame her for that.

"You didn't tell me you'd be on the second floor. I've been looking all over for you."

At Delia's loud stage whisper, he startled, frowning down at the laptop screen as he quickly backed out of the page and the search. He'd nearly been caught in the act of snooping into her past when he should have been looking for information to save his own neck. But that was only one reason he was so anxious right now. The rest had to do with the woman standing only a few feet away from him. He'd hoped for a few more minutes to mentally prepare himself before meeting with her again.

"And you didn't tell me you'd be almost a half hour early." He made a point of touching his eyelid to adjust his contact lens instead of looking up from the screen. So what if he was stalling? He deleted his search history and closed the browser.

"Is it a problem?"

"That you're early?" He shook his head, still avoiding looking up. "I just meant that I didn't get the chance to text you with my location. I would have done that in a few minutes."

"Well, I would have been grateful…in a few minutes."

Ben straightened his shoulders and finally looked up at Delia, who was grinning over her joke. His breath caught at just the sight of her. How naive he'd been to think he could just pretend that nothing had changed between them. And preparation? Nothing could have prepared him for the jolt of seeing her again.

She'd gone back to wearing her tight bun, which reminded him of a helmet in her protective armor. But he already knew how silky her hair felt and how soft she could be in his arms. Her absolute-coverage turtleneck under her open coat might as well have been a negligee for how ineffectively it shielded images of her curves now imprinted on his tactile memory.

As if she could read his thoughts and was shocked by his depravity, she yanked her coat closed and crossed her arms in an exaggerated shiver. "It's cold in here."

That she licked her lips in a nervous gesture didn't help. It had him thinking about her tongue, which only led to more forbidden thoughts. How was he supposed to forget about the other night? To pretend that kiss had never happened when he could still feel every feature of her mouth? How was he supposed to wash from his memory those touches that he'd cataloged among the best in his life?

"It's just cold by the window."

"And you had to be by the window at the back of the room."

"Training," he said with a shrug. "I have to sit here." And he needed to keep right on sitting, too, because if he stood up now, he might embarrass them both.

"Sometimes the training is downright inconvenient."

She made a production of opening her satchel

and pulling out her own laptop. Sitting opposite him with her right shoulder nearly touching that chilly glass, she didn't look up as she plugged the computer into the outlet built into the desk. He waited for her to say something, but she only logged on and started typing. She didn't even peek over at him though he watched her, just to be sure.

If he'd ever needed a reminder that it had been a bad idea to kiss Delia, she was providing him a hands-off signal now. Had it just been wishful thinking when he'd convinced himself that she'd been a willing partner in that kiss? Now she seemed determined to forget that anything had happened between them, something he just couldn't do. It was like unlocking a box, filled with all of the things he shouldn't want and could never have. Now he was supposed to lock it up again and destroy the key.

But he *did* want. More than he'd ever wanted anything or anyone.

Delia didn't want him, though. She'd made that abundantly clear. He could deal with rejection, but something about the *way* she'd reacted to their kiss hadn't sat well with him the other night. And it still bothered him. She'd seemed too upset about something as insignificant as a kiss, even a great one. Stranger than that, she seemed more upset with herself than even him.

Was she frustrated that she'd lost control with him? Or was it something more than that? Had she experienced a bad breakup in the past? Was that why she was afraid to trust others? There had to be something to it. His questions and his justifications made him grin. The male ego was a fragile thing. A man would make any excuse to explain away the truth—that a woman just didn't want him. And *he* needed to come up with some good excuse now because Delia Morgan didn't seem to want him at all.

"Thanks for suggesting this place," she said after a few minutes.

"As long as no other troopers pop in, we're good." At the question in her eyes, he explained, "You remember that since the cuts, some troopers are operating out of city police departments instead of only at their posts? The Novi department is just down the street from here."

"Oh. Right." She turned toward the stairs as if she expected to see blue uniforms at any moment.

"Is it bright enough for you in here?"

He meant it as a joke to distract her from worrying, but he regretted his words when she shifted and stared up the long tracks of suspended fluorescent lights. As if those weren't bright enough, each of the workstations had its own desk lamp, as well. He couldn't have suggested a brighter, less intimate place, without asking to meet her in the middle of a parking lot at high noon.

Delia turned back to him and shrugged, her gaze shifting to the side. "We'll definitely get more work done here."

"Definitely."

Of course, he would accomplish a lot more if he could stop staring at her, so he looked past her to the opposite side of the room. Unfortunately, his gaze landed on a teenage couple seated on one of the sofas in the reading area. He'd noticed them earlier, making too much noise and earning two warnings from the librarian at the reference desk. Both were at least pretending to read now, but it was clear that they were more interested in each other than their books.

Delia followed his gaze to the young couple. For a few seconds she only sat watching them, but then she turned back to Ben. "Guess other people need the bright lights, too."

He decided not to point out that she'd included the two of them in that group. Instead, he closed his laptop. "Why don't we start by updating each other on any new information we've found. Anything you haven't told me already?"

He expected her to look relieved that he was back to business, so her immediate smile surprised him.

"Well, there is one thing," she said.

He frowned. "So spill. The suspense is killing me."

"I'd rather show you."

Oh, she could show him, all right, but the library probably wasn't the best place for that. Missing the innuendo in her own words and his willingness to leap to such licentious conclusions, she reached into her backpack and withdrew a thick yellow clasp envelope.

He stared at the package she set on the desk in front of her. "Is that what I think it is?" Strange how he suddenly hoped it wasn't. As much as he needed what could be inside that package, the envelope only served as a reminder of all the risks Delia was taking. For him.

"I told you I'd get it. Aren't you going to open it?"

"Not here. You never know who might get nosy."

"You're probably right." She frowned. "You'll have to let me know if anything jumps out at you as significant."

"You haven't read it already?"

"I scanned it after I got home last night, but I don't have enough history to recall many of the cases."

"Scanned it?"

The side of her mouth lifted. "Okay, I pored over it for hours."

"That's my girl."

As soon as the words slipped out, he wished he could draw them back in. She slanted a glance to the side rather than to look at him. But was that an idiom or a Freudian slip? Had he just admitted to the both of them that despite all of the reasons he shouldn't be with someone like Delia, he wanted just that? No one had ever frustrated him more, or challenged him, or downright entertained him like she did. Did that mean something? Should he let it?

"Anyway, nothing jumped out at me."

"Makes sense. I told you that even I don't know which cases are involved."

Ben reached for the envelope and, though she bit her lip, her gaze shifting from side to side, she pushed it his way. After he'd placed it in his computer satchel, he folded his hands on the desk.

"Anything else?" He asked it quickly, before she had the chance to start asking *him* questions. He didn't look forward to explaining that he'd made no progress at all…other than digging for bones among the skeletons in her closet.

"Well, I've gone out with the others a couple of times."

"That's good," he blurted. "I mean, that's a good way to find information. No one's going to come out and announce, 'Hey, you should consider me as a suspect.'"

"You're probably loving this." She chuckled as she closed her laptop. "You've been encouraging me to get to know them better. Bet you never planned for it to happen this way."

"Might as well kill two birds with one stone."

"That's one way to look at it."

It wasn't a full-blown endorsement, he decided, but she hadn't shot his idea down this time, either. "When they're stuffing their faces, they're more relaxed. You'll get to overhear more conversations than you ever would at the post."

"I hope so."

And he hoped for more than that. Even if this investigation didn't turn out so well for him, if it ended his career—or worse—at least Delia would have built relationships with other team members. At least she would be all right. That this suddenly meant more to him than his own future demonstrated just how off his game he was around Delia and how much he needed to regain his focus.

"So you went to the Driftwood," he prompted when she didn't elaborate on anything she'd learned.

"Not the Driftwood. We've been going to Casey's Diner."

"That's a switch."

"Nobody wanted to go to the Driftwood," she explained, "because, well, things are different now."

He wasn't there. She didn't have to say it aloud for him to catch her meaning.

"Oh. Well, that's nice of…everybody." He cleared his throat, emotion threatening over that small sign of support. How soft had he become lately?

"It is kind of strange," she began, but stopped herself from saying more.

When their gazes met, she pointedly turned away. Unfortunately, the lovebirds in the reading area had become downright cozy by this point, snuggling up together, textbooks untouched in their laps. No matter how hard he tried to ignore the couple, he couldn't help picturing himself and Delia on that sofa instead, oblivious to everyone else.

When she looked back to him again, Delia swallowed visibly. "Anyway, I have some questions about Trevor Cole. What do we really know about him other than that he came from the Manistique Post?"

"Why? Did he say something suspicious?"

She was still wearing her coat, but she crossed her arms as if suddenly cold. "Nothing per se. But he just keeps—I don't know—watching me."

Ben pressed his lips together to keep from smiling, but from her frown, he could tell he'd failed.

"You told me to look for anyone behaving strangely."

"And you'd never noticed him *watching you* before?"

As much as it gave him an itchy feeling inside to know that someone else was staring at Delia, he could hardly blame the guy. Oh, he was tempted to call Trevor and tell him he'd be sorry if he didn't knock off the staring, but he couldn't blame him for seeing what Ben had somehow missed at first. Now he didn't know how that could ever have been possible.

"I'd never paid attention before," she said, also answering Ben's question without realizing it.

But that Delia hadn't noticed men's reactions to her didn't surprise him. She didn't know how beautiful she was.

"Maybe he thinks you're attractive."

She shook her head. "That isn't it."

He wouldn't be so sure. Strangely she'd failed to recognize some men's reactions to her, but she'd seemed keenly aware of the effect she had on Ben. Or had he read too much into that, as well?

"He did ask me what I was thinking when I was daydreaming last night at Casey's," she told him. "He said, 'Penny for your thoughts.'"

"Sounds like a bad pickup line to me."

"It felt more like the beginning of an interrogation. I was worried he'd seen me borrowing the file from Polaski's office. Or maybe he saw me return it after I'd made the copies."

"You had to sneak in there twice?"

"What did you expect me to do, steal it and hope no one missed it?"

"You're right." Clearly, he hadn't thought that through before he'd let her get the file. Let her? This was Delia Morgan he was talking about. She would have done as she pleased no matter what he'd said.

"Let's say that Trevor was behaving strangely," he began again, pushing aside his protective, and probably sexist, tendencies. "How do you suggest we check that out?"

She relaxed finally and wiggled out of her coat sleeves. "I just thought we should check to see if there were any cases of evidence irregularities at Manistique."

"I can hunt for any news stories suggesting that. Truthfully, I haven't looked at Trevor or Jamie too closely yet since they weren't in Brighton when some of the cases that I suspect were involved came through."

"I wasn't, either."

He only nodded. He couldn't admit that though

he hadn't looked into their backgrounds, he'd been scouring hers.

She pointed to his bag next to the desk. "That will answer your questions about which cases are involved, but I wouldn't rule those two troopers out yet. Just because they weren't around when the arrests were made doesn't mean they couldn't have messed with evidence by the time the cases went to trial."

"True." He hadn't thought of that, but she was right. "That means we can't rule anyone out yet."

"Except me."

"Not even you."

CHAPTER ELEVEN

DELIA COULD ONLY stare at Ben, though she'd promised herself she wouldn't. It was hard enough facing him after the other night—after the shameful way she'd behaved—without having kids on the verge of tangling their braces right in front of them. Now Ben had made it worse by revealing that he still suspected *her*.

"What do you mean, you can't rule me out?"

"Can you rule me out?" he asked.

She frowned at him but didn't answer.

Ben was the one under suspicion, and she had to keep reminding herself that she shouldn't clear him as a suspect without proof, either. So why was it so easy for him to continue suspecting her?

"You have a motive." When she shook her head, he only nodded. "Sure, you do. You're ambitious. You're looking to make your mark. You would benefit from having some of your superior officers out of the way. The question is how far you'd be willing to go to see that happen."

He was grinning as he said it, but she could only frown. Did he think this was funny?

"You really think I'm capable..."

He shook his head. "If I had answers to all of my questions, I wouldn't still be sitting here asking them. Maybe I'd even be back behind my own desk, grumbling about how small my office is."

He swiped his hand across the air in front of him. "Slash that. If all of this blows over, I'm not going to complain about my small office *or* the slow computers. For at least a week."

Ben was smoothing over the tense moment like he always did, but Delia couldn't let it pass so easily. Though she couldn't fault him for still having questions, when she'd never really explained why she was helping him. Or anything else.

"I have career aspirations, sure," she began, carefully planning her words. "And I am trying to make my mark. But my goals have nothing to do with any other officers. I don't want to shoot anyone else down."

She winced after her last comment. In a career where they all carried weapons, she shouldn't be talking about *shooting* anything. She expected him to make a joke about that, but he didn't even smile.

"So what do these goals of yours have to do with?"

To stop from fidgeting, she opened her laptop and swirled her finger on the mouse pad to bring up the screen again. Though she wasn't used to opening up to anyone, maybe it was time. She wanted to believe that it was only so Ben could eliminate her as a suspect, but she couldn't help wondering if it was something more. Did she finally want someone to really know her? Should she take that kind of risk, even if he might be the only person who would ever understand her?

She forced herself to look at him as she spoke. "I just see myself moving on to a higher-profile law enforcement agency where I can help crime victims. Especially kids."

Ben nodded and opened his laptop again.

"And in order to make the move to this high-profile agency, you have to make an impression where you are. Like the one I made at the bank?"

"Well, something like that couldn't hurt. Something with a commendation. But I didn't begrudge you your moment in the spotlight."

He lifted a brow. "Oh, really?"

Her stomach tightened. He'd seen right through her all along. Did he know her other secrets, as well? Had she given away hints without realizing it?

"Okay, I was jealous for about a minute. But even if I was still jealous, I wouldn't try to sabotage you. I wouldn't even benefit from damaging your credibility or from causing a scandal at the post."

"Why is that?"

"You know why that is. It's like earning top honors from the worst medical school in the country. Not exactly a résumé builder." She glanced down at her screen again, typing MSP Manistique Post into the search box. Somehow that was easier than seeing more questions in his eyes. Questions she wasn't prepared to answer.

"That's why you wanted to help me clear my name. So you could boost your own career."

Delia blinked. Was that really why she'd done it? "When you put it that way—"

"Is there any other way to put it?"

She stared at her hands as they rested on the keys. "I guess not. There was more to it, though." But how could she explain that to him? Could she tell him that she'd never witnessed that kind of valor before, and she couldn't bear the thought that she would have been wrong about him, too?

"Sure. You said it was the right thing to do. You just didn't say right for whom."

Delia's fists squeezed. So much for opening up to him. He'd taken what she'd said and twisted it until it looked ugly and selfish and—

"Wait." She jerked her head up. "Where that argument falls short is in assuming that the post's reputation could be cleared, as well. That's not going to happen because someone at the post or with access to it has committed these crimes."

"Valid point," he said finally.

"Valid point? That's all I get?"

"What do you want? A cookie?" At her frown, he continued, his hands held up in surrender. "Fine. There's a possibility that you were simply being magnanimous."

"Hmm, magnanimous. I like the sound of that."

"Figured you would."

But somehow winning the argument wasn't enough this time. She needed to understand him. So as she scanned through the headlines of articles about the Manistique Post, she casually asked, "If you questioned my motives, why did you agree to work with me?"

"You said it yourself. I didn't have many options."

She nodded toward the screen. Of course that was it. She didn't know what she'd expected, and that she'd expected anything wasn't a good sign.

"That wasn't the only reason," Ben said after a few seconds. "I let you help me because I admired your boldness. You were taking a huge risk, and you took it for me."

Though it didn't seem wise, nothing could have stopped her from looking back to him now. He was smiling, his eyes crinkling at the sides, those too-appealing dimples of his flashing unfairly. Their gazes caught and held in what felt like a caress. It was too tempting. Too sweet. And it had to stop.

Somehow she managed to look away, but she made the mistake of looking out into the open area of the room instead of turning to the safety zone of the window. That little blonde and her dark-haired boyfriend, the nemeses of her ability to stay on task tonight, picked that moment to steal a kiss.

It didn't seem right to watch, but she couldn't look away. Where she usually would have been annoyed that they didn't take their kissing elsewhere, she envied them the moment. Just once she wished she could have that, a normal relationship where kissing and touching seemed natural, instead of a cause for shame.

The reference librarian must have noticed the kiss, too, because she crossed to the pair and spoke to them in low tones. Whatever she said caused them to pack up their books and leave. After the tops of their heads disappeared from view on the staircase, she turned back to Ben. She caught him watching her, but he quickly looked back to his computer screen. Had he been observing her the whole time, and if he had, what did he think he'd seen?

"Well, good thing the PDA police was on that one."

She could almost hear the smile in his voice this time, but she kept looking at the screen. It was safer.

"Wonder if their parents knew how much studying they were doing at the library."

He chuckled at that. "Or what subject they were studying."

She tried to focus on her computer screen, but she couldn't stop peeking over at the sofa the young couple had vacated. Only it wasn't the kiss she and everyone else in the library had witnessed that kept replaying in her mind. She pictured a cold night and a burned-out street lamp. Two other hungry lovers coming together under a cover of darkness. But the images were as clear to her as if they'd acted out the scene on that same empty sofa, under a set of UV lights.

It took all of her energy to expel the thoughts. Though she was finally able to look at her computer screen and see more than letters swimming around in Times New Roman and Calibri Light, she was left feeling empty and frustrated. Was that how she'd left Ben the other night? Was she sorry she had?

After several minutes, Ben cleared his throat. "Find anything interesting?"

"Maybe." Delia quickly clicked out of the link that led to a blank screen on the state police website and then moved on to another. She had to find something. She wasn't about to tell him what she'd really been thinking while she was supposed to be researching.

"Hopefully, we're not searching for the same thing," he said. "I just did a general search on Trevor's name."

"We're not. I'm looking at his former post." She scanned down the page. "Wait. Listen to this. Did you know that the Manistique Post never technically closed?"

Ben partially stood and leaned forward as if he would be able to see over the top of her laptop. "It was on the list of post closures."

"But it says right here that it was just consolidated with the St. Ignace Post." She tapped the screen several times for emphasis. "Even the old building is still what's called a 'detachment post.' It's closed to the public, but troopers can begin and end their shifts there."

"So why was Trevor transferred to Brighton?"

She nodded. "He said he was transferred because the post closed, which we now know technically isn't true. And the total number of officers in the state is the same, so there weren't even any head-count cuts."

Ben pressed his lips together, squinting. "You know, this is one of those things that might be explained away with something as simple as the MSP needing to shift a few officers to rebalance numbers according to population shifts or something."

"But do we have that explanation yet?"

He shook his head.

"So it's something, right? More than we have on anyone else so far."

"It's something." He pulled a notebook from his bag and jotted down a few notes.

"Did you find anything?" She leaned forward toward his computer just as he had done to hers.

"Not yet. Only that there are dozens of uncreative parents in Michigan who gave their babies the same names. And about fourteen different arrest records for one of those pay sites."

"Also, we don't know if he has always lived in Michigan."

He nodded. "Looks like I have my new assignment."

"It would be great if we had access to the personnel records."

At that, Ben shut his laptop with a click. "Don't even think of trying to dig through those. You've taken enough risks for one week."

She considered arguing, but nodded. "You're right. I shouldn't push my luck."

Taking his closed laptop as a signal that he was finished digging for the night, she stowed her own computer in the bag.

"So tell me," Ben began as she straightened, "why kids?"

"What do you mean?" she asked, surprised he'd returned to the earlier subject.

"Why do you specifically want to work with child victims when there are so many types of targeted groups? The elderly. Gays. Women."

Delia gave the loosest shrug she could muster, though every muscle in her body was tight. Should she tell him it would be like fighting for her own cause every time she made an arrest? That each conviction would be like Lloyd finally receiving the steel bars of justice? Could she ever say those words out loud?

"They're all vulnerable groups, but children are the most defenseless. And the people who target them are the vilest of any. They treat them as prey." She should have stopped there, but she couldn't. "Someone needs to stand up for them. Society owes them a chance to grow up without being the target of someone else's sick perversions."

"So you want to focus on child predators?"

"Maybe." It probably wasn't a good idea to be too specific. "There are so many areas. Kidnappings. Violent attacks. Sexual abuse. Online predators."

"You could deal with any of those types of cases locally or even through joint task forces with other local agencies."

"But I want to make a bigger statement. To focus on that exclusively. The big guns. The FBI Violent Crimes Against Children program."

When he grinned, she knew she'd said too much. Would he ask why it meant so much to her? When she made up some answer, would he know she was lying?

"No one can say the lady doesn't have goals."

"Go big or go home." She chuckled, but it sounded awkward, even to her.

She appreciated the timely interruption as a female voice came over the loudspeaker, announcing that the library would close in fifteen minutes.

"So go home it is," Ben said with a grin. "At least for tonight."

He tucked his cord into his computer bag as Delia slipped on her coat and pulled her bag over her shoulder. She waited for him to grab his coat.

"You're not going to make some crack about me being an FBI wannabe?"

He tugged a scarf from his pocket and wrapped it around his neck. "Why would I do that?"

"Because it's probably an unrealistic goal. Or because I want to do something beyond working with the state police."

"There's nothing wrong with that."

He started for the stairs, and she fell into step behind him. When he reached the ground floor, he spoke over his shoulder.

"We all have our own reasons why we chose to go into law enforcement."

He watched her for so long that she was convinced he knew exactly what her inspiration had been. She held her breathing, waiting for him to announce it. But as they started through the sliding glass doors, he finally continued as if he hadn't just given her a heart attack.

"Some of us, like me, have something to prove or need to give something back." He shrugged. "You know my dad and all. Some of us just want to make a difference."

"That's what I want to do. Make a difference."

He nodded. "And you will. You have good goals. Honorable goals. It takes a special kind of person to work in that type of law enforcement. Just don't be in too much of a hurry to get there. There are probably a few lessons you need to learn first."

"Um, thanks."

It was a lame response to all of the things he'd said, but she was too overwhelmed to say something more profound. She wasn't accustomed to anyone believing her, let alone believing *in* her. Ben offered that belief so effortlessly, as if he didn't know what an honor it was.

The parking lot wasn't as dark as the one the other night, its lights all in working order, but Delia felt awkward anyway, from the moment they stepped outside. Would Ben walk her to her car again? Would he take her in his arms as he had before? Would she beg him to if he didn't?

"Which way is your car?"

They started in the direction she pointed. It wouldn't do to argue with him that she didn't need him to walk her there. She didn't really want to anyway. He didn't touch her, didn't come close to touching her, but she still felt the warmth of his nearness.

Once she reached her car and opened the door, she smiled as she caught him checking the backseat. For once, it was nice having someone looking out for her. Only after she was in the car with the door closed and the engine running did he start toward his own car.

She waited until he was inside his SUV before starting out of the parking lot. Though the heat was beginning to warm the car's interior, she suddenly felt cold and alone. Maybe it was good that he'd given her a wide berth tonight. After the sweet things he'd said to her, she was feeling vulnerable, and this time it involved far more than her body.

She might have just fallen in love with him a little bit.

"Trooper Morgan, do you have a minute?"

Delia stopped just inside the door leading to the station parking lot. So close. She'd almost made it through one more day of working under a magnifying glass without messing up and getting pinned like the rest of the insects, but her good luck may have just run out.

Pasting on a smile, she turned to find Lieutenant Campbell waiting behind her. He was already out of uniform and wearing his coat, but he didn't appear to be in any rush to go out into the two inches of snow that had collected on the parking lot since dinnertime. The uncomfortable feeling she'd had all during her shift settled at the base of her neck.

"Sure, Lieutenant. What's up?"

"You said you weren't able to go to Casey's tonight, so I wanted to catch you before you left."

She was caught, all right. But in case she was overreacting, which had become her habit these days, she fussed with her coat buttons and waited as if she had casual conversations with her boss every day.

"Yeah, I'm just a little tired tonight. Maybe I'm coming down with something." She held the front of her neck between her thumb and forefinger to suggest that her throat hurt.

Scott watched her for so long that she had to hold herself in place to keep from squirming.

"I just wanted to make sure you're continuing to include Kensington Metropark in your patrols."

That seemed like an odd thing to say given the

way he'd been studying her, but she was grateful. "Yes, I've been making a pass through all the main roads at least twice each shift though I haven't seen much new activity there. It's been pretty empty after dusk. Just a few die-hard ice-skaters and ice fishermen and a handful of cross-country skiers brave enough to ski paths at dusk."

"I would expect that as cold as it's been. With so little snow, I bet the toboggan run and the sledding hills are deserted even at the beginning of your shift."

She nodded. "I haven't seen anyone there. Maybe a few tomorrow." She tilted her head toward the door leading to outside where the snow continued to fall.

He pressed his thumb to the base of his nose, closing his eyes and then opening them again. "I just feel like we're missing something there."

"I know. Captain Polaski told me that no new leads have been discovered on the car we found there a few weeks ago. But someone went to a lot of trouble removing the plates and several sets of VIN numbers before setting it ablaze so that even if it didn't burn completely, it would be untraceable."

"All we know for certain is that the fire was intentionally set," he said. "Fire investigators found accelerants."

Delia shook her head. "If someone wanted to

dump a car, there are plenty of other places to do that. Places where it might not have been discovered for months."

"Yeah, I keep going back to that, too. Just keep an eye on the place. I know both Milford and South Lyon police departments have increased patrols, in addition to park police, but we need to continue to watch." He turned to the map on the squad room wall and gestured widely to the Kensington area. "We don't want more trouble there. It's a nice place for families, including mine. We have to make sure it stays a place where parents want to take their kids."

"I'll stay on it. Maybe I'll add another trip through during each shift."

"Great. Thanks. Well, you head home then and get some rest."

"I will." Clearing her throat for effect, she started toward the door again.

"Just a second, Delia."

She stopped again, noting the superior officer's switch to her first name.

"You've been spending more time with the rest of the team lately." He glanced over his shoulder as if to ensure that no one else could overhear. "Ben would be glad to know you're making the effort. He always said you just needed some encouragement. You're becoming a very solid member of our team."

"Thanks, Lieutenant."

Strange, a few weeks ago, she would have loved hearing that, especially if it meant good marks on her record. Now she didn't know how to feel. She wasn't really a team member. More of a mole infiltrating it. The team wasn't really a team, either, when one of its members was trying to destroy another.

"And Delia?"

She'd only taken a step, but she stopped again, this time looking over her shoulder.

He stepped closer and lowered his voice to a whisper. "Whatever you're doing to help Ben, please be careful."

For a few heartbeats, Delia only stared. How obvious had she been? And how many people knew? No point in lying now, she nodded, pushed open the door and practically ran to her car.

CHAPTER TWELVE

THE DARKNESS WAS so complete in the parking lot near Kensington Metropark's Possum Hollow picnic area that Ben had to flip back on his headlights just to make sure he wasn't there alone. It took him several seconds before he located Delia's car. Even in this remote area that formed a dead end off Park Route 4, Delia had managed to find the most hidden spot in the whole lot. So much for driving in unnoticed.

He had just put the car in Park when a person wearing a heavy coat, who he hoped was Delia, popped out of the other car and banged on the window of his SUV. When he unlocked the door, she jerked it open, allowing only enough light for him to confirm her identity beneath the coat's hood, before she slid inside and pulled the door closed behind her.

"Now drive."

"Why? This place is so remote. No one will see us here."

"Just drive. And keep your headlights off unless you absolutely need them."

"I'm going to need the lights." But as a concession to her, he didn't turn them on right away as he turned the car around and started for the parking lot exit. When they reached the road, he flicked them back on. "Sorry. I can't see the road."

She didn't answer as she stared out the windshield and pulled off her hood. Even with her gloves on and her coat buttoned to her throat, she shivered, despite the fact that he had the heat cranked and the fancy seat warmers set to maximum bun toasting. After flipping the switch for four-wheel drive, he retraced the directions she'd given him earlier back to one of the park's secondary entrances.

"How did you know to send me this way into the park?" he asked as he turned onto a narrow dirt road. "Doesn't the whole park close at ten?"

"You told me to patrol the park," she answered in flat tones.

"Right. You probably know all the cool paths by now."

She didn't answer as they continued down the road that didn't even have tire tracks to guide them.

After a few long minutes, he couldn't take it anymore. "So, you never really told me what happened at work."

"What didn't happen?" She puffed up her cheeks and blew out a breath.

"Want to be more specific?"

She only crossed her arms and turned toward the passenger window, tapping her booted foot so vigorously that her bucket seat shimmied.

He gripped the steering wheel tighter with his gloved hands, doing his best to keep the car out of the ditch. "If you don't tell me what happened, I can't help you."

"You can't do anything to help, anyway."

Ben swallowed, feeling that low blow just where she'd intended it to hit. "That might be true, but talking about it might help."

Still, she didn't say anything as she cranked the volume on the oldies radio station, and John Mellencamp crooned about something hurting "so good." But there was nothing good about what she'd said or how he felt, knowing that whatever had happened to her was his fault. It hurt, and that was all. Worse than that, she was right. He couldn't do anything about it.

Finally, he shut off the radio, the clock providing the only light in the car's interior.

"Delia, you called *me*."

"I know." She sighed. "I didn't know what else to do."

His spark of excitement that she'd finally called on *him* for help was doused as he realized that there wasn't exactly anyone else she could tell. Just past an area of heavy brush, he caught sight of a narrow drive. He pulled off the road and stopped, but he left the car idling. He couldn't afford to startle her by shutting off the engine.

"It was nothing. I'm probably overreacting. Again. It's just that lately it feels as if the walls at the post have eyes…and ears."

"What happened? Did you find out something new about Trevor? The Manistique Post maybe? Or did you figure out something about one of the others and manage to single-handedly break the case?"

Her chuckle was so low and throaty that he felt it deep in his gut. *Too* deep, especially when what he should have been feeling was concern for Delia. Only concern. But how was he supposed to do that while the two of them were sitting there in his SUV?

Alone. And in the dark.

"Well, there were a few things, but that's not it. One of them figured out what I'm doing."

Ben's breath caught, earlier off-topic thoughts vanishing. "Who? What did they find out?" His pulse pounded in his ears, his hands slippery inside his gloves.

"That I've been helping you. It was Scott."

"Scott?" He heard the chuckle in his own voice, so he held no hope that she'd missed it.

"What's so funny?"

"We shouldn't be surprised that he figured it

out. He's my best friend at the post. And I already told you he's the one who offered to help clear my name."

"But if he figured it out, how do we know the others haven't, as well? I already spent the whole shift feeling as if I was being watched. Even out on patrol."

Just the thought of it settled like a rock in his stomach. "We don't know that, Delia. And don't you think since Scott offered his help, he might have been watching more closely than the others?"

That sudden shift of hers must have been a shrug.

"Maybe," she conceded finally. "He told me whatever I was doing to help you to just be careful."

Ben peeled his gloves off his sweaty hands. "Sounds like good advice. Anyway, it could have been worse. It could have been Polaski."

"Or whichever one of them might be targeting you."

He didn't have an answer for that, but the knot inside him twisted tighter. The reasons for letting Delia help him were becoming flimsier by the minute.

"When did Scott tell you this?"

"Right before I left. By that time I was already

coming out of my skin." She shivered. "Seeing shadows everywhere."

"Why were you so upset before that? You said you found something on Trevor."

"Just a few things about his time in Manistique," she told him. "It's going to be harder coming up with any official records since the post was absorbed by St. Ignace, but the local weekly newspaper was pretty vocal about questions involving post investigations and a growing crystal meth problem. Trevor's name popped up several times and not in the most positive manner."

"Any charges against him?"

"More a cloud of suspicion as far as I could tell. But two different posts. Drug issues. One trooper at each. Could just be a coincidence."

"And we don't believe in those. So do you feel as if Trevor was the one watching you patrol tonight?" The need to protect that he'd been struggling to keep at bay peeked out once again. He knew Delia could take care of herself. So why was he determined to rush in on his white steed?

"I don't know," she said. "It was just a feeling. And wouldn't the GPS on the patrol cars have shown if we were in the same vicinity? No one mentioned that on the radio or in any of the calls tonight."

"Do you think someone followed you to the park now?"

"Yes. No. I don't know." She blew out another breath. "Obviously, I'm overreacting. To everything. All of this *watching* is starting to wear on me."

"That and the *collecting* of certain police files."

"Thanks for reminding me."

The frown in her voice only made him smile. "It's a good thing that gray areas don't sit well with you."

"But black-and-white wouldn't have helped you at all."

She must not have been freezing anymore because she slid off her gloves and unbuttoned her coat halfway.

"It is getting warm in here." He shut off the engine and loosened his jacket. Warm didn't begin to describe how he was feeling.

Immediately, the atmosphere inside the SUV changed. Became smaller, more intimate. Delia must have noticed it, too, because her breathing became uneven. Was she nervous around him again? Would she insist that he start the ignition or, worse yet, demand that he take her back to her car? That was what she *should* do. Or if she didn't, he should do the gallant thing and take her back anyway. But he hoped she wouldn't, and he knew he wouldn't. If he ever needed proof that he was no hero, there it was, right in front of him.

He cleared his throat. "Well, besides the stuff

about Trevor and the heads-up from Scott, did you find anything else?"

"Since yesterday? I thought that was plenty."

There was that chuckle again. So low and sexy he could barely keep himself from reaching for her. Did she realize that? Was that the reason she'd shifted closer to the door?

"What about you?"

"Nothing really." He cleared his throat again and broached the subject that had been weighing on his thoughts all day. "You'll find this funny, but I was so desperate to find any sort of lead that I did a search on your stepfather. I know it's a stretch, but Lloyd Jackson was accused of several high-profile crimes when he was county commissioner and—"

She interrupted him by throwing open the door, casting light over the SUV's interior. "Why did you have to go there? You know I'm not involved in the case at the post, but you just couldn't resist digging into my family, could you? Titillating reading, wasn't it?"

"Come on, Delia. I knew it was a stretch, but—"

"But nothing. You should have been trying to save your own sorry ass instead of digging into places where you have no business looking."

With that, she climbed out of the car, slammed the door and stomped off, leaving him staring and wondering what had just happened.

He climbed out as well, but he left his door open to keep the light on. "Wait, Delia. I'm sorry. I didn't mean…"

He let his words trail off because he had no idea why he was sorry or what he didn't mean. He'd always planned to thoroughly research the backgrounds of each team member. He'd told her that. Had she really believed he would skip hers?

"Come on," he called after her. But after Delia rounded the car's back bumper, even the light coming from the interior wasn't enough to help him see her as she kept walking.

Reaching across the driver's seat, he opened the glove box and pulled out a flashlight. He flipped it on and started after her, at least the way he thought she'd gone.

For a few heart-stopping seconds, he couldn't see her and wondered if she might have fallen somewhere, but he finally caught sight of her about twenty feet ahead. She had flipped on the flashlight app on her phone and was walking carefully in the tire tracks he'd made only moments before.

"Please stop. Let's talk about this." He hurried after her, not expecting her to listen to him.

But then she stopped and whirled so quickly that he had to move his flashlight beam that pointed directly at her face. At least she'd put gloves back on the hands she was using to shield her eyes.

"There's nothing to talk about."

"I think there is." He took advantage of the moment to close the distance between them. "You knew I had to look at everyone's family, right? It was just a starting place. We talked about it."

"Everyone else's history isn't as interesting as mine."

"Are you kidding? You're talking to *me* here."

Her breath came out in white puffs when she chuckled. "You've got a point." She paused for a few seconds. "But my history isn't all that pretty, either."

"Nobody's is if we dig deep enough. Families like the Huxtables and the Cleavers only exist in TV shows."

He didn't get the laugh he'd hoped for, but she didn't run away, either. She did shiver, however.

"Any chance we could continue this conversation in the car. It comes fully loaded. Heat and everything."

Instead of answering, she turned and started back toward his vehicle. He still wasn't sure what had made her so angry. It was the second time she'd made a big deal over something that should have been minor.

"Tell me," he said as she opened the car door. "Did you plan to walk all the way back into the park to your car?" He climbed in on the driver's side, turned the ignition and cranked the heat, shivering as freezing air blew on his face. The windshield and his glasses immediately fogged.

"If I had to." She closed the door, crossing her arms and rubbing her upper arms.

Slipping off his glasses, he wiped them on the hem of his shirt. He could still see her from the glow of the dashboard lights, but just barely. "How did you plan to find it in the dark?"

"The flashlight in my phone."

"Right. You think of everything."

"I try."

As he rubbed his aching hands together to warm them, he couldn't help watching her out of the corner of his eye. She had pulled off her gloves but was blowing into her cupped hands.

"Now can we discuss Lloyd Jackson without the two of us having to run out into the snow again?"

Delia nearly laughed with relief over Ben's question. He could have asked so many more difficult ones. She turned to face him, her left leg coming up on the seat.

"What do you want to know?"

"Just the overview."

She nodded. "Marian thought she'd hit the jackpot when she met her boss, Lloyd Jackson.

A rich corporate attorney with political aspirations." She took a deep breath, finding even this part of the story tough to tell.

"She'd been struggling for too long, I guess. My father died when I was two. So with Jackson, she got it all. Big house. Private schools for me. And he got an idyllic blended family for his political campaigns."

"But everything wasn't what it seemed, was it?"

She had to cough into her elbow to cover her sharp intake of breath. He couldn't possibly know how true his words were. She was shocked to find that she was tempted to tell him the ugliest part, too, something she hadn't shared with anyone since that one time so long ago. When no one had believed her.

No, she couldn't go there. Couldn't rip open old wounds, still hidden beneath the flimsiest of scars. Even if she suspected that this time someone would believe her and would help shield her from the hurt. Wasn't it bad enough that she couldn't be anywhere near Ben without imagining his hands on her, without remembering the taste of his kiss? Was her mind, maybe even her spirit, susceptible to him, as well?

She cleared her throat and started again, choosing to answer only what he'd asked. It was safer that way. "You saw the charges. Racketeering.

Mail fraud. I guess being loaded and powerful wasn't enough entertainment for him. Eventually he was forced to resign while he faced charges, but not a single one—"

"Stuck," he finished for her. "All of the charges were dismissed on technicalities, right?"

"It helped that his attorneys were more accustomed to defending mobsters than crooked commissioners."

"That was the connection I was looking at this afternoon," Ben admitted. "Was it possible that the attorneys who defended Jackson could be the same ones hired by some of the defendants facing narcotics charges? The ones with the evidence against them that magically disappeared."

"Sounds like you're grasping at straws."

He pounded his fist on the steering wheel. "I thought so, too. But at this point, I'm desperate for any connection."

"I get it." She couldn't blame him when she'd been so freaked out by her conversation with Scott that she'd insisted that Ben meet her tonight. "Well, to get this over with, so you can finally rule me out, you might as well ask me about Marian, too."

"From the few things I read about her, she sounded like the dutiful wife."

"A *Stepford* wife."

"Don't hold back or anything." He chuckled before becoming serious again. "I take it you didn't get along with her."

She shook he head. "He was guilty. Everyone knew it. His attorneys. The prosecutor. Letter-to-the-editor writers who called for his resignation." She paused for a second and then added, "Me."

"Everyone except your mother."

"Either she didn't know it or refused to see what was right—" she paused, coughing "—in front of her."

"A lot of people are like that."

She swallowed, realizing he was talking about his own mother now. If only Delia's story didn't force him to Ben to relive his.

"I'm sure she thought she was doing the right thing," Delia said.

"I guess so."

Neither needed to specify which "she" they were speaking about now.

"So when did Helen Miles become your legal guardian?" Ben said, returning to his questions as if he and Delia hadn't just slipped away on a tangent.

"How do you know about her?"

"Her name was in your file. She passed away when you were in college, right?"

"Yes. How many times did you read my file?"

She didn't mention the obvious truth that he only could have seen her file before he was put on leave.

"A few, I guess." He cleared his throat. "How long was it after the charges against Jackson were dismissed before your parents left you?"

For several seconds, Delia couldn't answer. She'd told herself she would never cry over her mother again, and yet a knot the size of a golf ball formed in her throat, and her eyes burned, smoldering with the embers of a childhood lost.

"A few weeks later," she began finally in a voice that sounded flat in her ears. "The media refused to go away, still parked outside our house. Lloyd started saying how much he hated southeast Michigan. That there were opportunities for them in Ohio or Illinois."

"He didn't include *you* in his plans?"

Delia swallowed, staring at her hands, which she gripped together in her lap. In all of these years, no one had asked her about those awful days. Even with Helen, who'd fed, clothed and sent her to school for seven years, Delia had learned that it was in her best interest not to mention any of the things that had happened to her. So it felt strange when something inside her, something wound so tightly that it had cut off the circulation to her heart, started to unwind in slow, halting turns.

"I didn't realize they weren't including me at first, even though I hadn't been silent about my belief that he was guilty." About more than just those charges, but she didn't clarify that. "So they sold the house, scheduled the movers and we all started packing."

She squeezed her eyes shut and then opened them again, pushing through the pain. "Until my clothes and bedroom furniture were the only things left in the house, I didn't know that I wouldn't be going with them."

"You've got to be kidding."

The anger in his voice startled her. The man who'd refused to blow his top, even when someone targeted his career and his freedom, was furious on her behalf.

"I probably shouldn't ask, but who was Helen Miles to your family?"

"Would you believe me if I said she was my mother's hairdresser?"

His jaw flexed. "No, I wouldn't."

"Then she was her distant cousin *and* her hairdresser."

"That makes it so much better."

"When Helen showed up that day with a truck, I was told she was to be my legal guardian and that I would be going to a new school. And that was that." She brushed off her hands the way they'd wiped her out of their lives.

"How old were you?" He paused to calculate. "About thirteen?"

"Twelve."

He blew out a long breath. "And I thought losing my mom was a tragedy."

"What are you saying?" She stared at him, sure she hadn't heard him right. "Of course your mom's death was a tragedy. And the accident was a tragedy. Even your dad's addiction—"

He only shook his head. "But they deserted you."

"I was okay. I wasn't on the street or anything."

"But they left you intentionally. What kind of parents do that?"

"Come on, Ben. We work in law enforcement. We see things like that all the time."

"Delia, your mother chose a man over her own daughter."

At the last, her breath caught. "I know."

She wasn't even sure why she'd defended them, but she'd never been in this position before. Ben had taken her side. Not with conditions like the support that Helen had always offered. But her side. Even without knowing the whole story, he was wholeheartedly in her corner. She'd never had that. Had never known how much she'd craved it. Until now.

"It was tough at first. Like living someone

else's life. But then you start at the new school, learn to eat some iffy cooking and, well, just get on with it."

"I know what that's like," Ben said as he stared out into the snowflakes fluttering on the windshield. "Sometimes I don't know how we survived it. My grandparents or me."

Delia nodded, remembering her own early days. "The first few months were the worst. I used to wait for Helen to go to sleep each night, and then I would close the door to my room and just let go."

"Let go?"

She could feel him watching her, but she couldn't look at him now, not if she planned to say the rest. For a reason she couldn't explain, she wanted him to know. At least this much.

"I would sob so loud that the walls must have shook. I felt so abandoned, and I wasn't even allowed to talk about it. Not unless I wanted Helen to give me the silent treatment."

"Did no one hear you? None of the neighbors?"

"None that I know of. But then I was used to no one listening or—" She somehow stopped herself before using the word *believing*, but the rest seemed to fall from her lips of its own accord. "I'd never felt so alone."

Something rustled as he shifted, and suddenly

Ben took hold of her hand, entwining their fingers. Her breath froze as she stared down at their hands.

"Delia, you don't have to be alone."

CHAPTER THIRTEEN

A MISTAKE. THE WORDS filtered through Ben's mind as he leaned across the console and touched his lips to the mouth he'd been dreaming about. But he didn't care whether it was a good idea or not. Not even handcuffs would have been enough to keep him from her this time. She'd been alone, likely even before her mother had chosen someone else over her own child. Even with all the tragedy he'd experienced, he still couldn't imagine that kind of betrayal.

Ben couldn't let her sit next to him, away from him, not realizing that she no longer needed to be alone. Whatever it cost him.

He didn't know what he expected as he sank his lips into all the precious softness, the mouth that his memory hadn't come close to accurately describing. But the way she nearly climbed inside of him with just her lips nearly yanked him out of his seat. Where was this coming from? This was the stuff that guys lied about in locker rooms, not the kind of thing that happened to a nice guy who seldom finished first. But she made him feel as if *he* was the prize instead of the other way around.

He tried to keep his clarity, but it was fogging fast. She'd said she never wanted him to touch her again, had sworn she wouldn't help him on the case if he did, and yet now it seemed as if she never wanted him to stop. Though well aware that he shouldn't be doing this, he was ready to oblige. He'd never been so ready.

Unlacing their fingers because his were trembling, he rested both hands on the bulky shoulders of her coat and tilted his head to deepen the kiss. But she was way ahead of him. No gentleness or finesse, she kissed him with an intensity that startled him. As if he was the only man she'd ever wanted. The only one who could begin to satisfy her needs.

He wanted to be that man for her…in all ways.

This crazy moment wouldn't last. She would come to her senses and would pull back from him in less time than it took to flip the switch in a patrol car for the lights and siren. So each time he kissed the corners of her mouth and each chance he had to nibble the softness of her lower lip, he considered a gift. Only instead of disappearing, the gift kept expanding until it felt like Christmas and a couple of birthdays were sitting there in his passenger seat.

And suddenly she wasn't sitting anymore.

Somehow Delia had lifted up on her knees, her hands landing on his shoulders. Releasing one side and then trading, she shrugged out of her coat before kicking off her snow boots. Ben was torn between closing his lids and just going with the kiss that he felt everywhere, and keeping his eyes wide-open because he wanted to see what she would do next. She must have recognized his quandary because she lifted his glasses from his face and rested them on the dashboard.

He was just adjusting to the new, slightly fuzzy image of her when she put her hands on his shoulders again. She pushed him back toward the window, but he steeled himself against the movement and shifted his hand to cover hers.

"Whoa. Whoa. Wait, Delia. Maybe this isn't such a…" Great idea? Who was he kidding? He couldn't think of a more perfect idea. It was the only thing that was clear to him when the rest of the world remained a transient blur.

But her disappointed moan as she wiggled closer to him shook him to his core. She kissed him with a determination that was so Delia-like, but with an abandon that seemed like someone else altogether. Delia was all about boundaries and rules, and she was crossing and breaking even her own.

He knew he should pull back. The timing, the situation, everything, was wrong about this. But she was so beautiful in the dashboard lights, and she smelled like flowers and tasted so sweet that the idea of becoming lost in her was sounding more rational by the second.

With a strength he hadn't known was inside of him, he pulled his mouth away from hers again. "Now, don't get me wrong. I want this. Believe me. I want this. But shouldn't we think about things before—"

"I don't want to think."

The words he'd been planning to say about regrets she would have later vanished as she dipped her head and caught his bottom lip with her teeth. He hadn't even tried to suggest that *he* would regret it. No sense in lying now when his racing heart would give him away. As Delia flicked her tongue over that sensitized spot on his lip and rolled it between her tongue and teeth, a sound emerged from his throat, more like a cheer than anything resembling dissent.

She released his lip and began a love affair with the sensitive dip at the base of his throat.

Ben swallowed, losing ground with each brush of her beautiful lips. "Come on, Dee."

"I like when you call me Dee."

"But remember what you said before?"

"I don't care what I said."

Ben would have offered another token argument, but he could only stare as she climbed across the center console onto his lap. Then digging down next to him, she found the seat controls and jerked the seat back. All the way back.

His resolve was crumbling fast. How was he supposed to behave like a gentleman when she was so insistent about what she wanted? What they both wanted.

He searched his spinning thoughts for one more decisive excuse, one more attempt to stop the roll of water amid a tidal wave. But Delia picked that moment to scoot closer, straddling him. She leaned back slightly and fumbled with his belt buckle.

"Now," she said as she leaned in and breathed a word against his lips. "Please."

She'd said "please," after all. Ben did the only *other* thing a gentleman could do: he helped her to undress him so they could get started on her.

SOMEONE ELSE MUST have been in that car tonight. That was the only way that Delia could explain this out-of-body experience. Someone else had been frenetic as she shoved away his clothes. And tore off hers. That other person had demanded and pleaded, seeking heat and relief.

So how could she explain that she was the one lost in a sea of sensation and emotion? That the five o'clock shadow abraded *her* tender skin. Calloused hands welcomed and touched her everywhere at once. Two hearts pressed so close beneath sweaty skin that they chorused their frantic rhythm.

A voice called out as they fully joined, and Delia recognized it as her own. Ben heard it, too, immediately stilling beneath her instead of beginning to move as her body implored.

"Are you…okay?" he managed between halting breaths.

He pressed his forehead to hers, the hands that had left a trail of tingles and heated skin in their wake dropping to his sides.

"We can stop," he whispered. "Tell me what you want to do, sweetheart."

But she couldn't answer as the tender way he'd spoken to her played in her thoughts. How could she tell him that the sound she'd made had come from a place so far from pain that it defied description? How could she let him know that his offer to stop was amazingly sweet? Though her absolute certainty that he would stop—even now when they were far beyond the point of no return—terrified her, it thrilled her, as well. Maybe there really was a man she could believe in after all.

She answered with her body instead of with the words she could never say aloud.

ENFOLDED IN A cocoon formed by fogged windows and a backdrop of night, Ben held Delia to him, her partly clothed form still draped over his lap, his face buried in a curtain of her hair. He'd pulled out every last restricting pin and would probably find those tiny metal hindrances all over his car for months, but he didn't care. The freed mass had fallen so beautifully past her shoulders, just as he'd imagined it would. He hadn't been able to keep his hands out of the waves, and even when spent, he continued sliding his fingers through the silky strands.

She was so beautiful, so sexy in her dishabille. Here with him. Like this.

Ben traced his free hand along the curve of her neck to the dent near her collarbone. Her skin felt like satin beneath his touch, still slightly damp. In the light, would she discover marks where his hands had touched her and where his lips had brushed? Even in the dark, he could tell that she'd left her mark on him. Only hers was beneath his skin.

Okay, the event hadn't unfolded the way he'd imagined it would, or hoped, even after he'd sworn it would never happen. Tonight wouldn't make the record books in the romance department. Or ever warrant any description beyond *hot* and *embarrassingly fast*.

But he couldn't bring himself to regret it. Not when making love to Delia had felt like finding home after he'd spent a lifetime of never belonging anywhere, at least in his personal life. He'd been certain he would never be worthy of belonging.

Now the idea that he'd ever tried to resist Delia, not just physically but in every way, made no sense to him. Even if it was dangerous putting his heart on the line, he no longer had any control over that. The heart wanted what it wanted, and his wanted her. He couldn't deny the truth that he cared about her. He would be with her to whatever extent she would allow. Would accept whatever level of trust she was able to put in him.

Was it enough? He refused to listen to the unwelcome voice inside of him that asked questions he wasn't prepared to answer. Anyway, she'd proven that she trusted him at least a little. She'd welcomed him into her body, after all.

As if she'd read his thoughts and wanted to vehemently disagree, Delia shuddered and pulled back from him then. Her movement and the immediate chill on his chest from the loss of her skin's warmth snapped him out of the spell of the moment. The perfect breasts that Ben had so recently memorized, she covered with one of her arms as she used the other to shift herself from his lap. He tried to help her, but she backed away from his touch all the way to the car door.

It would have hurt less if she'd slapped him. With her gun. Was he the only one who saw any magic in their lovemaking? At once, the bright beauty of the moment melted away like a perfect photograph as flames lapped at its edges.

"Sorry. Are you cold?"

Are you cold? Was that the best he could do? On the other hand, he had several things to apologize for tonight, so maybe it was best to start with a small one.

"No. I'm…fine."

She appeared to be a lot of things as she yanked up the bra that had ended up around her waist, pulled that strappy tank thing over her head and then struggled with the buttons on her sweater, but *fine* wasn't one of them. Maybe infinitely uncomfortable, quietly furious or just ashamed, but she was not fine. The woman who'd always seemed to have a chip on her shoulder, a solid block of resentment that made more sense now that he knew about her mother's desertion, was curling both shoulders inward toward her collarbones.

Though her reaction confused him, he couldn't blame her for being upset. What had seemed to him to be an amazing, inevitable moment probably had reminded her of two desperate teenagers fooling around in a car. He'd been desperate, all right. Enough to make himself believe that he wasn't the only one.

He cleared his throat, trying to ignore the lump

that had formed there. "I don't know about you, but I'm freezing."

It was a stretch since he had on far more clothes than she did. There hadn't been time to remove all of his. He had to do something now to help her stop shivering. Especially since he guessed that if he reached over to warm her with his hands, she would jump out into the snow again. He leaned forward and flipped the heat on high.

Delia was too busy wiggling back into her panties and jeans to notice anything he did anyway. She didn't stop when she had those on, either. She slid into her coat and jammed her feet back into her boots. Even then, she still crossed her arms, continuing to shiver.

What was he supposed to do now? He dug for the controls next to him and moved his seat forward, stalling. This was so confusing. She'd seemed willing. Enthusiastic even. She'd raced toward her own release with a fervency that had sent him careening over the edge along with her. But now as she cowered in the corner, nervously finger-combing her hair into some semblance of order, he figured he must have imagined her eagerness, as well. Even that sigh of what had sounded like bliss.

Shame filled him over remembering those details when she was so obviously upset. This wasn't about his pitiful performance insecurities.

It was only about the act he should never have allowed to happen in a car, whether she'd seemed to be on board with the idea or not. He wasn't some rutting teenager. He was a man who'd just taken the woman he adored in a way that made her feel ashamed.

He'd proven once again that when the chips were down, he was no hero. Another selfish loser. Just like his old man.

"This road seems deserted." He'd said it to fill the silence as he pulled his dark T-shirt over his head and shoved his arms into the sleeves of his flannel shirt, but he was immediately sorry as she stared out the steamy window as if she was being watched. She'd believed that earlier after all.

"Third shift hasn't been patrolling the park area since it's closed at this time," she managed.

He would have said illegal activity rarely took place when establishments were open, but he was so glad she'd spoken at all that he kept it to himself. Besides, as he repositioned his boxers and jeans that had never made it past his hips, he discovered a bigger surprise that could signal a more significant mistake than even the event in the car.

Telltale dampness.

He would have asked himself what he'd been thinking to take a risk like that, but it was clear he hadn't been thinking. Even with all the chances he'd taken in his youth, on those rare occasions when he'd been lucky enough to have sex with someone, he'd always used condoms. So why now? Why with Delia had he lost all claim to his good sense?

Backing the car onto the snowy road that was becoming slicker by the minute, he flipped on the high beams and crept in the general direction of the park. She sat as still as a Da Vinci sculpture, and though he couldn't tell for sure, was probably as pale as some of them, too.

"Delia, I'm really sorry." He paused, not even sure how to phrase this one. "If it turns out that—"

But she shook her head sharply to interrupt his apology and his promise. Maybe she was so freaked out by the possibilities that she couldn't bear to hear them spoken aloud. Didn't she realize he was a stand-up guy, who would be there for her if she was pregnant? But then nothing about tonight would suggest that he *was* a decent guy.

"Just talk about the case."

"But we really should talk about this—"

"Please!"

The word she'd used before to beg him to make love to her had now become a plaintive cry for him to forget it had ever happened. Didn't she understand that those shadowed images, her sounds, the sweet scent that was uniquely hers, all those things had engraved themselves on his brain and burrowed beneath the layers of his senses?

But because he would do anything to relieve her obvious discomfort, he cleared his throat and started again. "Okay. The case."

Strange how none of that mattered now, even if it was probably naive of him to look at his own future through such a cavalier lens. Still, in this moment, nothing was as important as finding a way to relieve her distress. To convince her to forgive him for causing it. As he entered the park and continued down the curvy roads back to the Possum Hollow area, he searched for anything to say that would give her the distraction she craved. When he backed into the space next to her car and shut off the engine, he turned in the seat to face her.

"Now, I know that some of the business owners that Jackson dealt with were eventually convicted and served time for other crimes." He stopped, watching the side of her face, since she wouldn't look at him. "But I want you to tell me once and for all, am I grasping at straws to think there might be a connection between the current investigation and Jackson, or any of his associates?"

Of course he was grasping. Reaching like his dad always had when he tried to explain away one more drink and one more pain pill. If anything, he expected a flat denial from Delia. From the beginning, she'd said it would be a waste of time to look at her family. But he'd only kept looking.

For what? Something that could explain the puzzle that was Delia Morgan? Something that would lay flat on the table the hand of cards that, until tonight, she'd always kept so carefully to herself?

But she didn't answer. Since she was the one who'd insisted on this conversation, he tried one more time.

"Could it maybe have been revenge against you because you didn't believe in him?" As he said it, he knew how nonsensical it sounded. Even if the man were targeting Delia, and that was a stretch, then why set up Ben? Could he have gone after him to get to the both of them? But that only sounded crazier. There wasn't really a *them* yet, except in his mind.

Still, she didn't answer. The temptation to reach over and shake her out of her stupor was so strong that he had to grip the steering wheel to stop himself. If he touched her at all, she would probably just run to her car and drive away. And he would be left with those questions...and more. So he waited.

Finally, her head shifted, and her mouth opened as if she was going to speak, but instead of answering his questions, she buried her face in her hands and sobbed.

CHAPTER FOURTEEN

"I'M FINE TO DRIVE. Really." Delia's voice cracked, but only a little this time. That was progress at least. Her voice sounded almost normal in her ears. Well, not too far from it.

She rubbed at eyes that felt as if she'd been through a sandstorm. Her lids were thick, swollen, leaving only slits of openings behind. Why it mattered after everything that had happened tonight, she wasn't sure, but she had ugly cried, and she didn't want him to see the splotchy results.

"Besides, we can't leave my car in the parking lot." She rubbed her upper arms over her coat, but the gooseflesh beneath the material refused to settle. "It would be as suspicious as the one we found several weeks ago."

"You think a parked car will raise as much suspicion as a charred one with all the serial numbers filed off?"

She could almost picture his eyebrow sneaking above the rim of his glasses. "Well, maybe not that much."

"And you said yourself that forty-five hundred

acres was a lot to patrol at once for the Metropark Police, even with the state police providing extra patrol."

Delia frowned. She had said that, on another day that was nothing like this one, so it wasn't fair for him to use it against her now. "That doesn't mean we should leave the car here."

The discussion had been going on that way for about fifteen minutes, with each side volleying, but neither gaining points. Ben had never seemed especially stubborn to her before, but he was digging his heels in this time in a disagreement that had more to do with worry than any car left in a parking lot.

She could feel Ben's gaze on her now just as he'd pretended not to watch her earlier, waiting while her sobs had turned to cries and then trickled to sniffles. The process had taken so long that he'd been forced to start the engine and flip the heat back on—twice—so they wouldn't freeze to death.

As if he'd guessed that she would shy away from his touch if he tried to comfort her, he'd kept his hands to himself the whole time. But he'd gripped the steering wheel so tight that his hands had to ache now.

"I told you we could get your car as soon as the park opens tomorrow." His gaze shifting to the dashboard clock, Ben cleared his throat. "I mean today. Still, it's unlikely anyone will even see it before then."

"But with my luck…"

She didn't finish her comment, but from the way he shifted in his seat, his back braced against the door, she could tell that he'd filled in the blanks himself. With something about the kind of luck it had taken to end up with a guy like him, surrounded by steamy car windows.

"Anyway, the two of us," she continued to fill the awkward pause, "probably shouldn't be seen together."

"You have a point," he said finally.

But his tone hinted that he wished she didn't have one. He was still trying to make right what had happened between them tonight, and she couldn't tell him that the truth had nothing to do with him. Most of it, anyway.

"At least let me follow you. Just to make sure you get home okay."

"I keep telling you I'm okay. Really."

His silence told her what he thought of that.

So she pulled the one card she had left. "Lieutenant Peterson, I go out, alone, in a patrol car every day. If I can't drive myself home, maybe I shouldn't…" She let her words trail away because his sudden shift suggested he'd already gotten the point. Even if he was convinced she was headed for a breakdown, he would have to let her go now.

The last thing he would ever do was to question her competence as a cop.

But if she hadn't painted him into a corner, he would never have given in. He would have followed her, insisted on protecting her, on being there for her, whether she wanted him there or not. She wasn't sure what to do with that certainty as the lump in her throat that had finally decreased in size had another growth spurt. She should have been cried out by now, for today and probably a few lifetimes, but her eyes and nose burned again.

So sorry. So sorry. So damn sorry.

His whispered words settled as heavily on her heart now as they had when he'd said them while she cried. What did he have to be sorry for? He wasn't the one who'd…pushed *her* seat back. And yet he'd apologized. With profanity, too, though he didn't usually talk like the rest of the trash mouths at work.

At least he hadn't asked her to explain why she was crying. She would have had to lie, and he would have seen right through her. It must not have made sense to him. She'd made the first move, after all. Well, maybe not the first, but certainly the second. And the third. So she had as much of an excuse as a grappler who'd started the fight and then whined over his bruises afterward. She probably had a few of those, too, if her sore tailbone from the steering wheel and her knee from a pesky seat belt buckle were any indication.

Her stinging eyes suddenly filled again. What was happening to her? She felt as if she were being ripped in two by slow, excruciating increments instead of a quick, merciful tear.

Now. Please.

Her own words sliced through her recollection with a razor-sharp knife of blame. She'd never initiated sex before. Never even wanted it really. Yet in that car, the cliché of settings for a romantic tryst, she'd begged Ben for it. She'd wanted him, all right, so much so that she hadn't been able to get close enough. She'd needed to touch every part of him with every piece of her. Inside and out.

And for a few minutes, she had. She'd never experienced such sweetness or such pleasure as she found in that tender dance. He'd breathed in every breath she exhaled, and she, his. It had all seemed so right. So magical. So perfect.

And then the event was over, and suddenly, it wasn't any of those things. She couldn't get covered up fast enough, as if he wasn't already aware of what was hidden beneath her clothes. As if any amount of clothes could cover her shame. For wanting it. For *enjoying* it.

What had she expected? Had she really believed that by climbing inside of Ben that she could fix all her broken pieces? The saddest truth of all was that on some level she *had* believed it.

She didn't know how long she'd been staring down at her hands, but when she lifted her head, she caught him watching her again. Waiting. For what? An explanation as to why physical intimacy turned a strong, reasonably sane woman into a blubbering mess? She swallowed. If only she had an explanation to give.

With a sudden shift, Ben turned away from her and reached up to brush at the condensation building on the windshield to see something beyond it. At first it just looked like a flash of light, but then a pair of headlights came into view, drawing closer. The car pulled in on the far end of the lot.

"Who's that? Is that a patrol car?" she whispered and sank low in the seat as though either action would help now, especially if the driver turned a patrol car's spotlight on them. At least Ben had shut off the engine again, so no one would see the parking lights. She strained her eyes, trying to make out the vehicle's shape. It didn't appear to have a gumball on top, so it probably wasn't a state police vehicle, but that didn't rule out other agencies.

"How are we supposed to explain our presence here?" She would have asked whose bright idea it had been to meet at the park in the first place, but they both knew who was to blame for that. The same one who should have known better since she'd been patrolling the area herself.

"Undercover surveillance?"

"Funny." They'd been doing something "undercover," all right. That is, if coats counted. But that wasn't something she was prepared to confess if an officer asked for their statements for trespassing after park closing.

"Better get our story together because he'll be over here soon."

Delia nodded. "I guess we could—"

"Keep our heads low and our mouths shut," he finished for her.

"What?" She swiped at her side of the windshield and tried to see what he saw. The other driver must have parked and turned off his ignition as his headlights faded away, and his vehicle disappeared into a blackness that the sliver of a moon and the steady flutter of snowflakes weren't enough to fracture.

"Do you think he saw the two cars down here?" she whispered. "There's kind of a dip in the lot at this end, and it's awfully dark."

"Hard to say."

"But there's a chance he didn't, right?"

"Can you see *him* now?"

That she couldn't came as a relief. There was hope that they would go unnoticed, too. Of course, that meant that they couldn't risk turning on the engine or the heat again, so they were stuck there for now, shivering in the dark.

"Do you think they'll be here long?" She wiggled her coat up next to her ears and buttoned it to just below her chin.

Ben flipped up his collar and rubbed his hands together. "Hope not."

But just as they settled in to wait it out, another set of headlights came into view. Delia's breath caught. Maybe the first driver had seen their two parked cars and had called for backup.

"You don't think—"

"I don't know. Do you have your weapon?"

"Of course." She glanced his way. "But you don't, do you?"

"It didn't seem like a good idea with everything else happening."

Since she was used to going in without backup, she was surprised by how much his being unarmed bothered her. After everything that had happened tonight, was she still tempted to rely on him?

She only hoped she wouldn't need backup as the second car flashed its lights and Car Number One returned the favor before its lights faded again. Once the second car parked next to the first, Delia took a deep breath.

"Here we go," she whispered.

Only they didn't *go*. For several seconds, nothing happened other than the lights on the second car going dark. The fear that both drivers were racing toward them in the cover of darkness was so overwhelming that she bent to retrieve her weapon from her purse while still gripping the passenger armrest with her free hand.

Finally, when she was certain she couldn't take this interminable pause any longer, the driver's-side door on the first car opened and closed. Thirty seconds later, the same thing happened on the passenger side of the other car. Interior lights disappeared in the same staggered order.

"Oh."

Such a tiny word, but when Ben said it, Delia's eyes widened. Two cars. A meeting place. She swallowed. Maybe they weren't the only ones with clandestine plans for tonight. Not that either of them had planned any of the night's events.

Trapped by scene and situation, they waited in a silence pulled taut with speculation. Though the chill had worked its way through the layers of her clothing, her face felt strangely warm. She didn't want to imagine what those other people might be doing in that car. Unfortunately, she could think of nothing else. Delia couldn't see inside it—or see the car itself—and yet her imagination did a great job of painting its own pictures. Vivid images that deepened her blush.

She felt like a Peeping Tom, but she couldn't look away. What if someone had been watching her and Ben not an hour before? As if working together hadn't been enough of a risk, they'd put themselves in an even more vulnerable position by becoming "otherwise occupied" when they should have been on their guard. Another excuse for frustration over what had happened between them tonight. Another reason for regrets. Holding herself in a protective hug now, she shivered from everything but the cold.

"Sorry," he said in a low voice. "Wish I could turn on the heat."

Red taillights flashed on then, saving her from having to answer when she couldn't explain. The passenger door winged open, and a figure she couldn't make out stepped outside and closed the door before entering the other vehicle. Soon one car raced out of parking lot, the second nearly hugging its back bumper.

Delia couldn't help but stare in the direction they'd gone for a long time after the dark and snow had swallowed them. What had happened inside that car? A lovers' quarrel? A call from a duped spouse? Or maybe they'd decided that this location was too crowded? The last had a chill scaling her arms.

"Well, that happened," Ben said as soon as the

two cars had disappeared somewhere along Park Route 4.

"It didn't take long, either." She pressed her lips together as she realized her double entendre. If he'd been uncertain where her thoughts had gone as they'd watched those two cars, she'd cleared that up. "I mean the cars weren't there very long."

"Guess not."

"Do you think they'll come back?"

"Shouldn't wait around to find out." He reached for the keys and turned the ignition.

"It's going to take me forever to thaw out." She paused and then added, "I should probably…"

"Yeah, you should get going." He cleared his throat. "In case they come back."

He was giving her a break, and she knew it. From him. From things she wasn't ready to face. From things he knew she regretted. It was such a *Ben* thing to do that it squeezed her chest and somewhere deeper inside.

She swung open the car door, snowflakes immediately landing on the interior, the wind stealing her breath. "Well, thanks for…for coming when I was worried."

He cleared his throat. "Sure thing."

Because she was tempted to believe he would be there for her, no matter what, she pushed herself out of the car and sank her boots into the accumulating snow.

He leaned over before she could shut the door. "You're sure you're—"

"I'm fine, Ben."

A sheepish grin spread on his face, and Delia's tummy did that familiar tumble.

"Drive carefully," he said.

With that, she closed the door and slugged toward her own car. It had been there long enough that snow covered the windows, and there was a fine sheet of ice beneath the snowflakes. She'd only started scraping when his door opened again, and he joined her, helping her without a need to comment. Ben just being Ben. When they were finished, he waved her off without another goodbye or delay.

As she pulled onto the lane that led to the park entrance, he moved his car into position behind hers, continuing to follow at a safe distance like that until they reached the highway. When she turned off at the ramp, he continued on straight, toward his own home in rural Livingston County.

Immediately, she missed his nearness. He hadn't pressed her for answers tonight, though his concern had settled on her shoulders with the weight and compassion of a touch. He deserved an explanation, for her tears, at least, if even she didn't understand the rest. She owed him answers. Needed to explain. And she would.

Later. When she was ready. She only hoped that *later* didn't come too soon.

BEN SHOOK THE snow off his coat, stepped out of his boots and turned the dead bolt on the door behind him. In the living room just steps away, his sweatpants that served as pajama bottoms still hung over the wing-back chair where he'd tossed them after Delia's call. That she'd been worried enough to ask him to meet her had concerned him so much that he'd changed out of his night clothes and raced out the door without bothering to lock it.

Strange how long ago that call seemed now. Only a few hours and so much had changed. He'd been almost asleep when she'd called, and now he doubted he could go to bed if the fate of humanity rested on him catching a few z's.

As he hung his jacket on the coat tree, he glanced down at the blue flannel shirt he'd thrown on over his T-shirt and the well-worn jeans he'd paired with those boots. If he'd had any idea what would happen with Delia tonight, he would have dressed nicer. Perhaps been prepared in the safe-sex department. On the other hand, if he'd known that tough-as-nails Delia Morgan would end up in despair after what had been the most amazing physical experience of his life, he would have thought twice about showing up at all.

Oh, who was he kidding? He would have gone if she'd needed him, even if he'd known that he would end up as miserable and confused as he was right now. He only wished he could have made whatever it was better for her.

But why had she been so upset? That same question that had nearly ripped him apart earlier, while he'd waited, praying for her to stop crying, clamored for answers again. He'd thought it was tough keeping his cool during the bank robbery attempt. That was nothing compared to the white-knuckled strength it had taken him to keep from pulling her into his arms and soothing her distress.

And after he'd comforted her, he would have demanded that she tell him what was wrong or at least *urged* her to tell. The truth this time. Could it have been only that they'd made love? Or could he have hurt her? He couldn't bear that thought. Still, something told him that whatever it was, it had to be more than that.

Shaking his head, he grabbed the pants off the chair and then his state police sweatshirt from the rocker opposite it. His lovemaking skills might not have earned him a standing ovation—or even polite applause—but they couldn't have warranted her sheer devastation, either.

I keep telling you I'm okay.

Just as his instincts had told him she was lying

every time she'd said it, he was convinced that there was more to the story. He would bet every minute left in his career that there was. He grimaced as he pounded up the stairs. That wasn't much of a bet when his career might have a shorter shelf life than a banana in the sweltering heat.

Tossing his sweats on the bathroom counter, he twisted on the shower faucet. He stripped and dropped his clothes into a pile, trying to forget how Delia had helped him remove at least some of them earlier. How he'd helped her peel away hers.

He stepped under the spray, hoping to wash away all thoughts of Delia, all of the questions. But just as the steamy water splashed his face, another thought struck him so hard that his head jerked back.

The two cars. A quick meeting. Sure, it could have been an illicit tryst, but it just as easily could have been a drug deal. Or some other illegal exchange. Anything. Because of the awkward moment they were experiencing, he and Delia had jumped to that one conclusion instead of considering all of the possibilities.

How could he have missed that? Delia at least could blame her rookie status. What was his excuse? Maybe he didn't deserve to be a police officer. First, he'd allowed himself to be set up regarding alleged mishandling of evidence, and now this.

The truth was when Delia Morgan was in his line of vision, he didn't see anything else. He didn't even care. All he could think about was Delia and whatever she was hiding. He needed answers almost as much as he needed her, and he needed her so much it terrified him.

If he had any sense at all, he would run, not walk, in the opposite direction from her. Far enough away that he could reclaim his priorities. His career and his future were on the line, and his sense of self-preservation had fled the moment her heart thrummed against his chest, awakening tender emotions. Those fragile shoots that had no business sprouting on such unseasoned and unprepared ground.

He shouldn't be thinking about planting any kind of roots with Delia, or anyone else, when his whole life was nothing but rocks. Big rocks. But how was he supposed to get back to finding solutions to his own problems when he could still hear the sobs that had crowded that car with her misery and could still feel the aftershocks that had shook her even after her tears had dried? Maybe if he found answers to help her, he would finally figure out how to help himself.

CHAPTER FIFTEEN

BLURRY RIBBONS OF light trailed after Delia as her car grasped for purchase on the deserted, snow-covered streets of Brighton. When had the road conditions become so bad? But what did she expect? Even if the snow had been light when she'd first gone out, it had been falling for hours, and now it was close to 2:00 a.m.

It had taken far longer than the twenty minutes it should have to make it back to town. That was unfortunate because it gave her more time to stew over tonight's events. Somewhere between Exit 155 and Exit 147 on the interstate, she'd gone from regretful and humiliated to downright frustrated.

And then to hopping mad.

She wasn't even allowed to have this one moment. Why the hell not? Why couldn't she have been sated and amazed like any other woman who'd just had her world rocked? And Ben had definitely rocked her world. But she couldn't even relish the moment. Instead, she had to feel dirty and ashamed. Just for wanting Ben—the nicest guy she'd ever met—more than she'd ever wanted anything. Even more than she'd wanted to escape from the phantoms in her memories.

You're frigid like your mother. Not a real woman.

She stilled as Lloyd's words struck out at her from the past, spewing their acid and eating through layers of healed-over wounds. She reached for the temperature controls. Though earlier she'd been freezing, now she was starting to sweat.

But instead of letting the fog draw her in, she shook her head. She refused to listen this time. Refused to let Lloyd take even another tiny part of her. What he'd said was a lie, anyway, on so many levels. She hadn't been a woman at all. Only a little girl. A sweet, trusting child. An innocent who'd deserved better than the betrayal she'd sustained at his hands.

As she stopped at the traffic signal nearest to her apartment—one that should have been set on flashing instead at this hour—she pounded her hands on the steering wheel.

"It's not fair."

She hated Lloyd. Hated feeling damaged. Mostly just hated.

Other people probably took having normal sexual relationships for granted. She never would. If tonight was any indicator, there were a lot of *nevers* in her future, when for the first time she wished for possibilities.

She despised Lloyd for taking those away from her along with everything else. Forget being able to have a one-night stand if she'd ever wanted one, which she didn't. And she refused to call what had happened with Ben *that*. What she called it didn't matter because the truth remained that even in a committed relationship, she would never be able to make love with someone she loved and allow herself to enjoy it. At least not without hating herself for it later.

And if she wasn't careful, she might fall in love with Ben.

She swallowed, eyes blinking rapidly, as she pulled into the complex parking lot. She couldn't let herself start pretending she and Ben had a relationship just because of one crazy night of passion. That was all it was, right? It didn't have anything to do with a man who challenged her, surprised her and frustrated her and then *touched* her with the gentlest hands she could imagine. Or did it?

What she felt didn't matter anyway. Ben deserved to be involved with someone who could have a normal relationship with him. Someone who would love wearing sexy lingerie for him and leave him steamy messages, promising long nights of lovemaking. Someone she could never be. She couldn't even think those things without feeling a cold chill and a temptation to run. He deserved better than that.

Better than *her*.

Darkness and shadows surrounded her car as she pulled into her carport, but as soon as she shut off the engine, her cell phone starting ringing. Pushing back the dread that immediately sprouted inside her, she grabbed her bag from the passenger seat and dug for her phone.

"Please don't be. Please don't—"

She stopped as Ben's name appeared on the screen. Though she couldn't handle receiving another call from the throwaway phones her parents had started using, this wasn't any easier. But it was just like Ben to call to make sure she'd made it home. Sweet of him, in fact. She should have been more surprised that he hadn't called already.

But what would she say to him if he apologized again? Would she be tempted to stop making up more excuses and tell him the truth? Was she ready to do that? And what would he say if she did tell him? She couldn't bear to hear the silence on the line as he scrambled for words, finally understanding how much of a mess she really was.

Her index finger trembled, perched just above the phone screen, but she couldn't bring herself to answer. Not yet. After a few more rings, when the call went to voice mail, she let go of the breath she was holding. Maybe Ben would give up and go to bed. She wasn't sure it would be easier to talk to him tomorrow or the next day, but she could hope for the chance to find out.

No such luck. The phone started ringing again. Had she really believed he would give up so easily?

Frowning, she slid her thumb across the screen to answer.

"Oh, there you are," he said in a rush.

"Sorry. I, uh, couldn't answer fast enough the first time."

"Oh." His tone said he didn't believe her. "You're not still driving, are you? If you are, hang up."

"No, I'm parked. Just now."

"So you made it home okay?"

Good old Ben. Always watching out for her. He was making sure she was all right, after all. It surprised her how comforting his concern felt. She'd never needed that from anyone before, and she shouldn't start now, but the temptation to rely on him, to let him share part of her load, was strong. Even if she needed to resist for her own good.

"All in one piece," she said over the lump forming in her throat.

"That took a while. I've been home for ten minutes, but my place is a lot closer to Kensington, I guess."

She cleared her throat. "Well, glad you made it home safely, too. I'd better get inside."

"Delia. Wait."

Her hand gripped the door handle. He'd called her "Delia" this time, so she braced herself for whatever he had to say.

"I was thinking about this in the shower—" He stopped, coughing. "I mean, was thinking there's a chance we had that thing at the park all wrong."

"Excuse me?" They hadn't…well, you know… in the park, but that had to be what he'd meant.

"Anyway, I started thinking—"

"Yeah, I was thinking, too." She couldn't help saying something to delay him. What had she been thinking about that she could actually tell him? Did she really think that interrupting him would stop him from talking about *it*? From apologizing one more time when he'd already used up his allowance for apologies given in any one day?

"I mean about the other cars."

"Oh." She coughed into her hand. Obviously, Ben was capable of thinking of other things, so she'd better figure out some way to do the same. "What about them?"

"When they were parked across from us, I was thinking, well—"

"Yeah, I'd guessed that, too," she said before she could stop herself. Why couldn't she just keep that to herself? He had to think she had a one-track mind now, which, in regards to him, was probably true. Only not in the way a guy would appreciate.

"So," he started again, "it wasn't until…later that I thought it could have been something else."

Her stomach tightened. "It was a drug transaction, wasn't it? And we just sat there watching it. We might as well have let them use our scale to do their business or offered to make change for them."

His long pause suggested that he agreed with her.

"We don't know that's what it was," he said finally. "A drug deal is one possibility, but there are others. Like it could have had something to do with the deserted car from a few weeks ago. The shared scene might be circumstantial, but it's still worth looking at."

"What was I thinking?" She squeezed her eyes shut, gripping the steering wheel before opening them again. "How could I have not made that connection? I'm the one who's been patrolling there for days."

"We weren't really on our games earlier. And I have caught a few couples in…well…*flagrante delicto* in parks before, so it was easy to jump to that conclusion. You've probably had a few of those cases yourself."

"Can't say that I have." She would have died if

she had, but she didn't add that. "Anyway, there was no excuse for *me* to miss it. None."

"Beating yourself up isn't going to help."

"Probably not."

"Anyway, there isn't necessarily a connection to that case, but we should look at it." He paused. "I mean *you*."

He was just being a cop, even though he'd been sidelined, but he didn't realize how right he was. She was the one who should already have planned to look into it on her next shift.

Only she'd observed suspicious activity, and she'd been too distracted to even discern that it was suspicious. Now she was falling down on the job in addition to falling—

No. She couldn't allow herself to fall for anyone. Particularly not Ben. She was supposed to help save his career, swoop in with her cape and her superb investigative skills. Not become involved with him.

"Look, Ben—"

"Oh, no. Sounds ominous. Should I sit down for this? Because I'm not sitting right now."

"Would you please be serious?"

"Okay."

He said it so slowly that it sounded like two words.

"I don't know what came over me…earlier. But that was crazy. Idiotic. Unacceptable." She used her hands to emphasize her point, not even caring that he couldn't see her. "For so many reasons. And whatever this, um, *thing* is between us, well, it has to stop. Immediately. Before it's too late."

"Too late?"

She gritted her teeth over his question.

"You know what I mean," she said. "Too late for *you*. Can't you see it? You're already sidelined. Do you really want that to be permanent? They're going to need a scapegoat for the scandal at the post, if nothing else. Are you willing to be that guy?"

"Of course not. I don't—"

"Don't you realize you could face charges?" Delia rolled over his words like a car in Neutral on a downhill slope, momentum building, frenzy and frustration escalating, until she collided with the truth. "For crimes you didn't even commit."

For several seconds, neither spoke. Though she'd refused to admit it, even to herself, she'd always believed he was innocent from the moment the news report was televised. Now she'd announced it out loud.

"Is that what you really believe?"

For several seconds, she couldn't answer. "I guess it is," she said finally. She held her breath. Would he make some big statement about it? Would he claim that he'd known all along?

"Do you think—" he paused as if considering

"—it's possible that the thing at the park tonight, or even the damaged car from earlier, is somehow related to the case at the post?"

Delia smiled at that. He could have made a big deal about what she'd said. It was a big admission after all. But he'd given her a break. As always.

"You're reaching again. Those things have about as much in common with the investigation as my past does."

"You're probably right."

"I usually am." She couldn't help but add that to lighten the conversation.

"And the timing couldn't be worse."

She cleared her throat, understanding that he was talking about them now and not the case. "Uh. Right."

Again, he was quiet for a few seconds. "You know I really am sorry. For so many things."

"You don't have to—"

"For the location. You deserved better." He spoke quickly as if he wanted to get it all out before she could interrupt. "For the lack of, uh, preparation. For taking risks."

"I know," she sneaked in when he took a breath.

"For…after."

"Ben." She cleared her throat. "I know." She couldn't let him go there. Not yet.

"Just had to make sure you knew."

"Then we're good. No more apologizing, okay?"

She was still smiling when she clicked off the call. It wasn't until she tucked her cell phone into her purse that she realized he'd apologized for everything except that he'd made love to her. Had it been intentional? Was he really not sorry for that? Was she? But as soon as she asked the question, she knew the answer with a surety she seldom had in anything.

Even if it could never happen again, even if it was poorly planned and poorly timed, even if she would never be able to give Ben the normal physical relationship he deserved, she couldn't bring herself to regret it this one time. At least once in her life she'd experienced the type of passion she'd only dreamed of—intense, raw, absolute in both vulnerability and strength. She'd read about it in books and heard about it in songs, but had assumed it was only for other people.

Just that once, in a shielded pause from the sharp shards that marked the rest of her life, Ben had made her feel like a regular woman. No scars. No fears. But pauses were limited in length and depth, and she could accept that. Still, Ben had given her that one perfect moment, and she would forever be grateful to him.

With a yawn and a stretch for sleep long overdue, she pulled her keys from the ignition. But just as she shifted toward the car door, a hard knock came from the other side of the window.

Her training kicking in, she pulled her weapon from her purse and rested it in her lap, just in case, and then swiped at the condensation on the window. Of course, it didn't help any more than calling herself an idiot for sitting alone in the car at night did. She still couldn't get a good look at the two individuals standing right outside her window, so Delia pulled out her phone and used the flashlight app again.

The moment the beam illuminated the two hat-covered heads, she sucked in a gasp, her limbs frozen in place. Standing right there outside her home were the two people she'd hoped—prayed—never to have to see again.

CHAPTER SIXTEEN

"WELL, IT'S ABOUT TIME."

Lloyd's voice rumbled through the glass though Delia's car windows were closed. She couldn't imagine how loud it had sounded outside the car. Or how many of her neighbors heard it.

With robotic movements, she returned her weapon to its case and pulled her hat lower over her ears. Calling for strength, she pushed the door open, forcing her guests to step back so she could climb out. The narrow parking spaces made it necessary for them to scoot from beneath the carport into the lighted parking lot where the snow was finally beginning to slow.

Delia stalled by reaching inside for her purse, and then she closed the door. The snow crunching under her feet, she stomped toward them with crossed arms, as much to hold herself together as to shield her body from the cold.

"What are you doing here?" Her slow, measured words appeared as individual puffs of condensation in the air.

Dressed in a poufy parka with a faux-fur hood

pulled over her hat, Marian was the first to step forward. She'd always been tiny, but the years and gravity had been especially unkind to her. The coat seemed to swallow her frail body.

"Oh, sweetheart, you're a sight for sore eyes," Marian gushed.

Delia wished she could say the same about her parents. No, scratch that, she didn't even wish it.

Before Marian could reach her daughter, Lloyd stepped between them. Like always. Instead of shifting to the side, Marian stayed where she was, relegated to the back of the line.

"Look at what the cat dragged in at…" He paused to look at the lighted face on his watch. "After 2:00 a.m."

His smile was a sneer in sheep's clothing, his piercing eyes looted from Delia's nightmares. Though tufts of white hair poked out from beneath his cap, and time had drawn its own graffiti on the face that had once won him votes and a convenient bride, Lloyd was the same man Delia remembered. She would recognize that rotted wood beneath a shiny veneer anywhere. Even now he carried himself with the confidence of a man who could have anything he wanted. And had.

Marian peeked around him. "We've been waiting here for hours for you."

"Yes. Hours."

Lloyd regarded Delia for so long that no amount of cold could have prevented her cheeks from burning. He seemed to see right through her coat, hat and clothes to where Ben's handprints lingered on her skin. What did she care if the man she despised had guessed where she'd been or what she'd been doing? She was an adult. Nothing she did, or with whom she did it, was any of his business.

Delia cleared her throat. "I asked what you're doing here." Her jaw tightened, and she bit the inside of her cheek until she tasted the tin-can flavor of blood.

"You didn't answer any of our calls," her mother supplied as if that explained everything.

"I thought you'd get the message." She cleared her throat. "But since you didn't, I'll spell it out for you. I don't *want* to talk to you. I don't want you here." She indicated her apartment complex with a wide sweep of her hand.

"Well, hasn't someone become awfully full of herself now that she's a big police officer," Lloyd said, staring down at her again.

Delia drew her brows together, his comment seeming odd. He was baiting her the way he always had, and she refused to swallow the hook. But why did it matter so much that she was a cop? She lifted her chin and met his creepy stare, refusing to be affected by him, refusing to let him have control over her ever again. Yet her body betrayed her as a shiver settled at the base of her neck, her bowels becoming unsettled.

"Sweetheart, it's been such a long time."

Marian's voice was suddenly shrill, desperation creeping in, but Delia wouldn't be moved by this display. This was the same woman who'd called her own child a liar to avoid accepting the unthinkable about her precious husband.

"Yes, how long has it been since you abandoned me? I was twelve, so that's fourteen years."

"It wasn't like that. You know we—"

"Why come after all of this time? Why the calls? Why this ambush? Did you really think I would welcome you with open arms?"

"It was time for us to come home," Lloyd answered for the both of them.

"Oh, I see. You think that enough time has passed for the residents to have forgotten about the things you did. Some of us will never forget."

Her breath caught. She hadn't meant to say the last bit, to admit that she still carried scars. The corners of his mouth lifted in a self-satisfied grin. He still wielded power over her, and she hated him even more for it.

Marian stepped around her husband and held her hands wide. "We just wanted to sit down together and put all of that, uh, messiness behind us."

"Messiness? That's what you call it?" Delia stared at her mother until she looked away. "I call it a violent crime against a child. And if you think I'm inviting you in so we can all sit around and laugh about old times, you're both as blind as the judge who dismissed all of those charges."

Lloyd's expression remained pleasant, but his jaw tightened. "If I remember correctly, the charges were dismissed for lack of evidence." But then a smile spread on his lips. "And we wanted to let you know that we forgive you for making those false accusations."

"Forgive *me*? For telling the truth?" She didn't even care anymore if he knew he'd gotten to her. She stared into the face of her personal Satan, refusing to look away until he blinked. "You know what you did. You should be in prison until the day you die for it."

She turned to her mother. "And whether you're willing to admit it or not, you knew that I was telling the truth. You just couldn't lose your meal ticket."

"Delia, you're wrong—"

"Am I? I don't think so. You know, I should thank you two since you're the reasons I went into police work. I want to help take down child sexual predators and ensure that child victims have at least someone who believes them."

Lloyd's hands came forward, fisting at his

sides, as the remarkable cool he'd been known for in office began to crack. "I don't have to listen to this bullshit."

"Well that's good since you won't have to." Delia straightened, pushing her shoulders back. "In fact, I don't want to see either of you again. Ever. Don't call. Don't text. I'll help you with that by changing my number, but I don't want you to visit, either. Don't even write me a letter."

"But, Delia, I'm your mother."

"Yes, you are, Marian. Biologically. You also made your choice a long time ago. And it wasn't me. Now you have to live with that decision."

"I'm sorry," Marian said in a small voice.

A knot immediately formed in Delia's throat. As much as she wanted to throw those words back in her mother's face, she couldn't. After every mistake Marian had made, she was still her mother, and her tiny admission would cost her dearly.

"If you ever leave him—" she paused to glance at her stepfather "—call me then. Leave a message for me at the Brighton Post. But until then, you've chosen your life, so stay out of mine."

Lloyd shifted closer to his wife, wrapping an arm tightly around her shoulders. "You see, I told you she wasn't worth the effort. We extend an olive branch, and this is what we get?"

With each word, his hand appeared to tighten

on her mother's shoulder, though with the quilted parka, it was difficult to determine if he was hurting her. Delia pulled her gaze away from that gloved hand and focused on Marian's tight expression.

She reached into her purse and pulled out her cell phone. "If he's been hurting you, I can call—"

But Marian shook her head to interrupt her. "No. I'm fine. He would never hurt me."

Delia nodded and slipped the phone in her coat pocket, strangely disappointed that her stepfather *hadn't* abused her mother. That reaction was messed up on so many levels. Even after all of those years, she'd reached for the flimsy hope that her mother hadn't deserted her willingly.

"You said it yourself," Lloyd said. "My wife made her choice. She knows who's good to her."

Having just announced his claim much as he might have on a car or a big-screen TV, Lloyd patted Marian's shoulder.

"Quite a prize you got yourself there, Marian."

Lloyd slowly lowered his arm to his side. He hadn't threatened, hadn't moved any closer to Delia, and yet his stance seemed menacing.

"You think you're something now that you have that uniform and a gun." He made a scoffing sound. "You must believe you're untouchable, but you're the same nothing you always were."

And suddenly Delia understood why her parents would try to reenter her life now.

"This doesn't have anything to do with my mother wanting to see her daughter, does it?" She took the surprise in Lloyd's eyes as a yes and kept going. "You can't stand it that I've pulled my life together and have made a career for myself as a state trooper."

"Oh, you, little lady, just think—"

"That's it." She raced over his comment with a confirmation of her guess. She hadn't missed that he'd flung words back at her that he'd used during her childhood. Words that still made her skin crawl. Still, she continued to smile so hard her cheeks ached.

"You perceive the strength and confidence associated with my job as threats to the hold you once had over me. A terrified little girl." As much as she wished she could speak with calm, even tones, her last words became a growl. "Of course you'd feel threatened. You need me to stay weak because you're so weak. Only a powerless man would have to force himself on little girls, you sick bastard."

The bald rage on Lloyd's face had her touching the side of her purse just to ensure that her weapon was still there. His gaze moved over her as if he was sizing up an enemy. Maybe he recognized determination where physical strength might have failed her, or maybe he just assumed she was armed because he didn't take a step forward.

"Go ahead and feel bulletproof behind that little metal badge, but if you repeat any of your false allegations to anyone, I'll sue you for slander faster than you can—"

Delia planted her feet wide, straightened her shoulders and crossed her arms. "Go ahead and try. Those reports are a matter of public record, anyway, if anyone digs enough. But I'm putting you on alert that if you have other victims, and most sickos like you do, I will make it my life's work to ensure that you die behind bars."

His wide eyes and the flare of his nostrils told her all she needed to know. Gooseflesh appeared on her arms as she thought of all the research, all the pain ahead of her. Though Delia had been focusing only on Lloyd until now, she swallowed when she saw the horror on her mother's face, the woman's blinders having been violently ripped away. But Delia couldn't think about that now. She couldn't recall anything ever striking her stepfather silent before.

"Now get out of here, or I'll call for police backup." She pointed toward the parking lot. "And don't come back."

"Trying to come up with some more trumped-up charges?" His words didn't have the power they used to carry.

"Not at all. Heard of stalking laws? Just remember that I've kept recordings of most of those messages you left me. The ones that have become increasingly threatening." She tilted her head to the side and shrugged. "But I'm sure we can sort all of this out at the Brighton Post if that's where you want to go."

Lloyd didn't even look at her as he ushered Marian toward their car. "Let's go. Your daughter isn't worth it. Never was."

Delia turned and called after them, "If you change your mind, *Mom*, the offer still stands."

Marian's shoulders jerked as if she'd just been struck by the title that should have brought her comfort, and Delia grimaced over tossing another rock at someone who'd already been beaten down. A woman who'd made her bed and was too tangled in the piled blankets and stained sheets to escape it now.

Delia waited until the car pulled from the complex parking lot, but as soon as those lights disappeared, she hurried to her apartment. How she'd been able to handle the cold before, she didn't know, but she was freezing now. She couldn't stop trembling, and her teeth chattered no matter how hard she gritted them. With shaky hands, she unlocked her apartment building's exterior door and stepped inside.

Every creak startled her as she climbed the stairs, and as she stopped by her apartment door, she couldn't help but look behind her. Someone really had been following her this time. She opened the door just wide enough for her body to fit through and closed it behind her. Her heart pounding so hard that it had to be chiseling its way out of her chest, she flipped both dead bolts into place.

She should have turned on the lights, should have checked out the place before she entered and certainly before she locked herself inside, but she couldn't bring herself to reach for the switch. Instead, she turned and pressed her back to the door, allowing her body to slide down until she landed with a thud on the floor. And then she sat there, her limbs fluid and seeming to stretch in all directions, as she stared into the dark.

CHAPTER SEVENTEEN

BEN GROUND HIS fists into his gritty eyes, the words on his computer screen shifting in and out of focus. He'd read every article he could find. More than once. Now the sun was threatening to bleed over the increasingly brightening sky, and he was no closer to answers than he'd been hours ago when he'd rested his first cup of coffee on his desk and flipped open the laptop. He lifted his mug with a shaky hand, but only the dregs of his *fifth* cup remained, so he set it aside.

He hadn't even bothered going back to bed. It wasn't as if he could have slept anyway, with thoughts of Delia lingering, tantalizing, just outside his conscious reach. On the other hand, wide-awake, he didn't even bother trying to get her out of his head. She'd arrived and had made herself at home there, and he was getting comfortable with this new tenant.

Glancing back at the screen, he clicked on another article, this one he'd read a couple of times already.

Jackson Charged with Racketeering

What had he expected? That archived newspaper articles would vomit up the answers they'd been holding back previously just because Delia had finally opened up to him about her history? And after he'd connected with her in a much more personal fashion.

Ben scrolled farther down the list of search engine hits. What were her birth father's obituary and stepfather's jerk moves as a politician supposed to tell him about her anyway? She hadn't known the first, and she'd had no contact with the second since middle school. He'd looked at information about her mother again, as well, but the woman hadn't been mentioned at all except as Lloyd Jackson's spouse in a few links and on the telephone directory website.

Ben had even completed a general search on "Delia Morgan"—again—and this time, he'd *paid* one of those ridiculous records sites for additional details. Of course, he hadn't learned anything he wouldn't be able to find for free. Nothing about any relationships Delia had ever had, though he wasn't sure he wanted to know about those. Had a past boyfriend hurt her somehow? Was that the reason for her tears earlier?

It had seemed odd that Delia didn't have a social media presence, something he should have noticed before, but given the private person she was, it shouldn't have surprised him. He'd even searched for information on beautician/legal guardian Helen Miles and found nothing more remarkable than her obituary. The article hadn't even mentioned Delia, the girl she'd helped raise, though he suspected that Delia herself had helped to write it.

Charges against Commissioner Dismissed

Sure, he'd discovered a few details he'd missed the first few times he'd looked into her background, but Ben had also hit a lot of dead ends, and he'd hit them hard.

"Come on, Dee. What are you hiding?" He posed the question he should have asked *her*, and would have if she wouldn't have shut him down.

He hated to admit that so much of his curiosity had to do with her reaction to their lovemaking. But something about it continued to eat at him. He could accept that he hadn't blown her socks off, but the tears still didn't make sense. Why had she been so ashamed about it? Because it happened with a fellow officer? Because she had at least played a role in initiating it? Okay, there were a few reasons she might have been embarrassed, but that had not been an embarrassed cry. Mortified was more like it.

He didn't understand why she'd been embarrassed when she'd seemed to want it as much as he had. He might have misread her signals once before, but he couldn't have been wrong this time. And as for the part about her initiating, he'd been more inclined to celebrate that moment—that didn't usually happen to guys like him.

He didn't regret any of it. Well, most of it. Yet Delia was too humiliated to even talk about it in terms more specific than the "thing" between them.

For those reasons, he had to keep looking. He rubbed his eyes again and closed one internet browser only to open another. This search was probably as useless as any of the others he'd tried, but he had the sinking feeling that the answer was out there to find.

The headlines looked the same. He'd seen them so many times now that they all ran together in a tragic collage, the unraveling of the picture-perfect family. He clicked through several pages, but just as he was about to close the browser, he stopped on one that didn't look familiar.

Jackson Faces New Allegations

The date appeared to be more recent than some of the other articles, so he clicked on it and scanned it. What he read turned his stomach.

Oakland County Prosecutor's Office officials confirm that Jackson will face the additional charge of criminal sexual conduct involving a minor.

"Oh, God. No."

Ben covered his face with his hands, pressing his fingers over his eyes. He didn't want to read more, and yet like bystanders at an accident scene, he couldn't help himself. He removed his hands, his heart pounding, as he scanned farther down the article. It was unbearably vague. Of course, the victim's name wouldn't be listed. Print and television media were usually good about protecting victims' identities.

The dread welling inside him, though, told him he already knew who it was.

Farther down the page, the article was stingy with details. When had it happened? Where? Even the release of the announcement appeared to have been premature as the prosecutor hadn't determined what degree of the criminal sexual conduct charge Jackson would face. Was it first-degree? That one involved the worst of the nightmares and carried a penalty of up to life in prison. Or could it have been second-, third- or even fourth-degree? Those all carried horrors of their own but had lesser penalties. And the victim could have been anyone, right? It didn't absolutely have to be Delia.

He wasn't sure he wanted the answers to any of his questions now, but he'd been searching for so long, he had to follow through. When that article refused to cough up more specifics, he narrowed the search. A few headlines appeared.

As he combed through the articles, he found isolated details until he could piece together nearly a whole story. The charge was first-degree, meaning penetration. The location was in their home. The timeframe was a year before Jackson left town in disgrace.

Other details were equally compelling. Suggestions of false allegations. Suggestibility in child witnesses. Tainted evidence. Dismissed charges.

Ben scanned down to the last article. This one seemed to offer no more promise than the others. Just a brief from one of the newswires, yet it contained the one detail all of the other articles had held back. The one that Ben had been searching for all along.

"The case, involving a stepdaughter..."

Covering his mouth, Ben ran for the bathroom, all of that coffee backing up to his throat. But he could only retch over the commode for several minutes, finding no relief for his body or his mind. Finally, he sat back on his haunches and grabbed the hand towel from the sink, wiping at his sweaty forehead.

Retrieving his glasses from the counter where he'd tossed them, he shoved them back on his face, though at the moment, the last thing he wanted to do was to see clearly. Never in his life had he wanted more for a hunch to be wrong.

On rubberlike legs, he returned to his office and dropped into his desk chair, defeated. His laptop had gone dark, but as soon as he touched the keys, that last article popped up again, those telling words reaching out to him like a fresh strike. He closed all of the screens and shut down the computer.

He'd wanted answers. He'd looked for them even when she'd told him to stop. Now that he had them, what was he supposed to do with the heartbreak of knowing her truth? What could he do with the rage?

Planting his elbows on his desk pad, Ben pressed his hands together like a prayer and touched his fingers against his lips and nose. He squeezed his eyes shut, wishing he could exorcise the images his mind had conjured, yet realizing he couldn't escape them. Just as Delia couldn't hide from memories that were undoubtedly so much worse.

Finally, he opened his eyes and stared at the

closed computer. So many things he hadn't understood about Delia, from the fierce independence on the job to her strange reactions in private moments, made sense in the light of this revelation.

Of course she would have a tough time believing that other officers would have her back when the people she should have been able to rely on had hijacked her innocence and ability to trust. But Delia hadn't only been betrayed by Jackson and by the woman who gave her life. The system had failed her, too, allowing her abuser to go free.

Not for a minute did he question whether she'd been telling the truth. He believed every word she *hadn't* said to him. Yes, she should have divulged this information during her training and interview process, but she'd probably buried the truth so deep that even she couldn't see it.

Her competitiveness, her ambition, her determination to take down child predators, all of it made sense. Delia was a survivor. She'd walked through hell and emerged on the other side with only minimal help. But no one ever said survivors prevailed unscathed. While some wore their scars like badges of honor, Delia buried hers like dirty little secrets. Private wounds he only wished he'd known about earlier.

"Stop it!" He pounded his fist on the desk. "Don't make this about you."

No matter how hard he tried to push aside those thoughts of the two of them together, the images lingered there, accusing, convicting. He'd interviewed victims before, even knew some of the signs to look for. From Delia's strange reaction to that electric first kiss, he should have realized there was something wrong. But he'd been so busy wanting her, needing her, that he couldn't see it.

Love is blind. The old saying echoed like a social media meme replaying in his thoughts. With a jolt that had him sitting up in his seat, Ben realized it was true. Somewhere between that moment at the station when she'd become for him as much of a sexy, intriguing woman as a colleague, to the instant where they'd shared the most intimate thing two people could, he'd fallen in love with the beautiful and indomitable Delia Morgan.

It couldn't have been riskier or more poorly timed, even before this morning's revelation, but she'd climbed inside his soul, and he didn't want her to leave again. And he suspected that she cared about him, as well. It was the only explanation he had for all the risks she'd taken on his behalf.

As the memory of her sobs filled his ears again, Ben shook his head, trying to remove the sounds. He couldn't bear to think that Delia would ever see their lovemaking as anything other than beautiful and perfect, and it was obvious that for her, it had been neither of those things.

He hated Lloyd Jackson even more for that. He hadn't felt this kind of anger since right after his mother's death when his father had survived, but he seethed with it now, his teeth gritted so tightly that his molars ached. His fingers itched to curl around Jackson's neck.

For the first time, he understood where victims who sought revenge were coming from, when their loved ones felt entitled to vigilante justice. He wanted to make Jackson hurt the way Delia hurt.

An image of himself as a barbarian, complete with sword and shield, flitted into his hazy thoughts, making him smile. Delia would tell him she didn't need a protector, and she would be right.

Now that he knew, though, he had to do something. He just didn't know what. Should he give Delia her space? If she'd wanted him to know the truth about this part of her painful history, she would have told him a long time ago. Right? Or at least when she'd shared the story about her mother's desertion. But she hadn't.

Was she afraid that people close to her would walk away if they knew? Helen Miles must have known. Had she told Delia to forget that it had ever happened?

Ben didn't know what anyone else had done when they'd learned the truth, but he knew what he planned to do. He would be there for her in whatever way he could. He wouldn't abandon her, even if she tried to push him away.

He needed to convince her that any intimate moments between them would be perfect and right, but before he could do that, he had to tell her that he knew. They could talk about it then, and he would somehow make this right for her. He had to.

Glancing at the time on his cell, he considered waiting until a more decent hour, but he had to talk to her now. He clicked on her name from his contacts list and waited for the call to connect.

Finally, the phone started ringing. And ringing. After several rings, the call went to voice mail.

"Delia, it's me. We need to talk. Call me back, okay?"

He clicked off the call and rested his phone back on the desktop. She'd just missed his call. She would call back in a few minutes. So he waited, watching the phone screen and then touching it each time the screen went dark. She would call back, wouldn't she? Just like she would have earlier if he hadn't called her twice.

After five minutes had passed, he picked up the phone again and clicked on her name under recent calls. She would definitely pick up now.

But this time, the phone rang only once before the automated mailbox picked up. Had she really just sent him to voice mail? His first instinct was to worry that something else was wrong, that something else was preventing her from answering. But wasn't last night already enough of an issue? This was still the morning after, and maybe she just wanted to avoid him.

They had to talk, though. He was a patient man, but he could be as determined as she was when she wanted something. And he wanted her. Eventually she would answer. He would just keep calling until she did.

"Quit calling me!"

Delia shouted at the phone in her patrol car, but as she'd been doing for two days, she didn't answer. Instead, she continued on the long, slow drive around the perimeter road of Kensington Metropark, watching for anything unusual, anything like the scene she'd missed the other night.

She would have to talk to him soon, would have to find out if he'd discovered anything new in the case that had sidelined him, but she could wait a little longer, couldn't she? Until the humiliation wore off.

How was she supposed to face him after the things they'd done together? The things she'd loved doing but should never do with him again.

Could he ever respect her in uniform now that he'd clearly *seen* her out of it with eyes, hands and mouth? Could he pretend that it had never happened just as she intended to do when she finally saw him again? Two days weren't enough to prepare her for the role she would play. She hoped the time and distance would help because she was still worried that when she saw him again, she might be tempted to invite him home with her for round two.

Delia continued farther along Park Route 1, past the drive leading to Martindale Beach. She couldn't think about Ben now. Couldn't tell herself she would die if he apologized one more time on her voice mail. She hadn't heard from her parents even once during that time, but Ben had taken up the telephone-message slack.

She blinked as her radio crackled to life. She was so preoccupied that she was lucky she hadn't missed it.

"Radio 570," she said into the handset. "All set."

She had to keep her mind on the job, just as she'd been doing the past two shifts, looking for any possible connection between the abandoned car from a few weeks back and the suspicious activity from two nights ago. It would have been nice if she could compare the two police reports, but she couldn't file the second one when she couldn't explain why she'd been at the park at that hour.

At least focusing on this case and the other one at the post helped keep her thoughts away from Ben some of the time. His constant calls weren't helping, though.

She followed the huge loop in the road, crossing the Huron River, passing the Farm Center and the Nature Center buildings. At the parking lot near the administrative office and the Kensington Road exit, she caught sight of headlights. Her breath catching, she immediately shut off her own lights and slowly entered the lot.

The car she'd noticed flashed its headlights in her direction, letting her know she'd already been detected. When she flipped hers back on, she recognized the telltale profile of a state police vehicle.

"What is he doing here?" she asked and then shook her head.

Sure, she'd been avoiding Ben, but why would he take a risk of getting caught by driving out here in a patrol car? For that matter, how had he gotten one? Had Scott helped him out? They were friends, but Ben had already refused to let Scott risk his career for him. Ben had always talked about being cautious and taking risks only when necessary. This didn't fall in that category.

The vehicle approached from the other side of

the parking lot, and she turned her car, so they would pass on the drivers' sides. As the cars reached each other, she pressed her brakes and the window control at the same time.

"What are you doing here?" she asked as soon as the other window lowered.

"I was about to ask you the same thing."

She blinked. The voice didn't sound right, and the profile didn't match. She turned her spotlight toward the other car. Trevor Cole sat in the driver's seat, holding a flashlight of his own and staring back at her.

"ARE YOU GOING to answer my question?" Somehow Delia managed to shield the tremor in her voice.

She blinked several times, trying to adjust her eyes to the glare from Trevor's flashlight. Finally, she slid the beam of her floodlight to the side, out of his eyes, and he returned the favor. What did he want?

Trevor watched her for several long seconds, as he would have a suspect under interrogation, and then he smiled.

"I knew you'd be here, at least at some point during your shift."

She nodded, trying not to shiver. Now her assumption that it would be Ben in the other patrol car seemed ridiculous. He didn't even have access to the post, let alone official vehicles.

"This has been my assignment over the past few weeks, but what do you care about that?"

"Is this where you meet them?"

She shook her head. *"Who?"*

"Your contacts."

"I don't know what you're talking about."

"I think you do."

"I don't have any contacts." If Ben didn't count. Only she had the idea that he did count. A lot.

"You've been acting suspiciously ever since Polaski put Peterson on leave." He studied her for several more seconds. "Is it guilt that has you so worked up? It's not as easy as you thought to target someone when the victim's a nice guy, is it?"

Delia couldn't believe her ears. He had this all wrong. It was like a polar bear that preyed on its hunter. He was the guilty one—at least she suspected that he was.

"Look, I don't know what you think you know, but—"

"I know more than you think I do," he said. "Like that it just about killed you when Ben was named for a commendation. You wanted one of those for yourself, didn't you?"

"Don't we all?" Delia shrugged, his questions confusing her. Was he trying to throw suspicion from himself by going after her?

"No. Not all of us are trying to move up the law enforcement food chain."

She could only stare at him. "How do you know that?"

"You're not the only one who's been watching. Or the only one who's been hiding something."

He paused as if waiting for his words to sink in.

"You've been watching *me*?" The question was out of her mouth before she could stop it. She didn't even bother to deny his accusation.

A smile of victory slipped over his lips before he became serious again. "Some of us are just doing our jobs."

"Which is exactly what I'm trying to do." She wouldn't say anything more. Someone with secrets like she had was in a precarious position in a police department. "So I'd appreciate it if you would let me get back to my work."

"Oh, you do that. You might as well while you still can."

"Is that a threat, Trooper Cole?"

He shrugged, smiling. "It's whatever you'd like it to be. A threat. A warning. A promise. Whether you want the answers to come out or not, they will and in a way you're not going to like."

With that parting comment, Trevor rolled up his window and pulled out of the parking lot. Delia considered following him, but she was still trying to figure out his cryptic message. The answers would come out? Was he talking about the evidence-tampering case or that she'd helped Ben with the investigation? Or could it be that he knew about her more personal relationship with Ben?

He couldn't know that, could he? She'd caught him watching her at the post a few times, but just how much could he know? Could Trevor have been in one of those cars the other night? Could he have seen her and Ben together then or one of the other times they'd met?

She still suspected that Trevor was the one who'd targeted Ben. There were certainly unanswered questions swirling around his time back at the Manistique Post. Maybe he knew that she was on his trail and wanted to throw suspicion her way before she got too close to the truth. Did he believe that accusing her would keep her from finding the answers that would clear Ben's name?

Her questions followed her as she started back toward the post at the end of her shift. She only hoped she wouldn't cross paths with Trevor again tonight. There were still too many question about him, and she needed to be properly armed with facts before she faced off with him again.

After all of this time investigating, she seemed to have more questions than answers. She needed to talk to Ben to make sense of this new development. She had no choice—she would have to face him now.

CHAPTER EIGHTEEN

THE FIRST LOCK was already in place, and Delia
was turning the second, when a knock came from
the other side of her apartment door, causing her
to jump back. She peered out the peephole, but
with the light inside her apartment still on and
the one in the hall as dim as usual, she could only
see a distorted image.

Hadn't she checked the parking lot carefully
before entering? She still wasn't sure whether her
parents had finally given up or would pursue her
even harder now.

A second knock came before she could peek
outside again. She swallowed, reaching for her
purse where she'd just rested it at her feet. Could
Trevor have followed her home to drill her with
more questions or threaten her? Or worse?

"Delia," came a whisper through the hollow
door.

She would recognize that voice anywhere.
Flipping the lock, she jerked open the door.

"What the hell are you doing here?" she asked

with a grumble. "Right out in front of my apartment door where anyone can see you?"

She didn't bother waiting for his answer before grabbing his arm.

"Get in here." She yanked him inside and closed the door again. "You're the one who said no one could know we were working together, and then you pull something like this?"

She locked the door again and turned back to him, crossing her arms over her chest.

"How'd you get in the building anyway? Are you trying to make *sure* we get caught? Do you want me to get fired? I already had—" She shook her head, too angry with Ben to tell him about Trevor yet. "Oh, never mind."

Clearly having missed what she'd started to say, Ben unbuttoned his coat, the one she remembered from the bar. The night that seemed so long ago now.

"You left me no choice. The lock sticks. No. And no."

She drew her brows together. "What?"

"I answered all of your questions. And if you didn't want me to come here, you should have answered my calls."

"All fifty of them?"

"At least one. Just so I would know that you were all right."

"I told you I was. Several times. I wish you'd quit asking. I'm fine, do you hear me?" She hated that her voice cracked on the last word.

"You sound fine, too. After two days of unanswered calls, I started to worry."

She stopped, staring at him. "Don't worry about me. I can take care of myself. I've done a pretty good job of it for fourteen years, and I don't need someone coming in here and—"

"And what? Caring about you? Is that not allowed?" He slipped out of his coat and rested it over his arm, as if he planned to stay awhile. "For the record, I am well aware that you can take care of yourself."

She shook her head to clear her thoughts. He was confusing her. Was he trying to mess with her? Because he was doing a fine job of it. And what was he planning to talk about that would take long enough that he would need to take his coat off? She was still wearing hers though she was beginning to sweat.

"Then what do you want, Ben?" she asked on a sigh. The sooner he got what he came for, the sooner he would leave. The less she would be tempted to rely on him. To let him *care*. "Did you risk people finding out about us just so you could torture me?"

"No. I wanted to talk to you about Lloyd."

"What about him? We're not exactly good friends." She chose her words carefully, but her heart was beating so hard that it might pound out of her chest. What had her stepfather done this time? Would she ever escape him?

"Delia." Ben paused until she looked at him. "I know the truth about Lloyd."

A tinny ringing began in her ears. He couldn't be talking about *that*. No one knew about it. "We've already talked about my family. I told you they left—"

"I know what Lloyd did to you."

"Oh." It was as if he'd punched her in the diaphragm and was waiting there, watching, as she struggled for breath. For words. Somehow she found both. "How dare you, Ben! You had no right."

"I'm sorry. It was in old newspaper archives on the internet. Some of the more obscure ones."

"It was none of your business!" Her hands were shaking with the need to hurt him the way she was hurting. To split and tear and destroy. "I told you to stop digging."

"I'm sorry. I needed to—"

"To know?" She yanked off her coat and threw it over the chair as she paced across the living room. At the kitchen entrance, she whirled and marched back. "I told you everything you needed to know in order to take me off your suspect list. But it wasn't enough, was it? Nothing is enough."

"I was worried about you…after the other night."

She was within a few feet of him now, but when he shifted toward her, his hands held wide, she stepped back reflexively.

"So you wanted to justify your disappointing, uh, skills, right?" She ground her teeth, wanting to hurt him, push him away. "If there was something wrong with me, then…"

She let her words trail away.

But he didn't take the bait. "It wasn't about that, and you know it." He cleared his throat, his hands reaching for her, before he stuffed them in his pockets. "You know me, Dee. You know I care about you."

"Do I?" She did know, but she didn't want to believe it right now. Not when he was asking her to dig up her skeletons and arrange them around her living room like invited guests. "And if you think I'm going to talk to you about *that*…"

"Come on, Dee. It's a little late for us to act like strangers. You know me. And I *want* to know you. The real you."

"Quit calling me that. Quit…everything!" She didn't care about being loud, didn't care about paper-thin apartment walls and nosy neighbors who filed complaints. She had to make Ben stop. Stop trying to take care of her. Convincing her to trust him. Chiseling his way past her carefully constructed walls.

"I don't need you. Or anybody. And I don't want to talk about it. Can't you see that?"

He nodded, his smile a sad one. "I know it's hard. Really hard. But maybe it's time to tell someone who already believes you."

She opened her mouth and then closed it. The venomous comment she'd been prepared to say died on her lips as his words filtered through her resistance. *Someone who already believes you.* She'd always wanted someone, anyone, to believe her, and now without even hearing her side of the story, Ben had professed complete belief in her.

Whether it was just that one promise or a combination of all the things that were Ben Peterson, she didn't know, but a dam broke inside of her. One moment she was shaking her index finger at him, demanding that he stay out of her life, and the next, she was crumpling toward the floor. And letting him catch her in his arms.

BEN'S HEART SQUEEZED like a fist as Delia sagged against him, and he cradled her head against his shoulder. Her tears soaked the front of his sweater, their heat radiating through him along with his guilt. He'd hoped she would open to him, to let out the feelings she'd buried inside her for so long, but he'd never wanted her to hurt like this.

He'd withstood the agony of not being able to comfort her the other night, but now each sob hammered right against his chest, her pain and each dark memory seeming to seep from her heart into his. He braced himself, withstanding it all for her sake.

Shifting and slipping to her side, he lifted her into his arms, cradling her to him. She was so tiny, so light, but he didn't doubt for a minute how strong she was. She'd survived atrocities that should have crippled her and had channeled her pain into a way to help others. She was a lot like him. Only stronger.

Having never been to her apartment before, he scanned from the dinette to the living room grouping in the mostly darkened room before starting toward the sofa. Even with the only light coming from the ceiling fixture in the front hallway, he noted that the place was the polar opposite of his own country home. As stark as his was overly adorned. A sea of practical beige and obsessive tidiness, versus loud prints and deliberate clutter.

Once he reached the couch, he turned and carefully lowered himself, and her, to the seat, draping her frame across his lap. For several minutes, he sat there, rubbing her shoulder and brushing his fingers over the soft strands that had escaped her bun.

Only when he stretched to turn on the table lamp did her eyes blink open. Her gaze darted about as if she wondered when they'd moved from the doorway to the couch.

"Uh. Sorry."

Awkwardly, she shifted out of his lap and pushed herself to the opposite end of the tan sofa, pressing her back to the seat's arm. It was all he could do not to pull her back to him, the plush chasm between them stretching too far. But maybe she needed space, and he just had to give it to her.

Delia swiped ineffectively at her tears, and then brushed her face on her sweater sleeve. With a chuckle, Ben passed her the box of tissues from the table next to him. She pulled out a few and started wiping.

"What are you looking at?" She frowned at first, but then the sides of her mouth lifted slightly. "I never cry. Ever. And that's all I can do around you lately."

"I'm just lucky, I guess."

She chuckled now as she exchanged the soggy tissues for fresh ones. "If that's what you want to call it."

For several seconds, neither spoke, but it wasn't an awkward silence. Just quiet, calm.

"You don't have to talk about it if you don't want to," Ben said in a soft voice.

"You say that now." She smiled again.

She didn't speak for so long that Ben figured she planned to take him up on his offer to keep her story to herself.

"I think I wanted you to find it," she said finally.

He turned to her. "What do you mean?"

"I kept discouraging you from looking, but I hoped you'd find it."

"So you didn't have to tell me yourself." He didn't pose it as a question because he knew it was true. Sometimes he found it easier to let others learn about his history the same way. "You really wanted me to know?"

She only shrugged, but it was enough. She might not have been ready to share her story herself, but she'd wanted him to know her. That said a lot.

"The articles weren't that easy to find, you know, hidden behind all of that other corruption stuff."

"I know. People who hurt kids are a dime a dozen. But those who steal large sums of cash from government entities, now, they make for fascinating news."

"That's the world we live in." He frowned at the bare walls.

"My world was pretty much a nightmare."

Ben straightened, turning back to her. "Are you sure you're ready to tell this story?" He had to ask because he wasn't sure he was ready to hear it, but he would listen for her sake.

"It's time."

"Well, then, would it be all right with you if we got rid of this?" He gestured toward the space on the sofa between them. At her nod, he slid closer until he was right next to her, reached down and took her hand in his, lacing their fingers.

She watched their joined hands as if mesmerized by the rhythm with which he rubbed his thumb over the back side of her hand. "You already know a lot of it."

"The story about them leaving you with the hairdresser?"

"That was right after the charges were dismissed. And you know what the specific charge was and what it meant, right?"

He nodded, swallowing. This was harder than he'd even imagined it would be.

"Then we don't have to go into that part." She paused as if considering where to go next. "The rest of the story isn't even all that unique. Powerful man, used to getting what he wanted. And he wanted me. I was ten."

Ben squeezed his lids shut, heat burning behind his eyes. How could anyone do that to a child? Who could be so evil? When he opened his eyes again, she was watching him.

"Sure you're ready to hear this?"

He cleared his throat. "Sorry. Of course."

She nodded. "It had been going on more than a year before I told my teacher, and she filed the police report. That's when my mother called me a liar. She helped to discredit me as a witness."

"How could she do that to her own child?"

"Oh, I made it really easy for her. I *was* a liar." She smiled this time, but the expression didn't reach her eyes. "In the months since Lloyd had started abusing me, I'd started lying. About everything. Homework. Where I'd been. With whom. You name it. It was my coping mechanism, but it didn't make me a credible witness. All my mother had to do was suggest that I'd always been a liar, and…"

"So the prosecutor dropped the charges?"

"They hadn't exactly had a winning record with Lloyd to start with," she said. "And in this case, they had only the testimony of a confirmed liar and no other witnesses. They couldn't run away from the case fast enough."

"It's not fair!" He knew his words weren't rational, but he didn't care. "I know I'm supposed to assure you that none of the things that happened to you were your fault. That you deserved to have a childhood where you felt safe. Those things are definitely true. But I'm pissed. That creep should not be allowed to walk on this earth, let alone run around free after what he did to you. I don't care what else he got away with. He should have to pay for what he took from you."

He hadn't known what to make of her strange sound at the beginning of his rant, but by the end, he was sure she was laughing at him.

"Did I miss something?"

"No. Sorry." She shook her head. "It's just that I said something similar to him the other night when he was here."

"What do you mean 'when he was here'?"

"He and my mother have been hanging around lately, trying to shove themselves back in my life. A bunch of calls, messages and then that little visit the other night." She released his hand to brush her own together. "But I'm pretty sure I shut that down for good."

Ben shifted forward in his seat, immediately on edge. "You didn't mention this before. Maybe we should have more patrols around your complex for a while." He pointed toward the door. "I already told you that the lock on the outside door sticks. If they come back—"

"Ben, they're not coming back." She met his gaze directly, then shook her head to make her point. "I handled it, okay? They won't be back."

"How are you so sure?"

"Lloyd loves himself too much to take more risks, especially since I told him I'm looking for other victims. And Marian is too afraid of being alone to return without him."

"Well, if you're sure."

"I'm sure."

He was staring at the cheap interior door, wondering what it would take for him to repair the one on the outside of the building, when he had another thought. "Wait. What night did you say your parents came here?"

"I didn't say, but it was that night when I came home really late. You know which one. When we saw those two cars in the park."

"You mean the night we made love."

She coughed into her hand and stared at the floor, color staining her cheeks. "I wasn't going to put it that way."

"That's why you wouldn't take my calls. At least part of the reason."

She shook her head emphatically. "It didn't have anything to do with—"

"You know it did. You'd just come home after…everything, and there they were to drag you back to the past."

"It wasn't like that."

"Wasn't it?"

She was quiet for several seconds, and then she shrugged. "It was an unfortunate coincidence."

"You were having a tough time that night, even before you came back here. It wasn't your first...?"

She shook her head to interrupt him, and then she shrugged. "I've had a couple of, you know, relationships. They didn't work out so well."

But even if the thought of someone else being with her made him uncomfortable, at least the other night hadn't been her first real time.

"So the other night was different because...?"

"We don't have to rehash that, do we?"

"No, we don't," he said. At least she hadn't argued the point that the other night had been different. "But maybe that's something you should talk about with someone. When you're ready. A counselor maybe. Someone who can help you put your memories into perspective."

"Maybe."

"I know the grief counselor helped me a lot after the accident." At her surprised look, he grinned. "My grandparents dragged my butt to her office every week."

Delia shifted next to him and became extremely interested in whatever she saw on her spotless dinette table. He was sorry he'd pushed it.

She cleared her throat as if preparing to tell him where he could put all of his advice.

"I don't want you to think I didn't, you know,

want to. Or didn't, um, like it." She paused, looking back to the table. "Because I did."

Ben had to remind himself to breathe. He knew what a big deal it was for her to admit that she'd wanted him, and she'd gone even further, admitting she'd enjoyed herself.

He turned to face her, drawing his knee up onto the sofa, then reaching for both of her hands. Her gaze lifted to his, and she pressed her teeth into her bottom lip, but she didn't try to pull away. That was a good sign. He decided to take a chance.

"About the other night." He tried not to notice when she grimaced. "I understand a little better why you were so upset after everything. But I can't be sorry it happened."

"Ben, you don't have to—"

He shook his head to stall her. "Please let me get this out. I know the words are tough for you. You've probably been taught to associate them with something dirty. I want you to know that there was nothing dirty or wrong about what happened between us. At least not to me."

She started to answer, but he had to keep talking, before he chickened out. "I need you to know that I adored making love with you. You blew my mind. And I'd be happy to repeat the whole event, with more preparation and a better location, anytime you like."

He didn't mention what she'd said the other night about the thing between them needing to stop because he hadn't wanted to hear it then and he didn't want to believe it now.

"Look, Ben. You know my history now. You know how messed up I am. Why would you even want to deal with any of that?"

"Do you think those things make you a less intriguing and desirable woman?" He shook his head slowly. "After you learned about my father, did you suddenly think I wasn't a decent person? Bad blood and all of that?"

Even as he said it with confidence, he braced himself. Insecurities had a way of lingering long past their expiration dates, and he wasn't sure he would ever completely let go of his.

"Of course not." She shook her head as if she couldn't believe he'd asked. "Those things had nothing to do with you."

"I could say the same thing about you."

She shook her head. "I'm just so confused."

"I get that," he said. "So I'm making you a promise. I will hold you, support you and listen to you. But I won't touch you like that again until, or if, you tell me that you want me as much as I still want you."

He turned her hands over and rubbed his thumbs slowly over the soft pads of her palms.

She watched his thumbs for a long time and then finally met his gaze.

"Thank you. For everything," she managed.

He smiled. "No. Thank you for trusting me with your story. You don't know how important trust is to me."

"I do know. And I do trust you, Ben."

"And I'm in love with you." His breath caught, his thumbs freezing in place where they touched her palms. It was too soon. "Oh, man. Sorry. I wasn't supposed to say that. Yet."

Slowly, he lifted his gaze to meet hers. The alarm in her eyes made him long to gather those words back to him with both hands, to cradle them deep inside where he alone could cherish them and no one would get hurt. He licked his lips. "Let's just pretend I didn't say that. Okay?"

For several seconds, Delia didn't move. She didn't even blink. She just stared into his eyes as if searching for answers he wasn't sure he could give. All of his life he'd never believed he was good enough. The weak fruit from an even weaker tree. But he prayed that in this one moment, in this one place, he would be enough for the woman who deserved someone so much better than him.

Slowly, she pulled her hands away, his skin immediately chilled from the loss of her touch. Instead of scooting away from him as she'd done earlier, though, she leaned toward him. She shifted by such tiny increments that he wasn't sure at first whether she'd really moved or he'd just imagined it in his best dreams. But she had moved. Closer and closer still.

When her mouth was but a breath away from his, she lingered there, seeming suddenly unsure. Then, as if she'd thought it through and had made her choice, she tipped her head and timidly brushed her lips over his in a mere feather of a kiss. His hands had just settled on her shoulders, his eyes drifting closed in the sweetness of that perfect moment, when she pulled back slightly.

He opened his eyes to find her studying him. And then those lovely lips lifted in the brightest smile he'd ever seen, and she spoke the words he'd never expected to hear from her.

"As much as I still want you."

CHAPTER NINETEEN

DELIA'S PULSE POUNDED so loudly in her ears that she was convinced that Ben could hear it, too. He loved her. He'd said it out loud, whether he'd tried to back out of his confession or not. What was she supposed to do with that? So vast, so overwhelming, it made her feel small, like a bit player in the film of her life.

She'd only now confessed that she trusted him, a risk she'd never dared to take with anyone else, and now he expected her to trust him with her heart, as well. Could she tell him the terrifying truth—that she already had? That his quiet strength had breached her defenses more effectively than an armed assault? But as she stared into the deep brown eyes of her self-effacing hero, the words she longed to say, the words buried deep in her heart, wouldn't come.

"You're sure?"

Her gaze shot over to him. Had he just read her mind? No. Obviously, he was asking about that other thing she'd said. She was wavering on that, too, so she nodded to convince them both. She cleared her throat. "I'm sure."

"I'm glad."

Delia braced herself to be as swept away as they'd been the first time, with heat and need eclipsing their good sense. But Ben surprised her by simply enfolding her in his arms. Nothing had ever felt more perfect. He gently drew her head to his shoulder and settled back into the sofa.

Why wasn't she bristling more at his ministrations? It went against everything she believed in to rely on someone else, to give him the power to hurt her. It felt so nice, though, so safe, letting someone take care of her, just this once. Especially since that someone was Ben.

She didn't know how long they'd stayed in that spot, with Ben tracing hypnotizing little circles on her back and with that sporty scent she would ever associate with him filling her with a sense of calm. Her eyes drifted closed as she allowed her other senses to simply enjoy his presence. This was what love could be like, how sweet and tender it could be, if she could only allow herself to dive into the waves of it instead of just poking her toes in the surf.

She was still considering the possibilities they might find on white-sand beaches while wading together in the frothy tide when Ben pressed his lips to her temple. Her eyes popped open, but she resisted the temptation to pull away from his sweet touch. She needed him, and she refused to let Lloyd steal one more thing from her. This moment was hers and Ben's.

"Do you mind if I take these out?" He reached for one of the pins holding her bun in place.

Her hand went automatically to the back of her head. "It'll be an awful mess."

"God, I hope so."

His chuckle was so low and throaty, so sexy, that she felt a tingling all the way to her most feminine places. Should she worry about how easily her body responded to him? How she always wanted things she'd never wanted before with him? No, this was right. This was Ben.

Gently, he removed her pins one by one, dropping them on the side table. When all that remained were the two bands that held the knot in place, Delia removed those herself, her hair falling in a heap down her back.

She shifted, her gaze darting his way to check his reaction. "You know I warned you."

"Yeah, you did."

But the roughness in his voice suggested he didn't mind what he saw, and the way he sank his hands into the mess with relish confirmed her guess.

"And you were so right," he crooned.

As his fingers slid with hypnotic repetition

through the strands, Ben leaned in close and traced a line of kisses from her temple to her jaw. Then he brushed his thumb over her chin to urge her to lower it, before he lifted up slightly from his seat and kissed both of her eyelids and the tip of her nose. At first, she had to remind herself to relax, to let go and enjoy his sweet seduction, and then bit by bit, she gave herself over to the sensation and adoration.

By the time he touched his lips to the corner of her mouth, his tongue darting out for the tiniest of tastes, Delia couldn't help but turn in to his kiss, restlessness already building inside her.

He pulled back so he could look into her eyes. "Patience, sweetheart. We have all the time in the world." He brushed her hair back from her face then reached for her hand, kissing each knuckle. "I want to get this right this time."

She was pretty sure there was nothing he could do to get it wrong—except maybe to stop—but she took a deep breath and nodded.

"You deserve to be adored," he whispered against her ear. "Cherished. Treasured."

Each word blew a delicious warm breath over her ear and the delicate skin just beneath it. Her skin was so sensitized that she could hardly sit still.

"But I—"

"You won't regret it. I promise."

She wanted to believe him. Unfortunately, she'd never been a patient woman. She shivered and snuggled closer to him as he continued his hot trail of kisses over her ear and down her neck. This time when he reached her mouth, he traced his finger over curves of her lips and then replaced his hand with his lips. She gasped right into his mouth.

Ben stilled, his jaw tight as he lifted his head away from hers. She wanted to call out in protest, but it didn't seem fair when he was trying so hard to restrain himself. He squeezed his eyes shut and took a few long breaths, his hands trembling as he braced them on her upper arms.

Finally, he pressed his forehead to hers. "You're not making this easy. Trying to be gallant here."

"I do my best," she said with a chuckle.

Opening his eyes, he tried to frown at her, but it softened to a grin. "Then I'll have to do the same."

Without preamble, he bent his head and kissed her again, and she immediately decided that every woman deserved to be kissed that way. Sweetly. Coaxingly. Thoroughly. He sank into the softness of her lips as if finding a resting place, and when she opened for him and met his tongue with her own, he settled in as if he planned to stay. She definitely hoped he would.

By the time Ben pulled back far enough that he

could look into her eyes, Delia could only stare back at him, as out of breath as he was. She'd never been kissed before. At least never like that. And she would never kiss anyone again without thinking of this man and this moment. She didn't even want to kiss anyone else, ever.

"You're so beautiful," he whispered.

He paused to trace his thumb over her lips, now swollen and sensitive, and then ran the back of his fingers along the skin on her neck, already abraded by the surprising five o'clock shadow on his baby face.

"How did I get so lucky?" he asked.

Reaching up, she traced her finger along his jawline and then smiled. "You finally woke up and noticed me."

"I must have been wearing a blindfold." He shook his head and brushed his fingers over her cheek. "How could I not have seen you? Just look at you."

"Maybe you were too busy trying to keep your job?"

"Look where that got me."

He was trying to get a laugh, but she didn't go for it. Instead of kissing her again, he wrapped his arm around her shoulders and settled back with her, deep in the sofa cushions. She should have felt relieved. He'd given her an out, in case she wasn't ready. That's what she wanted, wasn't it?

With a jolt, she realized that it wasn't what she wanted. Not at all.

She cleared her throat. "Uh, Ben, why are you stalling?"

"I'm not stalling." He wouldn't look at her when he said it.

"What would you call it then?"

He shrugged. "I'm just…taking it slow. I told you there's no hurry. It doesn't have to be today. Or tomorrow. Or even next week…"

"Ben, do you, uh, still want me?"

"What?"

He looked at her as if she'd grown a third eye or told him she'd just seen Jimmy Hoffa at the local Target store. Maybe both.

"I asked if you *want* me. Do you?"

In some ways, she hadn't needed to ask that question. She'd seen his hooded, glazed eyes, felt the rush of his heartbeat and brushed up against the more obvious sign of his desire, which he'd tried to shield behind the bulk of his sweater. But this was about more than physiological responses. Ugliness and scars were involved, and maybe he'd decided he couldn't take on all of her baggage. She couldn't blame him. If the roles were reversed, she might have chosen the same thing.

He tilted his head to the side. "Is that a trick question?"

She crossed her arms and lifted her chin. "It's not funny."

He shook his head. "I'm sorry, but I just don't know how you could ask that question. Of course I want you. More than I've ever wanted anyone." He met her gaze steadily. "So much that I can't think of anything else."

"Then why aren't you…you know?"

"Because you can't even *say* it, Delia. You're not ready for this, sweetheart."

"But I am." She held her hands wide. "Those words. They're just words. Loaded ones for sure, but that's all. I'll talk to someone about all of this. I promise. I really want to work through these things so I can at least make peace with them."

"Maybe it's just too soon."

"This isn't exactly…our first rodeo."

He shook his head definitively. "It doesn't matter. That happened before I knew everything you went through. I would never do anything to hurt you. Or frighten you. Or make you feel anything less than perfect."

"I know."

But instead of tying up her hair and readjusting her clothes as he probably expected her to, Delia turned to him and slipped her cardigan sweater off her shoulders. Ben didn't say anything, but he didn't look away, either. Then her fingers moved to the top button on her blouse. With hands that were far less steady than she would have preferred, she undid the first few buttons. Her new lacy pink bra peeked out the top.

It wasn't until Ben swallowed so hard that she could see his Adam's apple shift that Delia understood why she'd purchased the bra in the first place, why she'd begun wearing it when she might see him. It was impossible not to feel desirable when she saw herself through his eyes.

"Delia, you don't have to do this, tonight or any other night."

"I know that."

"If, at any time, you decide you want to call it off—"

"I know you would."

When he didn't say anything else, she reached for his hand and guided it to the upper swell of her breast, just over her heart. He stared at his hand, but he didn't move it. Delia held her breath, waiting. Finally, when his hand shifted, and he appeared to be pulling away, she said the only two things that could make him change his mind.

"I know I can trust you because you're *you*. Now please—" she paused, willing the words to come "—make love to me."

Though the words were foreign and uncomfortable, she felt bolstered in being able to say them. More importantly, now she knew with absolute certainty that she was ready. They must have been magic words for Ben as well because he stood and reached out a hand to her. Without hesitation, Delia rested her hand in his, and he helped her stand up.

He led her down the hallway, but stopped suddenly when he came to three darkened doorways. "Uh, which way?"

She pointed to the room straight ahead, and before she knew what was happening, he reached behind her knees and shoulders and gathered her into his arms. It was so precious, so romantic, as he carried her through the doorway…until he whacked her head soundly on the door frame.

BEN SHOOK HIS head in the darkness as the woman in his arms tittered like a child with a secret while she rubbed her head.

"Oh man, that hurts."

So much for making this a perfect night for her. He tightened his arms around Delia to keep from dropping her.

"Well, that didn't go the way I envisioned it. Sorry about that." He paused to rub the tiny bump forming at her crown. "It looks a lot easier in the movies."

"Been watching Richard Gere pulling off that scene in *An Officer and a Gentleman*?"

"Maybe I'd better watch it again."

"You'd better be more careful, too," she said, still chuckling. "I carry a gun, you know."

"Thanks for the reminder. Now, hush, or I'll drop you on the floor. Not intentionally, of course."

He couldn't help grinning as he slowly carried her toward the shadow that had to be the bed. As nervous as she had to be, she was trying to make this easier on *him*. Did he really think he could erase years of scars for her with one perfect night? Talk about performance anxiety. And he'd thought facing armed suspects at the bank had been nerve-racking.

He carefully lowered her feet to the floor. When she sat on the mattress, he took a seat next to her, not too close, but not too far, either. He patted his hands across the bedside table until he located the lamp and then fumbled for the switch.

In the soft light that suddenly filled the room, Delia chewed her lip, glancing sidelong at him. Clearly, he wasn't the only one who was nervous.

He grinned at her. "We're a pair, aren't we? I'd like to be real smooth here, but it's not working out that well."

"You don't need to be smooth for me. Just be you."

He swallowed. Once again, she was making *him* more comfortable when it should have been the other way around.

Shifting closer to her, he rested his head on her

shoulder and surveyed the sparse room around him. Her bedroom was as barren as the rest of the house. Empty walls. No knickknacks. The whole place had a transient feel to it, a reminder that she'd never intended to stay too long.

Ben pushed aside the emptiness that even the thought of her leaving brought to him. He couldn't think about that now. With all that was going on in his life, it wasn't as if he had the luxury of planning for the future anyway. He might not even have a future. Nothing to offer anyone.

Delia moved next to him. "Would you mind if we turned the light off? I'm feeling a little awkward."

"After everything we've talked about, now you feel awkward?" He smiled at her profile until finally the side of her mouth lifted.

"I suppose that's fair."

Lifting his hand, he brushed his thumb back and forth along her cheek. "You have no idea how beautiful you are. You can't possibly see what I see, or you would want to not only leave the light on, but also open the curtains."

Her shoulders twitched as she chuckled. "How about we don't do that?"

"So just the light, then?" He waited for several seconds before continuing. "That's a good compromise."

"And you're all about compromise."

Putting his arm around her, he combed his fingers through her hair. "But seriously, I really want to *see* you. It was dark…before. Not at all how I'd planned it."

At her side-glance, he nodded. Of course, he'd planned on them making love eventually. Or at least he'd fantasized about the possibility of it far more often than he cared to confess.

"I want this time to be different, Dee. Are you okay with that?"

For several seconds, she didn't answer. He knew he was asking a lot of her. Not only did he expect her to choose to be with him without having the heat of the moment as an excuse, but he also wanted her in the light, where she wouldn't be able to hide anything from him, even her fear. But just when he worried he'd asked too much of her, she turned back to him and nodded.

He curled toward her and used his thumb to bring her face closer to him. Then he pressed his lips to hers. The desire he'd been tamping back all night flamed again. He had to remind himself to move slowly. He wanted to show her she was special and convince her she should always have been treated that way.

Rolling to his side, Ben drew her down on the bed with him, heart-to-heart and face-to-face. In the light, he could see the trust in her eyes; he only hoped she could see the truth in his.

When Delia reached for the hem of his sweater, Ben helped her pull it over his head, and then with unsteady hands, he worked his way down the remaining buttons of her blouse. The first real sight of her porcelain perfection, covered only by a mask of pink lace, took his breath away. And when he peeled away her soft leggings and all that lace, revealing all, he could only look at her with awe.

She licked her lips, her gaze darting to him and then away. How could she not know how beautiful she was? How precious.

"You're perfect," he breathed, the words as natural as his exhalation.

"Far from it." But a smile spread across her face and a pretty pink flush crept from her chest to her neck, then to her cheeks. "But thanks anyway."

"Not just pretty, either. You're smart. And strong." He paused to kiss the corner of her mouth. "Resilient." His lips brushed the other corner. "And a heck of a shot with a .40-caliber semiautomatic." He paused once more, staring right into her eyes. "And I'm the luckiest man in the world."

He caught her surprise as he covered her mouth with his again. And he was lost. He breathed her in and tasted and touched, each sensation more potent than the one before. But because this night was about Delia, not him, he held a tight rein on his desire. As he stretched her out on the bed, he focused on her alone, touching with worshipful hands and coaxing lips as he memorized each curve, each plane.

Her fire built slowly, from a pile of kindling, to those first flames, to the glowing embers that suggested it was time. Reaching for his wallet, he rolled on the condom to protect them both this time and then shifted so that he was above her, balancing himself while staring into her eyes.

"Are you ready? You don't have to…"

But despite her wide eyes, she nodded.

"Are you afraid?"

This time she smiled and shook her head. "I have nothing to be afraid of when I'm with you."

Ben brought them together then, resisting the overwhelming temptation to claim her all at once. He moved slowly, loving her body with the same determination that had helped him garner her trust. Her face became his focal point as he watched for any sign of pain or misgivings. She only smiled. Soon she was meeting him and matching his cadence, urging him forward.

As she cried out in relief and buried her face in the curve of his neck, Ben gave himself over to the spell that was Delia Morgan. Losing himself in her. Loving her. Making her his. If only for a while.

He held her for a long time afterward, trailing his fingers over her smooth shoulders, drawing the covers closer over the two of them. Still, he couldn't help but brace himself for what was to come. He'd been there before, had relished her beautiful passion and then felt the crush of her remorse. Would she be sorry this time, too? Would she hate herself for allowing him to love her and hate him for doing it? Would it destroy *him* if she did?

So he continued to slide his fingers through her hair, to follow the lines of her shoulder blades with his gentlest touch. Her scars had many layers, and he had to be strong enough to help her peel away each one. Or if he couldn't help her himself, he would be strong for her as she sought guidance from someone who could help.

No matter what it took, he would be that kind of man for the woman he loved. The kind of man that his father had never been. He wasn't like his father, after all. He should have known that all along.

Delia shifted against him, drawing him up short. He braced himself for whatever was to come as he looked down at her, pushing her hair back from her face. His throat went dry and his heart thudded at the lovely image before him. Her breathing had changed. Her long lashes lay resting against her cheek. Sweet Delia, who'd spent her life hiding from the ugly truth and had finally trusted him with the weight of it and had fallen asleep in his arms.

CHAPTER TWENTY

Light was already sneaking into the room through the cracks between the mini-blind slats when Delia blinked her eyes open. Where was she? She glanced from wall to window and then wall to door, trying to make sense of it. It might have been her bedroom—the comforter she'd pulled up to her nose smelled like her lotion—but nothing else felt familiar. Except maybe that other pleasant scent that triggered something in her memory, yet she couldn't quite put her finger on it.

But as she turned her head, all of her discordant thoughts snapped together in the discovery of her overnight guest. Her first male overnight guest. Ever.

She took in a sharp breath, but that only gave her a fresh whiff of that sporty scent that she now recognized as Ben's cologne. He looked impossibly handsome as he slept, his chest bare and the blanket riding low on his hips. She couldn't help but stare at him as memories from the night before rushed at her from all directions. Pictures, flavors and memories of sweet touches joined to overwhelm her senses again, warming her inside and out, just as Ben had.

She couldn't get over the fact that she'd spent the whole night with him. That seemed impossible. Physical intimacy was one thing, even if it was a formidable thing, but actually sleeping with a man? That was different. She'd never been able to trust anyone that much. To give someone access to her body when her guard was down, to her mind when she wasn't alert to protect it. She'd never allowed herself to be that vulnerable.

Until now. Until Ben.

He slept on, probably unaware that this had been such a pivotal moment for her. Did he understand that trust was a far bigger risk for her than sex ever could be? Shifting in his sleep, he turned toward her, his breathing slow and even. He looked so young and carefree as he slept, such a contradiction to the strong and steadfast man she knew him to be. A man who'd never let his scars prevent him from doing the right thing.

Had Ben watched her sleep last night as she was watching him now? Though it was already daylight, she shot a look at the lamp that he'd insisted on leaving lit earlier. Its switch had been turned off. As unsettling as the thought of being watched was, she wasn't as uncomfortable as she would have expected, knowing that Ben would have been the one watching.

Without thinking, she reached over and brushed her fingers through his hair. He hadn't had a trim since being forced to take administrative leave, and his hair was beginning to curl at his nape. Ben jerked from her touch, and his eyes popped open. But unlike her, he barely looked around, seeming to know exactly where he was.

"Well, good morning," he said with a wide grin.

"Good morning." She tried to be enthusiastic like he was, but her voice sounded strained. After everything that had happened last night, what were they supposed to say or do now?

Ben answered her unspoken question by popping off the pillow and kissing her soundly on the mouth before she even had the chance to warn him about morning breath. Apparently, he didn't care about that. Her swollen and probably mascara-smeared eyes didn't seem to bother him, either, even after he'd slipped on his glasses and could take a good look.

Clearly, he'd missed the memo that said guys were supposed to buy into that whole morning-after-awkwardness thing. Or should skip out before dawn to avoid it. But she couldn't be as laidback about this as he was. Especially since she wasn't wearing a stitch of clothing under that comforter. Her cheeks burned as she realized he was wearing—or in this case *not* wearing—exactly the same thing.

As she sat up and propped her pillow behind her head, she also discreetly tightened the blanket under her armpits so her breasts were fully covered. Ben's gaze slid to the side as he sat up and propped his own pillow. He never missed anything.

She was relieved that he didn't call her on it, though. He could have said that he'd already seen most everything she had to hide. And that what he'd missed enjoying visually, he'd explored by touch and taste. He could have said many things, but he didn't, thank goodness. Still, her face felt like it might burst into flames as a slide show of tantalizing scenes played inside her head.

"Got anything to eat around here? Don't know about you, but I'm starving."

Only instead of throwing on his jeans and stalking off to the kitchen on a hunting-and-gathering mission, he pulled her to him with a hunger of another kind.

"Oh, I want this," he murmured against her skin. "I want *us*. After all of this is over, I want…"

He didn't finish as he was suddenly preoccupied with the tender spot just behind her ear. But he didn't really have to because she understood what he meant. She wanted it, too. Wanted there to be a *them*, now and later, after Ben's name was cleared so he could return to the post, where he belonged.

So it made no sense to her that she couldn't stop squirming in his arms, even as tingles blossomed along the path of kisses he followed from her ear to beneath her chin. Why was she still nervous? She'd said the words. Well, not quite as many as he had. She'd participated in the act. Willingly. And it had been lovely. Transcendent. Even now her body reawakened effortlessly with his lightest touch.

So why was she feeling out of sorts? Was there such a thing as *too perfect*? She was being overly sensitive, but she couldn't shake the feeling that something wasn't right. Was she really never allowed to have something wonderful in her life, or had she just convinced herself that this was true?

Ben lifted his lips away from the skin beneath her ear. She shivered, but held her neck straight instead of stretching to provide him better access as she was tempted to do.

"You okay?" he whispered.

"Of course," she said, even if her stiff posture proved her a liar. "But shouldn't we be getting back to the case?"

"We will. Eventually." He continued to nip at her neck.

She was tempted to just go with it, to let herself be swept away just as she'd been last night. But they'd wasted enough time already worrying about her issues when they needed to address his. They had to get back to the case, especially after her run-in with Trevor yesterday.

"Come on, Ben. Last night was…well, last night, but this morning we have to get back to reality. I'd already planned to tell you—"

"Always the workaholic. I like that about you." He paused, pressing his lips into that spot on her neck where her pulse quickened. "You know, I like almost everything about you."

Despite her determination to stay on topic, she couldn't help asking, "Almost everything?"

"Isn't that enough?" At Delia's raised eyebrow, Ben answered her unspoken question. "I'm not a fan of the bun."

She frowned. "What's wrong with my bun?"

"Too tight." He reached for a handful of her hair that was spread in every direction against her pillow. "Now this, I like."

"It's a mess." She reached up with one hand to pat her hair down since she needed the other one to keep the blanket from slipping.

"I like messes." He dropped a kiss right in the middle of the rat's nest.

"You must."

His grin as he pulled back suggested that he understood she'd meant more than just her tousled hair. At least he understood that he would be taking on a lot if he wanted to be with her. More baggage than could fill the belly of a 747.

Maybe it was just the old scars that had her uncomfortable this morning. Had she really believed that one perfect night—or even two—would blot out years of painful memories? Well, maybe she had, but she should have known better. There was no magic elixir. Even time hadn't been a sufficient healer. So eventually she would have to take Ben's advice and talk to a professional counselor who could help her deal with her past instead of fleeing from it. But not yet. Right now she knew better than to allow herself to think about it at all.

"Ben?"

He must have heard the frustration in her voice, because he blinked and then raised both hands in surrender.

"Okay. Okay. Let's talk about the case." He frowned. "There just hasn't been anything new to tell lately."

"There was something last night."

"What? Why didn't you tell me?"

She cleared her throat. "I did try, but I didn't really have the chance…"

"Right." He swallowed, then nodded. "Well, can you tell me now?"

She glanced down at the blanket still tucked

under her arms. "Could you please hand me my robe first?" With a tilt of her head, she indicated the fluffy periwinkle dorm robe on the chair next to the bed.

"Sure."

He stretched and grabbed the robe, managing to keep the blanket from falling from his pelvis. If it seemed odd to him that she needed to cover up after last night, he didn't say so.

She sat up, shifted her legs over the side of the bed and slipped her arms in the sleeves of the robe, carefully lowering the blanket from where it covered her upper body. Only after she'd cinched it at her waist did she pull the blanket away entirely. As she turned back to Ben, she had expected that he'd been watching the whole graceless process, but he wasn't paying attention to her at all.

On the opposite side of the bed, he stood with his back to her. He was still shirtless, but he'd already pulled on his jeans and was zipping them. When he finished, he grabbed his sweater and yanked it over his head. He settled back on the opposite side of the bed, purposely avoiding brushing her skin this time, though she could still feel his gaze on her. As awkward as Delia had felt before, she missed the soothing weight of his touch now, even if neither of them could afford the distraction.

BEN WAITED AS long as he could, just watching her. She looked bewildered. He didn't want to admit that he'd hoped that one night with him would heal all of her wounds. Had he thought he had magic hands or something? Well, if he had thought that, the robe that she kept pulling tighter at the base of her throat suggested otherwise.

Finally, he couldn't wait any longer. "Are you going to tell me what you figured out?"

"That's the problem," she said, shaking her head. "I didn't figure out anything. But someone else found *me* out."

A shiver danced up his spine, but he steadied himself. He didn't even have the specifics yet. It wasn't like him to react without compiling all the facts and weighing his options. But then he'd never been able to stop and think about anything first when Delia was involved.

"You're not talking about Scott again, are you?" His words were rushed, as if by speaking quickly, he could make the answers come faster.

"It wasn't Scott." She pressed her lips together.

"Then was it Polaski?" He shook his head, squeezing his eyes shut before opening them again. "I should never have let you become involved in this mess. Look, I'll talk to him. I don't know how much help I'll be. Probably not much since I'm persona non grata. But I'll try to make this right—"

"Ben," she said in a firm voice. "It wasn't him, either."

He stopped, stared at her, his insides twisting in knots now. Had they miscalculated the risk of working together? Just how desperate was the person involved to keep the truth from coming to light?

"Then who was it? Tell me!" He gripped his hands together to keep from grabbing her shoulders and forcing her to spill it.

"I'm *trying* to tell you." She drew her eyebrows together and then blew out a long breath.

But she didn't say it immediately. Was this the answer to the question he'd had since that night when that reporter had appeared on the TV screen, gleefully describing the dismantling of his life? Was he prepared to hear the answer to the question that revealed which of his friends had betrayed him? Would he ever be ready for that?

"It was Trevor."

"Trevor?" Disjointed thoughts smacked at each other from all directions, none finding the proper connections. "He can't be the one who set me up. He wasn't even here when most of those arrests went down."

"Well, he's the one who came after me at the end of my shift last night. He tracked me down at Kensington, asked me a bunch of questions and basically accused *me* of setting you up." She paused and met his gaze. "Ben, he knows."

"What does he know?"

She shook her head, frowning. "I can't be sure. That I'm helping you? That I'm on to him? That we're sort of, uh…together." She sat straighter in the bed, tightening her robe over her chest.

She fidgeted, rubbing her palms together. "I don't know if he really believes that I did it, or if he was just trying to throw suspicion off him."

"I really wish you would have told me this last night." His jaw tightened as fury unfurled inside of him. "Did he scare you?"

Her lips lifted. "Maybe I shouldn't answer that. I'm a police officer. I'm not supposed to get scared. I'm just supposed to stay alert and take things as they come."

"Of course you're supposed to get scared. Fear is what helps you to proceed with caution. It prods you to call on your team members for backup."

He crossed his arms, forcing his words to stop. Even after he'd confessed to her about his own fear during the bank incident, after their discussions about the importance of the team, she still couldn't admit she'd been scared? That she'd realized she couldn't handle the situation alone?

"Okay, it made me nervous," she finally admitted with a tight laugh. "Particularly after the thing we witnessed at the park the other night. There are just too many coincidences."

"And definitely too much risk," he couldn't resist adding.

"Do you think Trevor might be trying to set me up, too?"

Ben shook his head. "I don't think so. How would he even know to target you?"

As soon as he'd said it, his insides gripped like a fist. *Target.* Had he unwittingly painted a bull's-eye on Delia's back to mark her for someone who already had it in for him?

How could Ben have been so reckless with Delia's safety? From the beginning, they'd known that their partnership was tricky, but had it been naive of them to believe that only her career was at risk if someone discovered they were working together? They were involved in something they didn't fully understand, tinkering in something that had to be bigger than a couple of guys escaping prosecution over selling a few dime bags of weed. And he'd sent a rookie cop in to investigate the case for him.

"If you still don't believe it was Trevor, then why did he come after me? And if not him, then who?"

Clearly those were the critical questions. If they could answer them, they would have this whole thing settled. "I don't know."

"But we still can't rule him out, either," she insisted. "There were those drug cases in Manistique."

"You're right. We still need to get answers to those questions. Look, Delia, I can't explain why Trevor asked so many questions, but my gut tells me it was one of the others who set me up. Someone I trust enough to make me vulnerable. Or, now, to put both of us at risk."

For a few seconds, she was quiet, as if she was digesting his words. When she finally spoke, she didn't look up at him. "Then I should tell you about the other things Trevor said."

"You mean he didn't just pepper you with questions?"

She shook her head. "When I told him I needed to get back to work, he told me to do that while I still could. Or something to that effect."

"And is that it?" He managed through gritted teeth. How dare Trevor threaten the woman he loved? How dare he believe he could even come near her without facing consequences?

"One more thing. He said something about the answers coming out and not in a way I would like. It didn't make a lot of sense, but it gave me the creeps."

Ben shivered. "I can't let you do this anymore. It's too dangerous."

Her eyes widened. "You didn't *let* me do anything. I volunteered."

He shook his head. He had to present this delicately, to make her understand.

"But you've just had a taste of how out of hand this could become. It was a mistake for me to let you put yourself at risk like this. I should have thought it through. I should have realized that anyone who'd go to such lengths to protect drug dealers and to set me up would have no qualms about going after anyone who would help me. The suspect won't hesitate to hurt you."

He stopped, squeezing his eyes closed and shaking his head. "I can't let that happen."

Why hadn't he considered that he might fall in love with her? That his need to protect her would be stronger even than his instinct to save his own hide. He glanced down at his lap, finding his hands almost in a stranglehold in the same way that his fingers ached to wrap around the neck of anyone who would dare to harm her.

He waited for some reaction from her, but when she didn't speak, he couldn't help but fill the silence.

"For your own safety, I'm asking you to stop digging for answers on this case, particularly at work. Just back away and let the state investigators do their jobs. I can no longer justify endangering you or your career to protect my freedom or my job."

When he looked up at her at last, he found her staring back at him, a storm raging in her eyes. He knew he'd made a mistake before she spoke a single word.

"Are you listening to yourself, Ben? Are you really asking me to back off on an investigation because you're afraid I'll get hurt?" She pushed off the bed and didn't even bother tightening her robe as she stalked around the room, the opening falling loose over her chest.

"I didn't mean…" Ben began, but he didn't finish because he'd meant every word. The worst part was that she knew it, too.

"How can you say that to me after I've had to work so hard to get where I am? You know a female officer has to work twice as hard as a male officer to be taken seriously in uniform." She turned back to him, trapping him with her stare. "I'm a cop. Just like you. This is my job. How can you ask me not to do it?"

He could have pointed out that this case wasn't part of her job since she'd been specifically ordered to stay away from it—and him—but he wasn't that foolish. She was already furious enough and, unlike him, she still had a gun.

Could he have said anything more disrespectful to a fellow police officer? Was being in love with her enough of an excuse for doing so? He shouldn't have bothered asking himself that question because he already knew the answer. There was no excuse.

"I'm sorry. I shouldn't have—"

"You've got that right. You shouldn't have." She paused from pacing to glare at him. "Do you have any idea how insulting it is for you to try to *protect* me?"

He swallowed and then nodded.

"This just shows that you never respected me as a fellow officer. It was all an act."

"You know that's not true."

"All of those words about teamwork were just background noise to give the female cop the illusion that she was really part of the team."

"That's not fair. I never treated you differently because of your gender." Until now, a voice inside him insisted. Did he believe she'd suddenly become less qualified because she'd stolen his heart? Just because she had become endlessly more valuable to him personally didn't mean he had the right to place her in a padded box and shield her from harm.

"I don't—" She suddenly stopped walking, tucked her chin to her chest and stared at the floor. After several heartbeats, she turned back to him and sighed. "You're right. That wasn't fair. But what *you* said wasn't, either."

"I know."

She frowned at him. "Then what were you thinking?"

"I was thinking that I— I mean, I just don't want you to get hurt. I don't want you to put your safety on the line just for my sake."

In a mere twelve hours, he'd told her he loved her once, had tried to take it back and then had nearly told her again. From the way Delia was watching him, she knew it, too.

"This is what we do, Ben. We put ourselves out there for somebody else's sake all the time. And just like you would, I want to finish what I started. To ensure that the proper suspects are charged with these crimes."

"Are you sure we can't just hide out together and wait for the whole thing to blow over? I know of a few pleasant activities we could take part in to pass the time." He planted on his best smile though he'd already lost the argument.

Delia didn't respond to his attempt at humor. "If you respect me at all as a fellow police officer, you'll let me do my job. And without second-guessing or micromanaging. Can you do that?"

Despite his worry that this was a mistake, he nodded. She needed him to have confidence in her as a police officer as much as he needed her to know she could trust him with her heart. So he would keep telling himself he was making the right decision in continuing to put her life at risk for his sake, until he finally believed the lie.

CHAPTER TWENTY-ONE

DELIA APPROACHED THE white sedan from the rear, careful to observe any sudden movements from the driver, presumably a male, and his passenger, gender undetermined. She'd already trained the spotlight on the car's interior and waited several seconds before climbing out of her car, so she could monitor whether either occupant was behaving erratically.

As Delia reached the side of the car, the window rolled down.

"Hello, sir." She blinked at the teenager behind the steering wheel. She'd prepared herself to meet a middle-aged man, based on the type of car and honor-student bumper sticker on the back window. "May I see your driver's license and registration?"

Delia had felt off all night, and it wasn't only that Trevor had been right across the squad room from her during announcements, either. Or even that he hadn't stopped staring until they were dismissed to head outside for another snowy shift. She'd dropped not one driver's license, but two, right in the gray sludge along the side of the road while making routine traffic stops, and she'd managed to get herself lost in one of the larger subdivisions, despite her GPS.

She needed to pull it together. She couldn't afford to be distracted when she was on traffic duty—traffic stops were one of the most dangerous assignments troopers completed. There was no way to know who would be waiting for them inside those cars they pulled over.

Delia reached for a notebook and pen in her pocket. "May I see your proof of insurance, as well?"

At least she could rely on her regular speech. Otherwise, she would have forgotten what she was supposed to say next. The driver produced the documents, and the passenger, another older teen, didn't balk when also asked to show his driver's license.

She glanced at the driver's documents first. "Mr. Franklin, just so you know, the reason I pulled you over is that you were going forty-nine in a thirty-five-mile-per-hour zone."

"Yes, ma'am."

Hiding her grin, she returned to her car to type up the ticket. At least the kid hadn't given her any trouble. She could, in turn, make it a little easier on him.

Still, as Delia swiped the boy's driver's license through the card reader on her laptop, it was difficult to stay focused. Nothing had felt right since Ben had asked her to stop looking at his case. She couldn't decide which had her more discombobulated—that he'd asked her to walk away from the investigation or that he'd wanted her to stop for her own safety.

Because he loved her. He hadn't said it the second time, but that was what he'd meant.

What did that say about love? At least Ben's version of it? Was it just an excuse to dictate someone else's life? Just another word for control?

She tightened her jaw. If only her heart and head weren't telling her two different things. Her head, the only part of her she'd ever listened to before, was telling her to run. From Ben. From the weakness of relying on another person. From the risk of pain she wouldn't be able to bear if someone she loved deserted her. Again.

Only she didn't want to pull away. Not this time. She wanted to be with Ben. She could even forgive him his momentary lapse—he'd only wanted to protect her. She wanted him that much. And though he hadn't said it in exactly those words, he wanted a relationship, just like she did. So why, instead of feeling excited and hopeful for this new adventure, did she feel like a game-show contestant, choosing between the prizes behind two doors while already certain that both rooms were empty?

She shook off the thought and the edginess as she pulled the long strip of shiny, white paper off the miniprinter and returned to give the boy his ticket and the bad news.

"Now, I gave you a break—only ten over instead of fourteen—so it will be fewer points on your driving record," she explained. "But, unfortunately, since you're under eighteen and have a graduated driver's license, your probationary-license period will be extended by several months."

The boy looked like he was about to cry, but he accepted the ticket and her warning to slow down. As she stepped away, she could hear him talking to the boy in the passenger seat.

"Man, my dad's going to kill me."

She could relate to how that kid must feel. Not that she gave even a small damn what her parents thought about anything she did. But his general unease, now, that she understood completely.

Shaking the snow off her coat and her cover outside the patrol car, she wished she could shake off her discomfort as easily. She climbed in the car and lifted her police radio control.

"Radio 570. Traffic," she said into the handset.

Delia was looking over her shoulder to merge into traffic when her personal cell phone rang.

She froze. Should she answer? Would it be Ben calling again to warn her to be careful? Would he muddle her thoughts even more by almost telling her that he loved her?

Well aware he would only hit Redial if she sent the call to voice mail or "missed" it, she reached for the phone that she'd tucked in a storage nook built into the dashboard. But she didn't recognize the number, so she allowed it to go to voice mail. She'd thought she'd made it clear she wanted nothing to do with her parents, but that didn't mean they'd gotten the message. They would probably continue calling until she finally changed the number and maybe even moved.

Either curiosity or a self-destructive streak made her shift the car back into Park and click on her voice mail. But before she could listen to the message, her phone rang again, that same mysterious number flashing on the caller ID. With a shrug, she answered it.

"Delia? I wasn't sure if you had your phone with you."

She squinted, trying to place the voice. "Trooper Maxwell?"

"Yeah, it's me, Grant. I didn't think my voice was so recognizable."

"I guessed," she said with a chuckle. And it was recognizable, whether he realized that or not. A few weeks ago she would have asked how he had her phone number, but lately she'd started trading numbers with fellow troopers as part of her effort to become more involved with the team. The plan that Ben had encouraged. She'd even received a few calls and texts from some of the others since then. "So what's up?"

She waited for him to explain why he'd called. Since her run-in with Trevor, she was a little gun-shy with her coworkers.

"I'm calling because I can help you."

Automatically, she straightened in her seat. "How's that?"

"I realize I'm not supposed to know this, but I think you're helping Ben."

Her breath caught. Had everyone and his second cousin, Marty, figured out that she'd been looking into the case? So much for being discreet and flying under the radar.

"You don't have to answer," Grant said when she didn't respond immediately.

Great, he didn't even need confirmation. Just how obvious had she been? She might have questioned the information coming from Grant, but they'd already looked into his background, just like all the other officers. He was one of the first they'd cleared as a possible suspect. Good cop. Clean record.

"Anyway, I've been trying to figure out a way

to help him, too. Ben doesn't deserve any of this, does he?"

She sighed, figuring she would have to be careful not to admit her involvement just yet. At least Grant wasn't trying to turn the guilt back on her the way Trevor had.

"No, he doesn't deserve it."

"Well, I finally know how I can help."

She gripped the steering wheel, drawing in a sharp breath. Was this how operators at tip lines felt every time a call came in? That moment of hope before realizing the thrill seekers were just stirring the pot again. "How's that?"

"I happened upon some information that might help clear his name."

"What is it?" The words were out of her mouth before she could stop them. Her desperation was as obvious as it was authentic. Still, was it possible that he'd found something significant? She'd been looking for answers for weeks, and one of Ben's other coworkers "happened upon" something she'd missed? It wasn't fair.

"*If* I were interested in finding some information like that, what would I need to do to come across it?"

"You're funny," he told her. "Ben was right. He always said he saw such potential in you. That you were going to become a great part of the team."

"Uh. Thanks?" It was the second time a co-worker had shared that Ben believed in her. Even then. She cleared her throat. "So. About that information…"

"When can we meet?"

"Isn't there anything you can tell me now?"

"Well—" he paused as if taking the time to look around wherever he was "—probably not right here. Besides, I have some papers to give you, so—"

"When and where?"

She sounded too anxious, but she couldn't help herself. He had answers, and she needed them. It was as simple as that. And besides, if he really wanted to help the way he said he did, he wouldn't care if she sounded desperate. Ben was probably sick of waiting, as well. He deserved to be released from this purgatory as soon as she found the key to this particular set of handcuffs.

"Do you know where the Brighton Recreation Area is? You know, the state park?"

"Of course. It was on the Livingston County tour Captain Polaski insisted on during my first day on the job."

"You know the rustic cabins by Caroga Lake?"

She frowned. It seemed like an odd place to meet. "I don't, but I'm sure I can find them."

"You can get there by taking Bishop Lake Road."

"But isn't there a less out-of-the-way place we can meet?"

She glanced out the windshield to the horizon, where the scant winter daylight was fading fast. The recreation area would be as dark as Kensington was all those nights she'd driven through, but at least she knew that location. The state park would be both dark and unfamiliar.

"I know I seem overly cautious," he said, chuckling. "But I don't have to tell you that there are people who don't want any information associated with this case to come to light, and as you've probably guessed, at least a few of them are working right alongside us."

"A few of them?"

She tried to keep her voice even, but it was obvious that the tentacles of this case stretched beyond even what she and Ben had guessed.

"The information I have is good, I swear," Grant continued. "I would just rather be careful as I'm passing it along, if that's all right with you."

"Fine," she heard herself saying. She couldn't blame him for wanting to protect himself.

They agreed on a time and ended the call. Eight o'clock was later than she preferred, but at least it was during her shift, so she would still have her patrol car. She could use the spotlight to hunt down the little cabins, she decided, as she tucked her phone back in the shelf.

She glanced down at the radar gun in the passenger seat. Other drivers would get a break tonight because she was finished monitoring traffic for now. She picked up the cell phone again. Ben deserved to know what she'd just learned, but if she called him, he might tell her to stand down over the case again, and she was in no mood for another argument.

Maybe if she texted him instead, she could provide minimal details and not have to hear the worry in his voice. Decision made, she quickly drafted a message with her thumbs.

FYI Grant has answers we've been looking for. Knows I'm working w/ you. Says possibly more than 1 suspect. Meeting at 8 @ Brighton Recreation Area. Cabins near Caroga Lake. Info TBD.

She'd expected him to respond, but hadn't figured it would come before she had the car in gear. Leaving it in Park, she reached for the phone again. It wouldn't do for a police officer to be seen texting and driving.

Why the rec area? Can't make it by 8. Will be there ASAP. Wait for me.

Delia had to grin as she set her phone aside. Of course he wanted her to wait for him. After all he'd been through, he would definitely like to be there when the answers were finally revealed. But he couldn't make it in time anyway. She glanced down at her dashboard clock and frowned. From her current location, she would barely make it there on time herself, especially if she had trouble finding Caroga Lake among all of the tiny lakes in the rec area. She hit Reply and typed again.

Can't wait. Don't want to be late. You shouldn't come anyway. You're on leave. Not good to be seen together. Got it under control. Details later.

His response was immediate and confusing.

No. Wait. Don't take any extra risks. Call for backup before going in. On my way.

Delia frowned at the message. Ben might have talked about her stubbornness, but sometimes he could be just as bullheaded and impractical as she was. Especially when it came to her safety. Silencing her phone so she wouldn't hear the *ping* and be tempted to look at another one of his overprotective messages while she was driving, she set it aside, put the car into gear and pulled out into traffic. She would see him soon anyway. Whether it was a bad idea or not, whether he would get in trouble about it later or not, he'd be showing up at that meeting point. He would be there as fast as his SUV could go without him becoming a suspect in a high-speed chase on Interstate 96 or US 23.

Her gaze lowered to the police radio as she considered Ben's insistence that she call for backup and then shook her head. Why would she call for backup when she was just meeting with a fellow trooper, and Ben would be there in a matter of minutes? What would she even have said, that she was meeting up with an officer so that he could report on one or more fellow team members? That would go over really well. And how would she even know whether she'd be calling in someone who would help or harm her?

She didn't need additional backup, anyway. Especially not with Ben on the way. Just as she knew she could count on him to be there for her, she planned to do this for the man she loved to prove that he could count on her.

She was going to get to the answers that would secure his freedom. Hopefully, she would make him proud.

"PICK UP THE PHONE!"

Ben shouted at his cell phone, through his

SUV's hands-free unit, as the call went to Delia's voice mail for the third time in a row. He ended the call and immediately dialed again. She wasn't refusing the calls, but she wasn't picking up, either.

"Delia, answer your phone!"

Ben pounded his hands on the steering wheel as he pulled to the side of the highway and flicked on his warning lights. He couldn't afford the time, but she had to know what she was driving into.

DON'T GO IN!! A trap! Grant is the suspect. Danger.

As soon as he pushed Send, he merged back onto the road.

"You touch her, and I will kill you," he called out to the man who used to be his friend.

Why was it taking him so long to get there? Rush hour was long over. Why was there so much traffic? He had to get to her. Had to let her know she was driving into an ambush. He wouldn't be so worried if he was certain she'd called for backup, but this was Delia he was talking about. After everything they'd gone through together, she still didn't fully trust him. Didn't trust anyone. Now he had to get to her before Grant did.

Why it had taken him so long to figure out that Grant was guilty, Ben still didn't know. But when

Delia had texted about meeting with Grant, all of those niggling little pieces of the puzzle fell into place for him. Why had he wasted so much time looking at Trevor and the other newer troopers, when he'd always known it would be one of his longtime friends? One who could hurt him the most.

Ben had to have been wearing blinders himself not to have seen it earlier. Now the evidence, though circumstantial, was enough to shame him. Of course, he knew about Grant's credit troubles last year after his divorce. Ben had even tossed him a few bucks when funds had been tight. That's what friends did.

None of them had questioned the brand-new quad-cab pickup that Grant had bought with his inheritance after his grandmother's death. They'd all attended the funeral. That's what friends did.

And they'd all rallied around Grant last summer when a run-in with a motorist had nearly got him shot along Interstate 96. That's what friends did.

Individually, none of those things raised many red flags for Ben, especially with such reasonable explanations. He'd even ruled Grant out as a suspect because he had a clean work record and, according to the internet anyway, came from a good family. A good cop. A good friend.

Apparently, setting friends up to take the fall for crimes was something friends did, too.

At least now that he knew the real suspect's identity, he also knew who was no longer a suspect. Ben pushed the button on the steering wheel to make another call with his hands-free unit. When the man answered, Ben didn't waste time with pleasantries.

"Trooper Cole, you haven't been conducting any off-limits investigations that I should know about, have you?"

"Yes, sir, Lieutenant."

"You realize you'll probably be in trouble for doing this."

"Yes, sir."

"Then, I'm going to need your help."

CHAPTER TWENTY-TWO

DELIA CAUTIOUSLY APPROACHED the enormous truck parked near a group of tiny deserted cabins. The white treeless void beyond the buildings she could only assume was Caroga Lake. If not for Grant's truck, which she recognized from work, she would have wondered if she was in the right place at all.

She probably should have waited for Ben, but it was already time for the meeting, and she couldn't afford to miss whatever Grant planned to share with her. Especially since he'd taken the time to meet with her even though he was off duty. When she reached the truck cab, she stood on tiptoes to see inside. It was empty, but the truck itself was clear of snow, unlike the surrounding trees and buildings, suggesting it hadn't been there for long. Footprint trails peppered the area, making it difficult to determine which to follow first.

She glanced around the area illuminated only by her patrol car's headlights. She'd left them on along with the engine, which had to remain running to keep the electronic equipment online. She wondered again why he'd insisted on meeting in the middle of nowhere anyway.

She and Ben had met at all kinds of places without anyone catching— Okay, maybe Grant did have good reason for being so cautious. She was losing count of how many people had figured out that she'd been helping Ben, and maybe Grant didn't want the same thing to happen to him. Seemed reasonable.

It was probably only a matter of time until she was called into Captain Polaski's office for disobeying a direct order. Maybe even to be fired. But she couldn't worry about that now, not when she might finally have the evidence to clear Ben's name.

"Grant, where are you?" she called out, struck by how hollow her voice sounded in the empty space. She rubbed her arms, suddenly cold despite her heavy coat and the gloves she wore over her uniform and the layers beneath it.

Pulling her flashlight off her duty belt, she started toward the cottages that appeared to be closed for the season. "Grant, are you out here?"

Suddenly uneasy, she touched the grip of her weapon, to assure herself it was still there. Had something gone wrong? Had something happened to Grant? Did it have anything to do with Trevor? She shifted her hand to the pocket on her duty belt where she usually kept her cell phone, but she'd left it in the car. She wanted to believe it had been an accident, but could it have been at least a little bit on purpose? If she didn't have her phone, she could avoid more of Ben's texts warning her not to be a hero and to call for backup. She wanted to be a hero, though, just this once. For Ben.

The snap of a branch nearby brought her up short. At her gasp, a puff of condensation shot into the air before her. Grant stepped around the west side of the farthest cottage, dressed in jeans, a black parka and a stocking cap.

"Oh, there you are," she said with a chuckle that she hoped didn't sound too nervous. "You startled me." She wasn't about to share with one of her male fellow troopers that he'd just scared the bejeebies out of her.

He tromped into the lighted area near their vehicles.

"Just checking out the cottages. They're not bad." If he'd noticed how nervous she was, he didn't mention it.

For several seconds, Delia waited for Grant to unload his information, but he only stared back at her. Why didn't he just spit it out? Was he holding back just to drive her crazy?

"You said you knew something that could help Ben?" she prompted.

"I did," he said with slow smile. "Looks like I'm not the only one who wants to help out old Ben."

She drew her eyebrows together, frowning. "Guess not." She waited.

"He's a good guy," he said finally. "Deserves to have people pulling for him. Such a team player. Damn humble, too, even after his big arrest at the bank."

"More so than most of us would have been," she agreed to keep the conversation going. Maybe if she did, he would finally tell her what he'd invited her here to say.

"He signed off on the evidence chains for so many cases over the years. For all of us. More than he ever realized." He added the last as an afterthought and then shot a glance her way to see if she'd caught his slipup.

Did that mean that at least some of those signatures had been forged? So Grant was the suspect?

Delia pretended she hadn't noticed what he'd given away, though he'd seemed almost proud of taking advantage of the man she loved. Her heart raced, her sweaty palms dampened the inside of her gloves as she madly tried to recall what she knew about Grant from their background research. Divorced father of two. Strapped from bad settlement and child support. The truck he blew his inheritance on. Had it really been from an inheritance? The shooting incident. Was there more to it than they'd realized?

She was such an idiot. Why hadn't she and Ben looked closer at Grant when they were excluding him a suspect? No wonder Grant had wanted to meet her in the middle of nowhere. And no wonder Grant had figured out that she'd been helping Ben in the first place. He would have been watching everyone closely since he had something to hide. And she'd been asking too many questions.

Despite the ice forming inside her veins, she carefully schooled her features and met Grant's gaze.

"You're right that he signed off on a lot of cases," she said. "Ben told me he'd signed off on so many that it was hard for him to remember the specifics."

"Know how that goes. They all run together eventually."

That was possibly the first true statement he'd made since she'd met him. His lies must have blended together by now like a set of watercolor paints dumped in a tub of water. The line between right and wrong probably had become just as blurry. How far would he be willing to go to make sure his secrets didn't get out?

As discreetly as possible, she scanned his form, looking for his weapon, but his coat was so thick that either a duty belt or a shoulder holster could easily have been hidden beneath it. If the need arose, she could draw her weapon on him, but she had to prepare herself to face fire, as well.

She took a steadying breath. She had to keep it together. Ben was on his way. She just had to avoid upsetting Grant until Ben reached them. Why hadn't she listened to Ben? He'd told her to call for backup. Now, in her rush to get answers that might help him, she'd put them both in danger. She didn't even have her phone on her. Without it, she couldn't warn him. She was sending him into this mess blind and without a weapon.

"So what information do you have that can help Ben?" she managed, hoping her voice sounded steadier than she felt.

This time Grant laughed. "A little anxious, aren't you?"

"I guess so. We haven't found many leads so far."

"Many?"

She sighed. "None."

It wasn't in her best interest to tell him she had a pretty good lead right now. Of course, she would need evidence to go along with his offhand admission, and she had to find a way to get him to tell her more without setting him off. She tucked her hands in her coat pockets to keep him from seeing them trembling.

Grant tilted his head, studying her. "It wasn't

like you to poke around for answers after Polaski said hands off."

"What do you mean?" This wasn't how she wanted the conversation to go, but at least they were still talking.

"Little Miss By-the-Book? I figured it would kill you just to make a personal phone call on work time, let alone this."

He held his hands wide to indicate the cottages at this unfamiliar location, illustrating the breadth of her departure from the security of rules. What he didn't know was that his example didn't begin to cover it.

"That's fair, I guess," she said.

"What made you want to go out on a limb for him?"

"It was the right thing to do." She couldn't help but smile as she recalled the first time she'd said that to Ben. It had been the right thing, for more reasons than she could have spelled out then, and she still didn't regret it, even knowing she would end up here.

"Sure you don't have a thing for him?"

"Why would you ask that?" she said to give herself a chance to come up with an answer. She was already at a disadvantage here. It didn't seem like a good idea to give him further ammunition to hurt her or Ben with, so she lied. "Of course not. I just knew he wasn't involved in the crimes, and he deserved to have someone help him prove it."

He stepped past her toward the lake and glanced back at her over his shoulder. "You never know what the people around you are involved in."

"I guess that's true." But because that subject wasn't one she was ready to explore just yet, she directed the conversation back to an earlier one. "So what can you tell me about the case that I don't already know?"

It was dangerous to ask, but if she didn't bring it up, that would make it more obvious that she was trying to avoid it. When he didn't respond immediately, she continued, "Do you think it was just one suspect from inside the Brighton Post, plus some outsiders, or was it an inside operation?"

Grant crossed his arms and seemed to consider before answering, but when he did, it was with a question. "Who do you think would benefit the most from a few low-level drug dealers having charges against them dismissed?"

She hadn't expected him to tell her anything of value, so she weighed his words for several seconds. "Those higher in the operation, I guess. The suppliers. They wouldn't have to recruit another round of grunts."

He nodded. "Well, someone had to ensure that the grunts didn't serve time."

The next question was obvious. She needed to ask him the identity of this someone, but she already knew the answer. And once he realized she knew, he might want to make sure she couldn't tell anyone else. Another look at the hazy, deserted scene her headlights painted and she could no longer keep from shivering.

Was that the point of their meeting at this deserted location in the first place? So he could threaten her? Or kill her? No, it didn't make sense. She was on duty. Dispatch had GPS on her patrol car. She would be found eventually. But would it be soon enough?

In the distance, Delia thought she heard the sound of a car engine. Her gaze darted past her car to the road beyond, but there were no headlights to indicate an approaching vehicle. Had she just imagined it? Grant must have missed the sound. He looked out toward the frozen water again and then glanced back at her.

"Aren't you going to ask me?" He didn't look at her as he spoke this time.

"Ask what?"

When he shot a glance back at her, she made a point of not making eye contact.

"Who."

"Well, sure. I'd like to know who set up Ben.

You invited me here to share information. Is that what you wanted to tell me?" She forced herself to remain calm as another sound filtered through a bank of trees. It sounded like the click of a car door, and this time she was sure she hadn't imagined it. "Or was it something else?"

"You know."

His voice was so low that Delia wasn't certain she'd heard him right at first, but when she met his gaze, a grim smile lifted his lips. "I do?"

"You know I didn't invite you here for a nature walk. You might be an overzealous rookie, but you're no dummy." Taking a step closer to her, he patted his coat pocket to indicate that he was armed.

"So it was you?" She forced herself to look him in the eye as she spoke. "What kind of coward does this to his own friend?"

Grant spread his arms and fisted his hands, puffing up like a much larger man and taking several menacing steps forward. "You don't know what you're talking about. You don't know what they—"

Delia planted her feet where she stood, refusing to back down though her instincts told her to run.

At the thud of a branch hitting the snow, as if it had been thrown, both turned to the line of trees. Ben stood there, a heavy-looking log at his feet.

"Let her go, Grant."

Before Grant had the chance to look back at her, Delia drew her weapon, pointing it at him.

"Get on the ground. Right now," she shouted. "Put your hands behind your head."

Out of the corner of her eye, she caught sight of Ben advancing. "Stay back, Ben. He's armed."

"Look who's suddenly gotten brave now that her boyfriend's here."

Delia startled, her gun shifting slightly. Apparently, Grant hadn't believed her when she'd said she and Ben weren't involved. Grant had his hands behind his head, but as he dropped to his knees near her, he lunged forward and grabbed her ankles. She toppled backward with nothing to catch her fall unless she released her support hand's hold on her weapon. He barely had to grapple with her to pluck the gun from her dominant hand.

As he scrambled to his feet, he yanked her police radio off her duty belt, dropped it to the ground and crushed it beneath his heavy boot. Delia dove for the weapon again, but Grant only hauled her to him and pressed her own gun to her temple. Ben, who'd been racing toward them with his 9 mm drawn, stopped and held up his hands, one still holding the gun.

"Want your little girlfriend to get hurt, Peterson?"

BEN HAD NEVER thought himself capable of murder until that moment, but now he easily imagined himself snapping Grant's neck. If he hurt her, Ben couldn't promise he wouldn't make good on that threat.

She looked tinier than normal, crushed in Grant's grasp, but she still held herself straight, refusing to give him the satisfaction of seeing her cry. Grant couldn't see her wide eyes, though. Her fear ate right through Ben, tempting him to throw himself between her and the gun.

"She's not my girlfriend." He kept his face blank, but the words tasted acidic on his tongue for so many reasons.

"She said the same thing, and she was about as believable as you. Women are poison, man. That's my free advice." Grant tapped the side of Delia's head with the muzzle. "You might want to toss your gun over there in the snow."

Ben didn't argue with his former friend, but he didn't meet Delia's gaze, either, as he tossed his gun. They had to keep their wits about them.

He rubbed his hands together, empty without his weapon. "You don't really want to do this, do you, Grant? Have you thought this through?"

Grant chuckled at that. "Look at us, Peterson. Does it really look like I could have thought any of this through?"

"Then how did we get here?" Ben held his hands wide, his mind racing. He had to find a way to get Delia out of this without setting off a man who had nothing to lose.

"Has anyone told you your skills are wasted behind a desk, Ben? You've got the whole thing down, dealing with the distraught suspect." Grant tightened his grip on Delia. "Next thing you'll be telling me that you can make everything go away if we just sit down and talk it out. 'Kumbaya' and all."

"Sorry, buddy, but we're not going to be able to make all of this go away—" Ben paused, shaking his head "—no matter how many campfire songs we sing."

"I take back what I said then." Grant leaned in close to Delia's ear. "You might want to tell your guy here that I have the gun."

"Ben…"

He tried not to hear the strain in her voice. He had to keep Grant calm for a little longer.

"So, what really happened, Grant? Because I know you don't just wake up one day and start tampering with evidence."

This time Grant loosened his hold slightly on Delia and pulled the gun away from her temple. "Always right, aren't you, Ben? It started small. I developed a taste for some of the product I was confiscating from drug dealers. Coke, mostly, just to get my day going, then a little Molly or Ecstasy, to make the weekends a little more entertaining. Pretty soon, the need exceeded the easy access, and I became more a customer and less a disruption of the trade."

Ben nodded as the answers lined up with his many questions, his father's story continuing to play on the fringes of his thoughts. He'd heard this story before. "It's a slippery slope, isn't it?"

"I found myself having to remove evidence that implicated their associates in order to make sure I got my next fix."

"What about the thing that happened last summer? Was it related?"

Grant stared off into the darkness before looking back at him again. "I wanted to stop. The bullet that whisked by my head was to remind me that I needed to continue removing evidence."

"So a lot of these things were connected?"

"You don't know the half of it." He waved vaguely at Delia with the gun. "Even the thing at Kensington with the burned-out car. Just another reminder to a middleman who, like me, wanted to walk away from the business. But there was no walking away. Ever."

Grant was so caught up in his story that he didn't seem to notice when Ben started shifting closer to him. From the slight shake of Delia's head, Ben knew that she'd noticed. He would say she would just have to trust him, but he already knew she couldn't do that.

"I do have one question, though," Ben said.

"You mean why you?" At Ben's nod, Grant shrugged. "Sorry, man, but you were just an easy target. Why'd you have to go and be a hero? You put the post under the microscope when we'd been doing just fine."

"You know it all would have come out eventually, right?"

"Maybe." Grant pressed the gun to Delia's head again, and she closed her eyes. He looked down at her head. "Too bad I couldn't just have implicated you instead. It would have been so easy. You've never been one of us."

"One of us!" Ben knew he should keep his words in check, but he couldn't stop himself now, no matter who held the gun. "How dare you even think of yourself as part of the team."

"Ben, stop it," Delia warned him through closed teeth.

He only shook his head. He had one more button to push, and he wasn't going to let her stop him. "Delia is more one of us than you ever could hope to be, you coward."

He braced himself, but he didn't have to wait for long. Grant lunged for him, allowing Delia to break free, and she bolted in the direction that Ben had tossed his gun. Another pair of headlights flashed suddenly, tracing along the row of cabins and throwing Grant off balance. Ben took that opportunity to charge him, tackling him to the ground and wresting with him for the gun. He had to get it from him, had to stop him.

Where was Delia? He had to make sure she was out of danger. Had she run back to the patrol car? He hoped so. He couldn't let anything happen to her. Not on his watch.

"Drop the gun, Grant," Delia called out.

But a shot pierced the night then, and Delia's anguished cry followed. Ben braced himself, waiting. For the pain. For the burn. Had he been shot? With so much adrenaline pumping through his veins, would he know right away? Or was it Grant? Or, God forbid, was it Delia? It was so dark, he couldn't tell. He'd done what he had to do. He'd tried to protect her. If he'd failed, he didn't want to live anyway.

CHAPTER TWENTY-THREE

"No! Ben!"

He couldn't die. He couldn't. The man she loved couldn't die for her ridiculous mistake. He didn't deserve that—she did.

Delia rushed toward the two men in a heap on the ground. She must have been running in slow motion because someone ran up behind her and overtook her, reaching them before she did.

"Radio 620," the man called into the radio microphone at his shoulder as he crouched over the two men. "Officer down. I need an ambulance at Brighton Recreation Area. Near Caroga Lake."

He turned back to Delia. "Are you going to help or not?"

"Trevor?"

"Yeah, it's me. Ben called me for backup. Now help me."

Delia shook her head to clear it, holstered Ben's weapon in her duty belt and crouched down beside him. Before they could even pull the two apart, someone moaned.

"Oh, Ben," she said under her breath.

"I'm fine," he said, though he winced.

He didn't sound fine, but he was beneath Grant, so they carefully pulled Grant to the side. There was so much blood on the both of them. Dark. Wet. Delia patted her hands along Ben's chest and shoulders, looking for the injury.

"It's not me, Delia," Ben said, pushing away her hands and sitting up.

Just then, Trevor, who'd been examining Grant for an injury, must have found something as the other officer grunted in pain.

"It's going to be okay, buddy," Trevor told him. "It's just the shoulder. Help's on the way."

But Ben didn't waste any time. He shifted over to crouch next to Grant, slipped out of his coat and yanked his sweater and undershirt over his head. After quickly rearranging his clothes, he folded over the T-shirt and applied direct pressure to Grant's wound.

Delia settled in next to him, trying not to notice when he shifted slightly away from her.

"Thanks for everything. For coming. For calling in Trevor."

"I knew *you* wouldn't."

She licked her lips. She'd deserved that, but she had to thank him, so she tried again. "I was so relieved when you got here. Who knows what would have happened if you hadn't shown up like the cavalry."

"You shouldn't have gone in alone."

"I know. But you were on the way. I was just so anxious to get answers that could help you—"

"Don't worry. You'll be officer-in-charge of this scene. I'm already in trouble for being here at all when I was supposed to be on leave."

She shook her head. "What are you talking about?"

"You'll get your chance to be in the spotlight, just the way you wanted."

For several seconds, she only stared at him. Was that really what he thought of her?

She didn't get to ask, though, as sirens announced the arrival of the ambulance. Grant would be headed to the hospital rather than a jail cell, at least initially, but his room would have an armed guard outside.

Just as the ambulance pulled away, Delia turned to find Trevor lumbering through the snow toward her.

"Helluva night, Trooper Morgan."

"Yeah, thanks for coming in for backup."

"No problem. Lieutenant Peterson called me in."

"I figured." Delia sneaked a glance at Ben, who looked away as soon as their gazes connected. Of course he would have called for backup. He'd asked her to do it, but hadn't trusted her to follow instructions. He'd been right not to trust her.

"Hey, sorry about our little conversation the other night," Trevor continued as she turned back to him. "I was doing some investigating of my own, and you were looking good as a suspect. Ben told me tonight that you two were investigating, as well."

"I wasn't doing such a bang-up job."

"The suspect's in custody."

She nodded. Their investigation had been a success at least on that end. "Tell me one thing. What was the deal with the drug cases in Manistique?"

"Oh, you were doing your homework on me. Well, let's just say when you arrest the daughter of the editor of the local weekly newspaper in a crystal meth sting, it's amazing how much unfavorable coverage you get on the editorial pages."

Well, she supposed that put one more mystery to rest.

Soon the area was overrun by crime scene technicians and other investigators, who needed to process the scene after the shooting. Delia tried several times to move closer to Ben, but he seemed to be avoiding her. After everything, was this how it would be between them now? Ben was right. She'd just gotten exactly what she'd wanted. She would be recognized for this case, which would affect dozens of drug cases, as well. She would have no trouble moving on to a higher-

profile agency, just like she'd planned all along.
Only now that she had what she wanted, it wasn't
what she wanted at all.

BEN RUBBED HIS temples as he hurried down the
hall at the Brighton Post, still stinging from
the tongue-lashing he'd sustained in Captain
Polaski's office. He just needed to get out of
there, reach his car and make it home where
he could treat his wounds, the ones that no one
could see, in peace.

But Delia caught up with him before he made
it out the door. "I need to talk to you."

"Come on, Delia. It's late. Can't we deal with
this later?" He was exhausted. Didn't she understand that? He'd only experienced the type of fear
he'd felt today one time before, and that was the
day he'd lost his mother. The woman he loved
could have been killed tonight.

"So you can avoid me the way you've been
doing all night?"

"I haven't been—" he began but didn't bother
finishing. He'd been doing exactly that. "What
do you want to say?"

The squad room was mostly empty as the
third-shifters were already out on patrol, but
Delia shook her head. "Not here. Maybe we could
go somewhere."

"I've got to get home."

She blew out a frustrated breath. "Then here."

Delia led him into the interview room and closed the door behind them. He lowered into one of the two chairs at the table, but he didn't want to look at her. The pain was too fresh, the fear a ripe wound.

She pointed to his sweater, still caked with Grant's blood. He didn't even want to think what might have happened if that gun had been pointed another direction or if the bullet had ricocheted.

"I guess I won't be keeping this sweater."

For a few seconds, Delia stared at it, as if she only now recognized how much danger they had been in tonight.

"I wanted to thank you for coming to my rescue—"

"You already did that earlier."

"And I wanted to apologize for going in alone," she said. "I should never have taken a risk like that."

"You could have been killed," he spat before he could stop himself.

"I know. It was an unnecessary risk. It won't happen again."

Fury burned within him as it had all night, impotent, pointless fury that had no place in his reality. Resignation would be easier. It wouldn't hurt as much. But no matter what he thought, no matter what he felt, he couldn't change the truth that she would never learn to trust others.

"I should have called for backup, just like you told me, Ben."

He shook his head, meeting her gaze across the table for the first time since they'd entered the room. "It doesn't matter now. With the recognition you'll receive from having broken this case, you can reach your goal. You've got your ticket out of here. You'll be able to move on to the larger agency of your dreams."

"I don't know if it's really what I—"

"I just hope you make your move soon."

Delia blinked. Clearly, she hadn't seen that one coming.

He should just shut up now. He'd said enough. But he couldn't stop. "I used to think I could help you become part of the team, even after I learned about your history." He closed his eyes, shaking his head, before opening them again. "It was naive. I know. But I understand now that you'll never be able to trust any of the troopers on the team to have your back. And for that reason, none of them, none of *us*, can trust you to have ours."

He'd wanted this conversation to remain emotionless, to state the facts with clinical sterility, but from the tears welling in her eyes, he could tell that he'd failed.

"You're wrong about me, Ben." She shook her head to emphasize her point. "I've changed. I've learned that I can trust the other officers. And I trusted *you* to be my backup. I knew you'd be there for me."

She raised her hands to stop him before he could argue. "I know. I know. I made a rookie judgment error. I went in too soon, and I went in without backup when I met with Grant. But I already knew you were on your way. You'd told me so in the text. I'd told you that you shouldn't come, but I knew you would anyway."

"You can't make mistakes like that, going in without backup in a job like ours," he said, shaking his head. "Officers get killed from mistakes like that. Citizens get killed."

"But this isn't just about my mistakes on the job, is it?" she asked quietly.

He wanted to shake his head no. But the reality was that his thoughts about Delia, on and off the job, had melded.

"You don't get it," Delia said when he didn't answer. "I don't even want to go to another agency anymore. I want to stay right here at the Brighton Post, and I want to be near you. Because I love you."

Ben swallowed. He'd wanted so much to hear her say those words, and now they only tore through him, maiming instead of salving wounds.

He'd always known people stayed true to form, so why had he convinced himself she could change? Just because he'd made her his pet project. Or because he'd fallen in love with her. Or that she'd claimed to love him. His father was supposed to have changed, too, and his mother paid the price for believing that lie.

"I'm sorry. I can't." He shook his head slowly with finality.

"What are you saying?"

But he just kept shaking his head. Trust was one of the things he'd tried so hard to teach Delia about, and it was the one thing he couldn't afford to give her now.

"This isn't about *us*." His voice caught on the last word, as if even his vocal cords recognized he was lying. "This is about the team. Only the team." It had to be about the post and not his trampled heart.

Her bottom lip was trembling, so she pressed her lips together before speaking again. "But you told Grant—"

"That you were more of a team member than he was? It wouldn't take much, if you think about it. He betrayed the whole team."

She nodded and then stared at her hands. When she looked up, her lashes were damp.

"You're wrong about me, Ben. You might not see it now, but I'll prove it to you."

"WELL, LOOK AT who finally decided to show up at work."

Ben glanced over to find Vinnie Leonetti grinning back at him.

"Right, Vinnie. I would do anything for a good, long vacation." Ben smiled at him, so happy to be back at work that he wanted to break out in a Seven Dwarfs' whistling tune. If he could whistle.

He was glad to not have been at the Brighton Post the early days after Grant's arrest when another media circus erupted, complete with the three rings of the local affiliate stations and a big top crowded with talking heads from the cable news networks. But now that the case was settling down, he was itching to get back in uniform. He'd never been so glad to pin on his badge in his life. Or to get out of the house. There was only so many times he could watch TV interviews where a certain brunette downplayed her role in bringing a fellow state trooper to justice.

"Hey, look who's back." Scott Campbell strode toward him with his hand outstretched, but the handshake ended in a hug with a hearty back pat. "You sure you want your office back? It's made a great broom closet while you were gone."

"It always did."

Ben had just stepped into the doorway of his office, alongside his fellow lieutenant, when the one person he dreaded seeing passed by them in the hall.

"Lieutenant Campbell. Lieutenant Peterson," she said with a nod.

"Trooper Morgan," Ben responded.

"Good to have you back, sir." Her gaze caught his in the briefest of contacts before she continued down the hall, her posture as stiff as a Kensington Palace guard.

Ben couldn't help but stare after her, his heart squeezing in his chest. He'd done the right thing by walking away from her, hadn't he?

"I'd bet there's a story there," Scott said when Ben turned back to him.

"Not one I'd be willing to share."

"Your call."

Scott's smile was the sly one of a family man. Someone who knew too much for his own good.

"Trooper Morgan's been making quite a hit on TV news lately, but she won't take credit for any of it," Scott told him. "Even after Grant agreed to testify in all of those cases against some of Detroit's biggest drug suppliers."

"Yeah, I know." It had shocked him, too. She was finally receiving the kind of attention she'd craved in order to boost her career, and she was pushing it aside to credit the team.

"Surprising, isn't it?" Scott asked, watching him closely. "I know she received minor censure just like you and Trevor did for freelancing on your case, but she's been more than trying to make up for that. You know how we both thought she was too independent for her own good? Well, now she's become the biggest team player I've seen in a long time. Almost as if she has something to prove."

Ben nodded, digesting that. She'd told him she would prove he was wrong about her, and it looked like she was trying to do just that.

"Well, I'll meet you in the squad room in a few. I'm sick of leading the briefings, so you'll be up."

Ben started to close his door. He needed a minute to decompress, to put things into perspective.

But Scott turned back before Ben had closed the door completely. "You know, none of us is perfect. Even you. Although you're pretty damn close since you're trying to make up for your dad. But if you spend your whole life shielding yourself to make sure nobody fails you again, you're gonna wake up someday, alone, and wonder what happened with your life."

With that, the other lieutenant strode away from him, leaving him with more questions than answers.

DELIA STOOD IN front of the mirror in the women's locker room at the end of her shift, adjusting her tie instead of removing her uniform, straightening her badge and nameplate and then brushing back a piece of hair over her ear. She'd started wearing her hair in a loose bun lately, just as she'd changed so many things at work in the last month. None of it had made any difference.

She swallowed the emotion clogging her throat and blinked back tears. She'd known that it all might have been too little too late, but she'd hoped. Sometimes hope could be a dangerous thing.

She'd told herself she could become that committed team member that Ben had always encouraged her to be. She'd believed she could learn to put the team's needs ahead of her own and play a solid role in the background. She'd even thought she could show him that in their personal relationship, too. Prove to him that if one of them was afraid to trust, to take a leap of faith for love, it wasn't her. And she'd been convinced she could do all of that even after he'd returned to work and her heart broke daily just from his nearness.

Unfortunately, she wasn't as strong as she'd hoped. The thought of being this close to him and knowing they would never be together was like ripping her heart out during every shift. She couldn't do it any longer.

With one last look in the mirror, she exited into the squad room and started down the hall to the commander's office. A transfer to another state police post was what she needed. At least somewhere else she would have the opportunity to use all of the lessons about teamwork that Ben had taught her without having to see him every day and wonder what might have been.

She stopped in front of the commander's office and knocked, pushing the door open when he invited her to enter.

"Captain Polaski, could I talk to you for a minute?"

"Sure." At his desk, Polaski crossed his arms. "Come in. Have a seat, but leave the door open a crack. It gets awfully hot in here."

Once she was seated across from him, he asked, "How may I help you?"

"I need to request a transfer."

He nodded, his lips lifting slightly before he pressed them together. "And why is that? The publicity is finally dying down."

She cleared her throat. "My reasons are personal."

"I see." He glanced down at his desk and shuffled a few papers, selecting one, before looking up at her again. "Unfortunately, I'm going to have to deny your request."

"Deny?" Her word came out sharper than she'd intended, so she tried again. "Could I at least have a reason, sir?"

"A higher-ranking officer has already made a request on your behalf."

"I see," she said, lowering her gaze to her lap. Obviously, Ben had wanted her out of the post so badly that he'd made the request himself.

"No, Trooper, I don't think you do see."

At the sound of Ben's voice behind her, she froze. Pulling the door fully open, he stepped around Polaski's desk so that both of them were facing her.

"You see, Trooper Morgan, Lieutenant Peterson has requested that I deny any request from you for a transfer," Polaski explained. "Additionally, he has requested that he never be in a position of direct authority over you."

She looked back and forth between them. "I don't think I understand, sir."

This time the commander didn't bother hiding his smile. "I'll let the lieutenant explain that himself. You two are dismissed to continue this discussion elsewhere."

In the hall, Ben extended his hand to shake hers. "Peace?"

"Peace," she responded, still not understanding.

But when he gripped her hand, he held on a few seconds longer than necessary—long enough to truly confuse her. Slowly, he leaned in so that his breath feathered on her cheek.

"I can't be your supervisor because, eventually, I plan to be something else." He paused before adding, "Your husband."

Her breath caught. Had she heard him right? Could everything she'd ever wanted be packaged in those two little words?

Ben didn't even look back but continued down the hall through the squad room and out the steel door toward the parking lot. Was she ready to put her trust in Ben, to put her heart in his hands? The answer to both of those questions was a resounding yes. Delia hurried through the squad room, not bothering to acknowledge the snickering troopers she passed.

In the parking lot, Ben sat in his SUV, off duty and waiting. Ignoring her own car, Delia threw open the door to his car, climbed up on the step and propelled herself toward him. His arms were there to catch her when she landed.

"I've been waiting forever for you to get here," he said, his lips already brushing kisses along her hairline.

She smiled at him, his lips and ecstasy only inches away. "That's great to hear because I've been waiting a lifetime for you."

EPILOGUE

Two Months Later

"GUESS YOU DON'T really need a best man when you have that thing with you."

Scott pointed to the plaque Ben still grasped under the sleeve of his dress uniform, despite the ceremony for the Michigan State Police Bravery Award having ended an hour before. Though some other recipients were still at the reception, his group had relocated to the Brighton Post squad room for a little celebration of their own.

Ben shifted the plaque so he could see where his name was beautifully engraved on the front. "It's a little hard to put down. I still need a best man, though."

"It's okay to be a little proud, you know," Scott told him as he pulled the rings from his pocket to make sure they were still there.

Delia stepped up next to them, looking beautiful though the only thing she'd changed about her dress uniform from an hour earlier was to trade her cover for a simple veil—and she also carried a small bouquet of flowers.

"Oh, he's proud, all right." She read the award and then brushed her hand across the engraving. "I wouldn't expect any less."

"Thanks, Dee." He leaned in and gave her a deep kiss that was not at all ceremony appropriate.

Rather than being embarrassed or shooing him away, Delia wrapped her arms around his neck and gave Ben another kiss that he felt all the way to his toes.

"Save it for the honeymoon, will you?" Shane called from the opposite side of the room.

Delia sent a frown his way before turning back to Ben and Scott. "Anyway, since I get to carry flowers, it's only right that he should get to carry something, too." She glanced down at the plaque and looked up again, waving her index finger at him. "But don't even try to bring that to bed tonight."

"Don't worry about that," he said, grinning.

As if she suddenly realized they had guests, Delia jerked her head toward the state police chaplain, who looked particularly embarrassed. "Sorry," she whispered.

"Let's get this show on the road," Vinnie called out. "We have partying to do."

With several murmurs of agreement, their

tiny group of guests took their seats, which had been arranged in the middle of the squad room. It was a select group. Only their closest friends and spouses, just the way they liked it.

"Want me to take those flowers for you?" Kelly asked as she stepped into her maid-of-honor position.

They'd joked that Delia had chosen Kelly because she was the only other female trooper on second shift, but it was great to see that the two of them had become close friends. In fact, Delia had become friends with all of the Brighton Post team members.

Ben and Delia joined hands as the chaplain began the ceremony. Two wounded souls had found hope and healing in each other, and now they could make a difference while serving their community together through the Michigan State Police.

* * * * *

LARGER-PRINT BOOKS!

GET 2 FREE LARGER-PRINT NOVELS PLUS
2 FREE GIFTS!

HARLEQUIN®
Romance

From the Heart, For the Heart

YES! Please send me 2 FREE LARGER-PRINT Harlequin® Romance novels and my 2 FREE gifts (gifts are worth about $10). After receiving them, if I don't wish to receive any more books, I can return the shipping statement marked "cancel." If I don't cancel, I will receive 4 brand-new novels every month and be billed just $5.09 per book in the U.S. or $5.49 per book in Canada. That's a savings of at least 15% off the cover price! It's quite a bargain! Shipping and handling is just 50¢ per book in the U.S. and 75¢ per book in Canada.* I understand that accepting the 2 free books and gifts places me under no obligation to buy anything. I can always return a shipment and cancel at any time. Even if I never buy another book, the two free books and gifts are mine to keep forever.

119/319 HDN GHWC

Name _____ (PLEASE PRINT) _____

Address _____ Apt. # _____

City _____ State/Prov. _____ Zip/Postal Code _____

Signature (if under 18, a parent or guardian must sign) _____

Mail to the **Reader Service:**
IN U.S.A.: P.O. Box 1867, Buffalo, NY 14240-1867
IN CANADA: P.O. Box 609, Fort Erie, Ontario L2A 5X3

Want to try two free books from another line?
Call 1-800-873-8635 or visit www.ReaderService.com.

* Terms and prices subject to change without notice. Prices do not include applicable taxes. Sales tax applicable in N.Y. Canadian residents will be charged applicable taxes. Offer not valid in Quebec. This offer is limited to one order per household. Not valid for current subscribers to Harlequin Romance Larger-Print books. All orders subject to credit approval. Credit or debit balances in a customer's account(s) may be offset by any other outstanding balance owed by or to the customer. Please allow 4 to 6 weeks for delivery. Offer available while quantities last.

Your Privacy—The Reader Service is committed to protecting your privacy. Our Privacy Policy is available online at www.ReaderService.com or upon request from the Reader Service.

We make a portion of our mailing list available to reputable third parties that offer products we believe may interest you. If you prefer that we not exchange your name with third parties, or if you wish to clarify or modify your communication preferences, please visit us at www.ReaderService.com/consumerchoice or write to us at Reader Service Preference Service, P.O. Box 9062, Buffalo, NY 14240-9062. Include your complete name and address.

HRLP15

LARGER-PRINT BOOKS!

HARLEQUIN

Presents®

GET 2 FREE LARGER-PRINT NOVELS PLUS 2 FREE GIFTS!

PASSION
GUARANTEED
SEDUCTION

YES! Please send me 2 FREE LARGER-PRINT Harlequin Presents® novels and my 2 FREE gifts (gifts are worth about $10). After receiving them, if I don't wish to receive any more books, I can return the shipping statement marked "cancel." If I don't cancel, I will receive 6 brand-new novels every month and be billed just $5.30 per book in the U.S. or $5.74 per book in Canada. That's a saving of at least 12% off the cover price! It's quite a bargain! Shipping and handling is just 50¢ per book in the U.S. and 75¢ per book in Canada.* I understand that accepting the 2 free books and gifts places me under no obligation to buy anything. I can always return a shipment and cancel at any time. Even if I never buy another book, the two free books and gifts are mine to keep forever.

176/376 HDN GHVY

Name	(PLEASE PRINT)	
Address		Apt. #
City	State/Prov.	Zip/Postal Code

Signature (if under 18, a parent or guardian must sign)

Mail to the **Reader Service**:
IN U.S.A.: P.O. Box 1867, Buffalo, NY 14240-1867
IN CANADA: P.O. Box 609, Fort Erie, Ontario L2A 5X3

**Are you a subscriber to Harlequin Presents® books
and want to receive the larger-print edition?
Call 1-800-873-8635 today or visit us at www.ReaderService.com.**

* Terms and prices subject to change without notice. Prices do not include applicable taxes. Sales tax applicable in N.Y. Canadian residents will be charged applicable taxes. Offer not valid in Quebec. This offer is limited to one order per household. Not valid for current subscribers to Harlequin Presents Larger-Print books. All orders subject to credit approval. Credit or debit balances in a customer's account(s) may be offset by any other outstanding balance owed by or to the customer. Please allow 4 to 6 weeks for delivery. Offer available while quantities last.

Your Privacy—The Reader Service is committed to protecting your privacy. Our Privacy Policy is available online at www.ReaderService.com or upon request from the Reader Service.

We make a portion of our mailing list available to reputable third parties that offer products we believe may interest you. If you prefer that we not exchange your name with third parties, or if you wish to clarify or modify your communication preferences, please visit us at www.ReaderService.com/consumerschoice or write to us at Reader Service Preference Service, P.O. Box 9062, Buffalo, NY 14240-9062. Include your complete name and address.

HPLP15

LARGER-PRINT BOOKS!
GET 2 FREE LARGER-PRINT NOVELS PLUS
2 FREE GIFTS!

H HARLEQUIN®

INTRIGUE
BREATHTAKING ROMANTIC SUSPENSE

YES! Please send me 2 FREE LARGER-PRINT Harlequin® Intrigue novels and my 2 FREE gifts (gifts are worth about $10). After receiving them, if I don't wish to receive any more books, I can return the shipping statement marked "cancel." If I don't cancel, I will receive 6 brand-new novels every month and be billed just $5.49 per book in the U.S. or $6.24 per book in Canada. That's a saving of at least 11% off the cover price! It's quite a bargain! Shipping and handling is just 50¢ per book in the U.S. and 75¢ per book in Canada.* I understand that accepting the 2 free books and gifts places me under no obligation to buy anything. I can always return a shipment and cancel at any time. Even if I never buy another book, the two free books and gifts are mine to keep forever.

199/399 HDN GHWN

Name	(PLEASE PRINT)	
Address		Apt. #
City	State/Prov.	Zip/Postal Code

Signature (if under 18, a parent or guardian must sign)

Mail to the **Reader Service:**
IN U.S.A.: P.O. Box 1867, Buffalo, NY 14240-1867
IN CANADA: P.O. Box 609, Fort Erie, Ontario L2A 5X3

Are you a subscriber to Harlequin® Intrigue books
and want to receive the larger-print edition?
Call 1-800-873-8635 today or visit www.ReaderService.com.

* Terms and prices subject to change without notice. Prices do not include applicable taxes. Sales tax applicable in N.Y. Canadian residents will be charged applicable taxes. Offer not valid in Quebec. This offer is limited to one order per household. Not valid for current subscribers to Harlequin Intrigue Larger-Print books. All orders subject to credit approval. Credit or debit balances in a customer's account(s) may be offset by any other outstanding balance owed by or to the customer. Please allow 4 to 6 weeks for delivery. Offer available while quantities last.

Your Privacy—The Reader Service is committed to protecting your privacy. Our Privacy Policy is available online at www.ReaderService.com or upon request from the Reader Service.

We make a portion of our mailing list available to reputable third parties that offer products we believe may interest you. If you prefer that we not exchange your name with third parties, or if you wish to clarify or modify your communication preferences, please visit us at www.ReaderService.com/consumerchoice or write to us at Reader Service Preference Service, P.O. Box 9062, Buffalo, NY 14240-9062. Include your complete name and address.

HILP15